THE GIRL WITH A CLOCK FOR A HEART

PETER SWANSON

THE

GIRL

WITH A

CLCK

FOR A

HEART

wm

WILLIAM MORROW
An Imprint of HarperCollins*Publishers*

THE GIRL WITH A CLOCK FOR A HEART. Copyright © 2014 by Peter Swanson. All rights reserved. Printed in the United States of America. No part of this book may be used or reproduced in any manner whatsoever without written permission except in the case of brief quotations embodied in critical articles and reviews. For information address HarperCollins Publishers, 10 East 53rd Street, New York, NY 10022.

HarperCollins books may be purchased for educational, business, or sales promotional use. For information please e-mail the Special Markets Department at SPsales@harpercollins.com.

FIRST EDITION

Designed by Jamie Lynn Kerner

Library of Congress Cataloging-in-Publication Data has been applied for.

ISBN 978-0-06-226749-8 (hardcover)
ISBN 978-0-06-232527-3 (international edition)

14 15 16 17 18   OV/RRD   10 9 8 7 6 5 4 3 2 1

For Charlene

And in loving memory of my grandfather,
Arthur Gladstone Ellis (1916–2012),
the kindest of men and an excellent writer

The Girl with a Clock for a Heart

PROLOGUE

I t was dusk, but as he turned onto the rutted driveway he could make out the perimeter of yellow tape that still circled the property.

George parked his Saab, but left the engine running. He tried not to think about the last time he'd been to this almost-hidden house on a dead-end road in New Essex.

The police tape was strung in a wide circle, from pine tree to pine tree, and the front door was plastered with red and white tape in an X pattern. He turned off the engine. The air conditioner stopped blowing, and George almost immediately felt the smothering heat of the day. The sun was low in the sky, and the heavy canopy of pine trees made it seem even darker.

He stepped out of the car. The humid air smelled of the sea, and he could hear gulls in the distance. The dark brown deckhouse blended into the woods that surrounded it. Its tall windows were as dark as its stained siding.

He ducked under the yellow tape that declared POLICE LINE

DO NOT CROSS and made his way toward the back of the house. He was hoping to get in through the sliding-glass doors that opened into the house from the rotted back deck. If they were locked, he would throw a rock through the glass. His plan was to get inside the house and search it as quickly as possible, looking for evidence the police might have missed.

The sliding doors were plastered over with police stickers but were unlocked. He entered the cool house, expecting to be consumed with fear once he was inside. Instead, he felt a surreal sense of calm, as though he were in a waking dream.

I'll know what I'm looking for when I find it.

It was clear that the police had thoroughly searched the property. On several surfaces there were the streaky remains of fingerprint dust. The drug paraphernalia that had been on the coffee table was gone. He turned toward the master bedroom on the east side of the house. It was a room he had never been in, and he opened the door expecting a mess. Instead, he found a fairly neat space, a large, low-ceilinged bedroom with a king-size bed that had been made up with floral sheets. There were two low bureaus opposite the bed, each topped with a plate of glass. Faded Polaroids were pinned under the grimy glass. Birthday parties. Graduations.

He opened the drawers, found nothing. There were some old items of clothing, hairbrushes, perfume bottles still in boxes, all with the dusty, floral smell of mothballs.

A carpeted stairwell led to the lower level. As he passed the landing by the front door he tried hard to keep the images out of his mind. But he looked extra long at the place where the body had fallen, where the skin had turned the color of not skin.

At the bottom of the stairs, he turned left into a large finished basement, musty-smelling and windowless. He tried the wall switches, but the electricity had been turned off. He pulled the small flashlight he'd brought out of his back pocket and cast its thin, dim light around the basement. In the center of the room was a beautiful vintage billiards table with red felt instead of green, balls scattered randomly across its surface. In the far corner was a high bar area with several stools and a large mirror engraved with the logo of GEORGE DICKEL TENNESSEE WHISKEY. In front of the mirror was a stretch of empty shelf that he imagined had once held an array of liquor bottles, long since emptied and thrown away.

I'll know what I'm looking for when I find it.

He returned upstairs and looked through the smaller bedrooms, both of them, searching for any sign of their most recent occupants, but found nothing. The police would have done the same, would have bagged as evidence anything that struck them as significant, but he had had to come and look for himself. He knew he'd find something. He knew she would have left something.

He found it in the bookshelf of the living room at eye level in a wall of books. It was a white hardcover book, slipcovered in plastic as though it had once belonged to a library, standing out among the other books, most of which were technical. Boating manuals. Travel guides. An ancient set of a child's encyclopedia. There was some fiction on the shelf as well, but it was all mass-market paperbacks. High-tech thrillers. Michael Crichton. Tom Clancy.

He touched the book's spine. The title and the author's name were in a thin, elegant red font. *Rebecca.* By Daphne du Maurier.

It was her favorite book, her one and only favorite book. She had given him a copy the year they had met. Their freshman year of college. She had read parts of it out loud to him in her dormitory on cold winter nights. He knew passages by heart.

He pulled the book out, ran his finger along the deckled edges of its pages. It fell open at page 6. Two sentences were boxed by carefully drawn lines. He remembered that it was the way she marked books. No highlighter. No underlined passages. Just exact outlines around words and sentences and paragraphs.

George didn't immediately read the marked words; the book had fallen open not by chance but because a postcard had been tucked between its pages. The back of the postcard was slightly yellowed with age. There was nothing written on it. He turned it over and looked at the color image of a Mayan ruin, standing untoppled on a scrubby bluff, the ocean in the background. It was an old postcard, the color of the ocean too blue and the color of the grass too green. He turned it back over. "The Mayan Ruins of Tulum," the description read. "Quintana Roo. Mexico."

CHAPTER 1

At five minutes past five on a Friday night, George Foss walked directly from his office to Jack Crow's Tavern through the gluey air of a Boston heat wave. He'd spent the final three hours of work meticulously proofreading a rewrite on an illustrator's contract, then staring numbly through his window at the hazy blue of the city sky. He disliked late summer the way other Bostonians disliked the long New England winters. The weary trees, the yellowing parks, and the long humid nights all made him long for the crisp weather of autumn, for breathable air that didn't make his skin stick to his clothes and his bones feel tired.

He walked the half-dozen blocks to Jack Crow's as slowly as he could, hoping to keep his shirt relatively sweat-free. Cars jockeyed along the narrow Back Bay streets attempting to escape the funk of the city. Most residents of this particular neighborhood would be planning their first drinks of the evening at bars in Wellfleet or Edgartown or Kennebunkport, or any of the seaside towns within reasonable driving distance. George was happy enough to be going to Jack Crow's, where the drinks were average but where the air conditioning, monitored by an ex-pat French Canadian, was routinely kept at meat-locker temperatures.

And he was happy enough to be going to see Irene. It had been over two weeks since he'd seen her last, at a cocktail party thrown by a mutual friend. They had barely spoken, and when George left first she had thrown him a look of mock anger. It made him wonder if their on-again off-again relationship had reached one of its periodic crisis points. George had known Irene for fifteen years, having met her at the magazine where he still worked. She had been an assistant editor while he was in accounts receivable. Being an accountant at a well-known literary magazine had seemed the perfect job for a man with a literary bent but no literary talent. Now George was business manager of that particular sinking ship, while Irene had worked her way up the ranks of the *Globe*'s ever-expanding website division.

They had been a perfect couple for two years. But those two years had been followed by thirteen years of diminishing returns, of recriminations, occasional infidelities, and a constantly lowering set of expectations. And while they'd long since given up the notion that they were an ordinary couple with an ordinary destiny, they still came to their favorite bar, they still told each other everything, they still occasionally slept together, and, against all odds, they'd become best friends. Despite this, there was the periodic need to clarify their status, to have a conversation. George didn't feel he had it in him this particular night. It had nothing to do with Irene; in some ways his feelings toward her hadn't changed in about a decade. It had more to do with how he felt about life in general. Approaching forty, George felt as though his world had been slowly drained of all its colors. He'd passed that age when he could reasonably expect to fall madly in love with someone and raise a family, or to take the world by storm, or to have anything surprising lift him out of his day-to-day existence. He would never have voiced these sentiments to anyone—after all, he was securely employed, living in the fair city of Boston, still possessed of all his hair—but he spent most days in a haze of disinterest. And while he was not yet pausing in front of funeral homes, he did feel as though he hadn't looked forward to anything in years. He had no interest in new friends or new relationships. At work, the paychecks had grown but his enthusiasm for his job had wavered. In years past he had felt a sense of pride and accomplishment with the publication of each monthly issue. These days he rarely read an article.

Approaching the tavern, George wondered what kind of mood Irene would be in tonight. He was sure to hear about the divorced editor at her office who had asked her out several times that summer. What if she agreed, and what if they became serious and George was finally thrown all the way to the curb? He tried to summon an emotion but instead found himself wondering what he would do with all the spare time. How would he fill it? And whom would he fill it with?

George pushed through the frosted-glass doors of Jack Crow's and walked directly to his usual booth. Later he realized he must have walked right by Liana Decter sitting at the corner of the bar. On other evenings, cooler ones, or ones when George was less dispirited about his lot in life, he might have surveyed the few patrons at his local tavern on a Friday night. There might even have been a time when George, catching sight of a lone curvy woman with pale skin, would have been jolted with the possibility that it was Liana. He'd spent twenty years both dreaming of and dreading the idea of seeing her again. He'd spotted variations of her across the world: her hair on a flight stewardess, the crushing lushness of her body on a Cape beach, her voice on a late-night jazz program. He'd even spent six months convinced that Liana had become a porn actress named Jean Harlot. He'd gone so far as to track down the actress's true identity. She was a minister's daughter from North Dakota named Carli Swenson.

George settled in his booth, ordered an old-fashioned from Trudy, the waitress, and removed that day's *Globe* from his well-worn messenger bag. He'd saved the crossword puzzle for this very occasion. Irene was meeting him, but not till six o'clock. He sipped at his drink and solved the puzzle, then reluctantly moved on to sudoku and even the jumble before he heard Irene's familiar steps behind him.

"Please, let's switch," she said by way of greeting, meaning their seats. Jack Crow's had only one television, a rarity in a Boston bar, and Irene, outranking George in her Red Sox loyalty and fandom, wanted the better view.

George slid out from the booth, kissed Irene on the side of her mouth (she smelled of Clinique and Altoids), and resettled on the other side, with its view of the oak bar and floor-to-ceiling windows. It was still light outside, a pink slice of sun just cresting over the brownstones across the street. The spread of light across the glass caused George to suddenly notice the lone woman at the corner of the bar. She was drinking a glass of red wine and reading a paperback, and a flutter in George's stomach told him that she looked like Liana. Just like Liana. But this was a flutter he'd experienced many times before.

He turned to Irene, who had swiveled toward the blackboard

behind the bar that listed the day's specials and the rotating beers. As always, she was unfazed by the heat, her short blond hair pushed off her forehead and curling back behind her ears. Her cat's-eye glasses had pink frames. Had they always?

After ordering an Allagash White, Irene updated George on the continuing saga of the divorced editor. George was relieved that Irene's initial tone was chatty and nonconfrontational. Stories of the editor tended toward the humorous anecdote, even though George was apt to detect a critical undertone. This editor might be chubby and ponytailed and a dedicated microbrewer, but at least with him there was a palpable future consisting of something more than cocktails and laughs and the very occasional sex that George offered these days.

He listened and sipped his drink but kept his eye on the woman at the bar. He was waiting for a gesture or a detail to disabuse him of the notion that he was actually looking at Liana Decter and not a ghost version or some doppelganger. If it was Liana, she'd changed. Not in any obvious way, like putting on a hundred pounds or cutting all her hair off, but she looked altered somehow, in a good way, as though she'd finally grown into the rare beauty that her features had always promised. She'd lost the baby fat she had in college, the bones of her face were more prominent, and her hair was a darker blond than George remembered. The more George stared, the more he became convinced it was her.

"You know I'm not the jealous type," Irene said, "but who do you keep looking at?" She craned her neck to look back toward the rapidly filling bar area.

"Someone I went to college with, I think. I can't be sure."

"Go ask her. I won't mind."

"No, that's okay. I barely knew her," George lied, and something about the lie caused a spidery ripple of agitation to race across the back of his neck.

They ordered more drinks. "He sounds like a little prick," George said.

"Huh?"

"Your divorcé."

"Ah, you still care." She slid out of the booth to go to the restroom, and this gave George a moment to really stare across the room at Liana. She'd become partially blocked by a pair of young businessmen removing their jackets and loosening their ties, but in between their maneuverings he studied her. She was wearing a white collared shirt, and her hair, a little shorter than it had been in college, hung down on one side of her face and was tucked behind an ear on the other. She wore no jewelry, something George remembered about her. There was an indecent creaminess to her neck and a mottled flash of crimson at her breastbone. She'd put away her paperback and now seemed, as she occasionally surveyed the bar, to be looking for someone. George was waiting for her to get up and move; he felt that until he saw her walk he could not be sure.

As though his thinking it had made it happen, she slid off the padded stool, her skirt briefly bunching at midthigh. As soon as her feet touched the floor and she began to walk in George's direction, there was no doubt. It had to be Liana, the first time he'd seen her since his freshman year at Mather College, nearly twenty years ago. Her walk was unmistakable, a slow tilting roll of the hips, her head held high and back as though she were trying to see over someone's head. George lifted a menu to cover his face and stared at its meaningless words. His heart thudded in his chest. Despite the air conditioning, George could feel his palms start to dampen.

Liana passed just as Irene slid back into the booth. "There's your friend. You didn't want to say hello?"

"I'm still not sure if it's her," George said, wondering if Irene could hear the dry panic in his voice.

"Got time for another drink?" Irene asked. She had reapplied her lipstick in the bathroom.

"Sure," George said. "But let's go somewhere else. We could walk a little bit while it's still light."

Irene signaled the waiter, and George reached for his wallet. "My turn, remember," Irene said and removed a credit card from her bottomless purse. While she paid the check, Liana walked past again. This time George could stare at her retreating figure, that familiar walk. She'd grown into her body too. George thought she'd been his ideal in college, but if anything she looked better now: long tapering legs and exaggerated curves, the kind of body that only genetics, not exercise, will ever get you. The backs of her arms were pale as milk.

George had imagined this moment many times but had somehow never imagined the outcome. Liana was not simply an ex-girlfriend who had once upon a time broken George's heart; she was also, as far as George still knew, a wanted criminal, a woman whose transgressions were more in line with those of Greek tragedy than youthful indiscretion. She had, without doubt, murdered one person and most likely murdered another. George felt the equal weights of moral responsibility and indecision weigh down upon him.

"Coming?" Irene stood, and George did as well, following her brisk heel-first pace along the painted wooden floors of the bar.

Nina Simone's "Sinnerman" rat-a-tatted on the speakers. They swung through the front doors, the still-humid evening greeting them with its wall of stale, steamy air.

"Where to next?" Irene asked.

George froze. "I don't know. Maybe I just feel like going home."

"Okay," Irene said, then added, when George still hadn't moved, "or we could just stand out here in the rain forest."

"I'm sorry, but I suddenly don't feel so great. Maybe I'll just go home."

"Is it that woman at the bar?" Irene arched her neck to peer back through the frosted glass of the front door. "That's not what's-her-name, is it? That crazy girl from Mather."

"God, no," George lied. "I think I'll just call it a night."

George walked home. A breeze had picked up and was whistling through the narrow streets of Beacon Hill. The breeze wasn't cool, but George held out his arms anyway and could feel the sweat evaporating off his skin.

When George got to his apartment, he sat down on the first step of the exterior stairway. It was only a couple of blocks back to the bar. He could have one drink with her, find out what brought her to Boston. He had waited so long to see her, imagining the moment, that now, with her actually here, he felt like an actor in a horror flick with his hand on the barn door about to get an ax in his head. He was scared, and for the first time in about a decade he longed for a cigarette. Had she come to Jack Crow's to look for him? And if so, why?

On almost any other night, George could have entered his apartment, fed Nora, and crawled into his bed. But something about the weight of that particular August night, combined with

Liana's presence at his favorite bar, made it seem as though something was about to happen, and that was all he needed. Good or bad, something was happening.

George sat long enough to begin to believe that she must have left the bar. How long would she really sit there by herself with her glass of red wine? He decided to walk back. If she was gone, then he wasn't meant to see her again. If she was still there, then he'd say hello.

As he walked back to the bar the breeze pressing against his back felt both warmer and stronger. At Jack Crow's, he didn't hesitate—he swung back through the door and, as he did, Liana, from her spot at the bar, turned her head and looked at him. He watched her eyes brighten a little in recognition. She had never been one for outsize gestures.

"It *is* you," he said.

"It is. Hi, George." She said it with the flat intonation he remembered, as casually as though she'd seen him earlier that day.

"I saw you from over there." George tilted his head toward the back of the bar. "I wasn't sure it was you at first. You've changed a little, but then, walking past you, I was pretty sure. I got halfway down the street and turned back."

"I'm glad you did," she said. Her words, carefully spaced, had a little click at the end. "I actually came here . . . to this bar . . . to look for you. I know that you live near here."

"Oh."

"I'm glad you spotted me first. I don't know if I would have had the courage to go up to you. I know how you must feel about me."

"Then you know more than I do. I don't exactly know how I feel about you."

"I mean about what happened." She hadn't changed position since he'd come back into the bar, but one of her fingers gently tapped on the wooden bar to the percussive music.

"Right, that," George said, as though he were searching in his memory banks for what she could be talking about.

"Right, that," she repeated back, and they both laughed. Liana shifted her body around to face George more squarely. "Should I be worried?"

"Worried?"

"Citizen's arrest? Drink thrown in my face?" She had developed tiny laugh lines at the edge of her pale blue eyes. Something new.

"The police are on their way right now. I'm just stalling you." George kept smiling, but it felt unnatural. "I'm kidding," he said when Liana didn't immediately speak.

"No, I know. Would you like to sit? You have time for a drink?"

"Actually . . . I'm meeting someone, in just a little bit." The lie slid out of George easily. His head was suddenly muddled by her close presence, by the smell of her skin, and he had an almost animal urge to escape.

"Oh. That's fine," Liana quickly said. "But I do have something I need to ask you. It's a favor."

"Okay."

"Can we meet somewhere? Maybe tomorrow."

"Do you live here?"

"No, I'm just in town for . . . I'm visiting a friend, really. . . . It's complicated. I would like to talk with you. I'd understand if you didn't, of course. This was a long shot, and I understand—"

"Okay," George said, telling himself he could change his mind later.

"Okay, yes, you'd like to talk?"

"Sure, let's meet while you're in town. I promise I won't call the feds. I just want to know how you're doing."

"Thank you so much. I appreciate it." She took a large breath through her nostrils, her chest expanding. George somehow heard the rustle of her crisp white shirt across her skin above the sounds of the jukebox.

"How did you know I lived here?"

"I looked you up. Online. It wasn't that hard."

"I don't suppose you're still called Liana?"

"Some people. Not many. Most people know me as Jane now."

"Do you have a cell phone? Should I call you later?"

"I don't have a cell phone. I never have. Could we meet here again? Tomorrow. At noon." George noticed how her eyes subtly moved, searching his face, trying to read him. Or else she was looking for what was familiar and what had changed. George's hair had turned gray at the sides, his forehead had wrinkled, and the lines around his mouth had deepened. But he was still in relatively good shape, still handsome in a slightly hangdog way.

"Sure," George said. "We could meet here. They're open for lunch."

"You don't sound sure."

"I'm not sure, but I'm not unsure."

"I wouldn't ask if it wasn't important."

"Okay," George said, again thinking that he could change his mind, that by agreeing he was only postponing a decision. Later George thought that there would have been times in his life when he simply would have told Liana that he didn't think they should see each other. He had no need for justice, not even any real need for closure, and for that reason George didn't believe he would have alerted the authorities. The mess that she'd gotten involved in was many years in the past. But it was bad enough that she must have been running ever since, and she would have to continue running the rest of her life. Of course she didn't have a cell phone. And of course she wanted to meet somewhere public, a bar at an intersection in a busy part of Boston, somewhere she could take off from right away.

"Okay. I can come," George said.

She smiled. "I'll be here. Noon."

"I'll be here as well."

CHAPTER 2

They had met the first night of college. George's RA, a gangly, nervous sophomore named Charlie Singh, had brought several of his freshman charges to a jam-packed keg party in McAvoy. George had followed Charlie up the crammed stairwell to a sweltering, high-ceilinged quad with window seats and scuffed hardwood floors. He drank a sour beer and made small talk with Mark Schumacher, one of the freshmen from his hall. Mark begged off, leaving George alone in a sea of attractive upperclassmen who all seemed engaged in making one another laugh riotously. He determined that he could leave the party, but only after he got himself one more beer. He mapped an approach across the room to the unmanned keg and picked his way through the flannel and khaki. He was edged out by a girl who took hold of the nozzle just as he was reaching for it; she pressed the knob, and nothing but foam and air sputtered into her lipstick-smeared cup.

"It's empty," she told him. She had flat, dark blond hair, cropped just under her jawline, and blue, blue eyes spaced far apart on *either side of a heart-shaped face. The spacey eyes made her look a little dim, but George thought she was the prettiest girl he'd seen so far at college.*

"You sure it's empty?"

"I don't know," she said with a drawl that meant she wasn't from New England. "I haven't really ever done this before. Have you?"

George hadn't, but he stepped forward and took her cup from her. "I think you pump this thing. I actually don't know either, but I've seen it done."

"Are you a freshman too?"

"Yes," he said as a stream of beer went half into her cup, and half over his wrist and down his sleeve.

They spent the rest of the evening together, smoking her cigarettes by an open window, then exploring the campus late at night. They made out under an arch that linked the college chapel to the main administration building. George told her how his father—a farmer's son—had invented a mechanized system for slaughtering poultry and had made more money in one sale than his grandparents had made in their lifetime on the farm. She told him how her dad was an ambulance-chasing lawyer in a small town, then added, as George slid a hand under her shirt, that she was a girl from south of the Mason-Dixon Line who had no intention of having casual sex just because she was at a college in New England. The way she spoke was not censorious but matter-of-fact, and her almost-innocent directness, plus the brief feel of her full breast held by a thin, satiny bra, was all it took to make George fall immediately in love.

He escorted her back to her dorm and dropped her off, then half ran across campus to get into his unfamiliar bed with the freshman orientation handbook. Her name and address were in it, but no picture. He stared at the name, though, and the blank space where her picture should have been. George felt he had never met a creature like her before. Unlike the alternately repressed and opinionated members of George's family clan, she had seemed wide open, talking as though the words were falling directly from her thoughts. When they had met by the keg, she had stared at George in a way that felt challenging and yet completely innocent. She stared at him like she had been newly born into the world. There had been something almost spooky about it. Then George remembered the hungry way she had kissed him, pushing hard against his lips, their tongues touching, one of her hands on the back of his neck. George's roommate, whom he had barely met, was snoring loudly from across their double room. George touched himself through his boxers and came almost immediately.

When he woke up the next day, he wasn't thinking about independence, or college, or the classes he'd be starting soon. He could only think of Liana. Hungover but giddy, he went and sat alone in Mather College's dining hall for three hours to make sure he'd see her. Liana showed at eleven, coming in with another girl and going straight to the cereal station. Her hair was still damp from the shower, and she was wearing a pair of tight-fitting khaki pants and a white cotton sweater. George's mouth went dry when he saw her again. He got himself coffee (thinking it would look more sophisticated than the grape juice he'd been drinking) and pretended to run into her as she was filling her bowl with Froot Loops.

"Hey, again," he said, willing his voice to sound sleepy and disinterested.

She introduced him to Emily, her roommate, a private school girl from Philadelphia who was wearing a faded Izod shirt and tennis skirt, then asked him to join them at their table. When he *did, Emily, out of either discretion or disdain, excused herself after eating half a bowl of Grape-Nuts. Liana and George looked at each other. She was, he thought, more alarmingly beautiful in daytime than she'd been the night before. Her skin, in the raw daylight of the high-ceilinged dining hall, looked fresh-scrubbed and poreless, her eyes a translucent blue, flecked with hints of grayish-green. "I've been waiting here for three hours," George admitted, "just to see you."*

He thought she'd laugh, but all she said was, "I'm glad."

"I've had a lot of cereal."

"I would have come earlier, but Emily asked me to wait for her and then took an hour getting dressed. I don't think I'm going to like her much."

They were together for the next three months, and while both made concerted efforts to develop other friendships, to spend some of their time apart, at the end of most nights they would find each other, even if it was just to stand and kiss in the cold black shadows of the college chapel, halfway between their two dormitories. She was true to her word about having sex—she had no intention of moving too fast in that department—but a steady progression of allowances led to an evening in late November, the two of them naked and nervous in George's single bed, his roommate, Kevin, away for the night.

"Okay," she said, and he fumbled with a condom he'd had since junior year of high school. He entered her slowly, one hand on her waist and one cupping the underside of her raised thigh. She lifted her pelvis to meet his and tilted her head back, biting her plump lower lip. It was that sight, more than the feel of her hips moving beneath him, that caused George, to his shame, to come almost immediately. He apologized, and she laughed, then kissed him deeply.

She said it was her first time, but thankfully there was no blood. Later in the month, when Emily, done early with exams, had left to return to her home in Pennsylvania, George and Liana had a week together in her dorm room. The entire Eastern Seaboard was hit by an ice storm so bad that half of Mather's finals were delayed. George and Liana studied, chain-smoked Camel Lights, occasionally left the dorm to go to the dining hall, and had sex. They tried every position, finding ways to make George last longer and the easiest ways for Liana to come. Each day felt like the discovery of a brand-new country hiding behind a low door in a wall. The intensity of that week bordered on an almost unbearable sadness for George. He'd read enough books to know that youthful love comes only once, and he wanted it never to end or go away. And he had been right: that week spent in Liana's single bed, not much bigger, or more comfortable, than a foldout cot, had seared itself into his memory.

He had been searching for it, or its equivalent, ever since.

They took their exams, and the bright ice from the storm that had temporarily locked the world underneath its shell melted into slush and rivulets of mud. Two days before Christmas they said their good-byes before leaving for their respective home states, Liana by car and George by train.

Liana had given George her parents' phone number in Florida but begged him not to call. "The chances of me actually being there are slim to none," she'd said. "Really, don't bother. If they catch wind of a boy calling me from college, there'll be about a thousand questions to answer. They'll send me back here with a chastity belt."

"You serious?"

"I am," she'd said with her pronounced Southern drawl, an accent that had never fit his conception of a Florida girl. He pictured surfers and convertibles, but she said the kids from her town

of Sweetgum—the white kids anyway, not the Mexicans or the blacks—listened to country music and drove pickups.

"You can call me," George had said, writing down his parents' phone number.

"I will."

But she hadn't.

And when he returned to Mather College in January, he heard the news.

She wouldn't be returning to Connecticut.

She had committed suicide at her home in Florida.

Chapter 3

At a quarter to noon, George was the first patron at Jack Crow's. One of the many things George liked about this particular bar was that it hadn't yet succumbed to the citywide brunch craze. It opened at lunchtime, even on the weekends. No lines outside the door for eggs Benedict and ten-dollar Bloody Marys. No jazz trio playing in the corner.

Even early in the day, Jack Crow's was cold as a meat locker. The smell of Lysol just barely edged out the smell of stale beer. There were no waitresses visible, so George walked up to the bar and ordered a bottle of Newcastle.

"You're here early," the owner said, returning to the lemon he was sectioning into wedges.

"I'm sick of this heat, Max."

"You and me both."

A rumpled newspaper sat on the bar, and George took it with him to a booth toward the back, sitting down where he could watch the door. He opened the paper but couldn't focus on the words, just peered over its top toward the entryway. By the time he'd finished his beer, it was ten minutes past noon. The front doors had opened three times—first to admit a young Japanese couple who were each pulling a suitcase on wheels, then the mailman, who quickly dropped a rubber-banded bundle of mail on the bar. The third time the doors opened a regular named Lawrence came in. George raised the newspaper slightly so he wouldn't be spotted as Lawrence went immediately to his usual seat at the distant end of the bar, closest to the kitchen.

George got up to order another beer. Kelly, one of the waitresses, was now behind the bar cleaning glasses. As George approached the wall phone behind her rang, and she snatched it, tucking the handset under her chin. George listened to her say, "Jack Crow's, how can I help you?" Then she paused, raising her eyes to look at George. "Yeah, I know him. I'm looking right at him. Hold on." She held the phone out to George just as he reached the edge of the bar. "Some lady. For you." Kelly shrugged as she handed over the phone.

George took it, knowing who it would be.

"Hello?"

"Hi, George. It's Liana."

"You okay?"

"I'm fine, but I'm not going to make it to meet you. It's a long story. I let someone borrow my car, and now I don't know where she is. I don't suppose there's any way you could come to me?"

"Where are you?"

"New Essex. You know it?"

"Sure. On the North Shore. I've been there."

"Do you have a car? Would you be willing to drive up here?"

Her voice sounded shaky to George. And she was talking abnormally fast.

"You okay?"

"I'm fine except for the fact that I don't have my car."

"You sure?"

"What was it you said last night? *I'm not sure but I'm not unsure.* Something like that. I won't lie. I'm in a little bit of trouble—not right this instant but in general—and I was hoping you could do me a favor."

When George didn't immediately say anything, she asked, "You still there?"

"I am. I'm listening."

"Trust me when I say that I am *well* aware that I am the last person who should be asking you for a favor. I'm hoping that maybe you'll hear me out."

"You can't ask me now, over the phone?"

"I'd like to ask you face-to-face. Do you have a car?"

"I do."

"I would appreciate it if you drove up here and at least listened to what I have to say. You can trust me. I'm trusting you. There's nothing stopping you from calling the police and giving them my address."

George breathed through his nostrils, looked at Kelly, the waitress. She glanced at his empty bottle of beer, mouthed, "Another?" George shook his head.

"Okay. I'll come up. Where exactly are you?"

"Thank you, George. Do you know Beach Road? I'm staying at a friend's house just behind St. John's, that old stone chapel."

"Okay. I might know where that is."

"After you see the church on your right, there's an unpaved

road called Captain Sawyer Lane. It's the house at the very end.
More like a cottage. I'll wait for you. Anytime this afternoon is
fine."

"I'll be there."

"Thank you. Thank you. Thank you."

George handed the phone back to Kelly. "Uh-oh," she said
in her strong Boston accent. "Starting to get phone calls at your
local bar. Never a good sign."

"Thanks, Kel. Maybe you'll take messages for me when I'm
not here."

"You wish."

George thought about ordering another beer, plus something
to eat, but decided instead to go immediately to see Liana. Talking to her had tightened up his stomach, not just because she was
back in his life but because she sounded genuinely scared. He
left Jack Crow's and walked the two short blocks to the garage
where he kept his Saab.

George would never have considered himself a car person,
but the Saab 900 was the first and only car he'd ever fallen in
love with. He'd bought one with 100,000 miles on it just after
graduating from college, added another 100,000 to its odometer,
and had then begun to look for a replacement. He'd been replacing his Saabs ever since. The current car was his fourth, the first
with the Special Performance Group option; Saab had made only
about fifteen hundred of them back in 1986, and they only came
in Edwardian Gray. Garaging his Saab was a major expense, but
he loved her far too much to leave her on the street.

Liana's location, on a traffic-free day, was about forty-five
minutes north of Boston. Tucked between inlets, New Essex was
an old quarry town by the sea. Half the granite in Boston origi-

nated there, and there was a massive hole in the ground to prove it, but the primary reason people went to New Essex was to eat fried clams and steamers, to gaze at the rock-strewn shore, or to visit the kitschy galleries that had replaced the old fishing shacks around the harbor.

George made it to the center of town at a little past one thirty. He wound his battered Saab past the granite statue of a quarryman that crowned the tiny rotary at the heart of down-town and took Beach Road north. It was another muggy day. The sky was a chalky blue, and the sea, glimpsed through gaps in the evergreens, was slack and gray. George slowed the car down to look for the markers. He rounded a corner and saw, up ahead at the next bend, a stone church fronted by a bell tower. He drove past it. There was a lone man sleeping on a bench in the church's garden. He was dressed in long pants and a long-sleeved shirt, each a navy blue; he sat rigidly straight, but his chin had drooped to his chest. George had the sudden and alarming thought that the old man had died on that bench and the world hadn't no-ticed, or had decided not to wake an old man sleeping in the sun.

After passing the church, Beach Road swung sharply inland, and the view of the sea was blocked by white pines. The green sign for Captain Sawyer Lane was bleached nearly unreadable, and the road itself was deeply rutted. George turned in and drove a few hundred yards, past a 1970s deckhouse that was camouflaged in the woods on the right. He kept going, and the road dead-ended at an old shingled summer cottage that would have looked abandoned had there not been a shiny white Dodge pulled up to its decrepit front steps. George parked behind the Dodge, killed his engine, and got out of the car. The driveway was a combination of pebbles and shells. Behind the cottage were a marshy inlet and a pier that appeared older and less reliable than the house. George climbed the steps and knocked on the unpainted door. Nothing stirred. The breeze from the sea gently rocked the surrounding pines. George knocked again; the wood felt hollow, as though it had rotted from the inside. He was about to try the door when a man came around the side of the house and said, "She's not here."

George turned. The speaker was a short, neat man wearing suit trousers and the type of silky expensive shirt that you don't see too often in Massachusetts. He had a smile on his face notable for its unfriendliness. "Who's not here?" George asked.

The man's smile got wider, and he took a couple of steps toward George. "Really?" he said. He had grayish-purple teeth, as though he'd drunk too much red wine for breakfast.

"Who is it that you're looking for?" George asked, hoping to turn the tables on him. The man was pretty small, but something about the way he carried himself made George almost physically recoil. He reminded George of a pit bull, the kind you'd normally see muzzled and straining against a leash.

"I was looking for Jane," Pit Bull said, as though she were a mutual friend. "She's been staying out here. What are *you* doing here?"

"I'm a salesman," George said. He came down off the steps so that he was standing on even ground with the other man. Pit Bull was at least a full foot shorter than George, if not more.

"What are you selling?" he asked.

"I'm glad you asked that. I'm selling everlasting life." George reached out his hand to shake Pit Bull's, aware that his palms were beginning to sweat but wanting to at least keep up the pretense that he didn't know Liana/Jane and that he wasn't particularly scared to be alone in the dark woods with a man who looked like he could snap George in half the way he could snap a towel in a locker room.

They shook hands. George was not surprised that the stranger's hand was dry and cool to the touch. He went to let go, but the man held on, digging into the back of George's hand with his thumb so that George had no choice but to straighten out his fingers. Pit Bull squeezed hard, jamming George's knuckles together. "Jesus," George said, trying to pull his hand away.

"Don't move," Pit Bull said, his smile now more of a smirk, and George did what he said. The way he was gripping George's hand made it pretty clear that if he squeezed just a tiny bit harder knuckles would explode like rocks in a crusher.

"I don't know who you think—"

"Shhh. Don't. I'm only going to ask you once, so I want you to give me straight answers or else I'll crush every bone in your hand. I've done it before, and I really hate doing it. I'm squeamish about some things. Not about blood, of course, but the feel of turning someone's hand into a limp glove filled with gravel makes me sick to my stomach. Even thinking about it, I don't feel too good. So I don't want to do it, and you *really* don't want me to do it, so just tell me everything you know. Okay? When did you last see Jane?"

George hesitated one brief fraction of a second, long enough to conclude that there was no decent reason to try to lie. "I saw her last night. In Boston."

"Where did you see her?"

"A bar in Beacon Hill, called Jack Crow's. She's an old friend. I knew her in college, and I asked if we could get together, and she told me she was staying here and I could come see her tomorrow. That's the whole story."

"Why'd you lie to me?" Up close the Pit Bull had tiny features on an acorn-shaped head and waxy skin that looked pinpricked all over with minuscule pores. His nose was flattened along the bridge like he'd lost a couple of fights, which was hard to imagine. His hair was short and heavily gelled, and he smelled of astringent aftershave lotion, something with a lot of alcohol in it.

"Look, I know that . . . that Jane has a history of trouble, although I honestly know nothing about what is happening right now. You looked like someone she might want to avoid."

The man laughed, and it was possible that he beamed a little, as though proud of George's assessment of him. "Look, if you see her before me, then tell her that she really ought to avoid me at all fucking costs. But she knows that already. What's your name?"

"George Foss," George said, willing himself not to lie. He could feel the interrogation winding to its close, and he wanted to keep the bones of his hand intact.

"Good, George. You've been telling me the truth, and I like that about you. Do you want to know my name?"

"Only if you really want to tell me."

Pit Bull tilted his head back and barked with laughter again. His chin and neck were incredibly smooth, as though he'd had a professional shave that very morning. George felt a slight loosening of the grip on his hand and almost considered trying to pull away and make a run for it.

"George, I like you, and I am going to tell you my name so that we're on a first-name basis. It's Donnie Jenks, and I hail from the state of Georgia, and I can always tell when someone is lying to me, and you haven't been lying to me, at least not since that bullshit session with which we started our friendship. So if you see Jane, you can tell her that Donnie Jenks is in town. Will you do that?"

"I don't plan on seeing her, but yes, I will if I do. I promise."

"So before I go I want to leave you with something, just so you know that I'm serious."

Donnie Jenks pulled George forward with his right hand so that George's hips spun, then turned his own hips and punched George in the kidney with his left fist. George felt the pain in an instant, a small detonation unleashing its ruin in his lower back. He dropped to the ground, a wave of blackness passing over him as though he were about to pass out.

"Donnie Jenks. J-E-N-K-S," the short man said. "Tell Jane she has one goddamned life left, and it's a short one. You try and help her in any way and I'll shorten your life as well. You remember all that?"

George managed to nod, and the man turned and walked away, loafers crunching on the driveway.

Spit flowed into George's mouth, and he turned his head and vomited violently, continuing to spasm even after his stomach had emptied itself of a distant breakfast and the beer he'd had for lunch. He heard the Dodge start up and drive away. He had enough strength to push himself a few feet over, turn onto the side where he hadn't been punched, and put his head down. He stayed like that for over ten minutes, staring at his own stomach contents on the crushed-shell driveway.

CHAPTER 4

George got back to Boston a little before three. He considered stopping at a hospital on the way back but kept driving. The need to be home in his own neighborhood seemed greater than his need to deal with a potentially ruptured kidney. The nausea and dizziness had passed, but every time he turned the steering wheel to the left it felt as though a small rip in his side was getting larger. He instinctively touched his side to make sure his insides weren't spilling out into the car.

He parked in his garage, tried to smile at Mauricio, the garage attendant, as he took the keys and asked how the Saab was running, then walked the long half block up the steeply inclined street to his building. His place was the minuscule converted attic of a luxurious town house, accessible by a stairwell, built onto the back of the brick building, at the end of a cobblestoned pedestrian walkway that was charming for three seasons of the year but smelled of urine and garbage for most of the summer.

Sitting on the bottom step of the back stairs, exactly where

George had been sitting the previous night, was Liana. She looked pale and nervous, her knees clamped together, an elbow on each knee, her chin on a hand. Next to her was a small black purse, a perfect square of well-worn leather.

"What the fuck are you doing here?" George asked.

"Look, I'm sorry, I—"

"Fuck off, please. Go away," George said and maneuvered around her.

"Look. I can explain. I tried to call you, but you'd left the bar. My friend came back with my car."

"Why didn't you stay there and wait for me? You knew I was coming to you." George kept walking up the stairs gingerly, trying not to pass out.

"That's what I need to talk with you about. There's someone who's after me, and I think he might have found out where I was."

"His name's not Donnie Jenks, is it?"

Liana took a large intake of breath. "Jesus. Was he there? Are you okay?"

"I'm okay. I just . . ." He stopped and turned. Liana was looking back down the alleyway.

"Did he follow you here?" she asked.

It was a possibility that hadn't crossed his mind. "I don't know. Maybe. He left before me, but I guess that doesn't mean anything. For all I know, he's on his way here right now. You should probably leave." He looked down at Liana, who seemed small and frail, her shoulders impossibly narrow.

"Did he hurt you? You're hurt. I can tell." She took two steps up toward George and put a hand on his arm. "What can I do?"

"I want you to leave here, that's what you can do. I've been beat up three times in my life, and each time it was by someone you knew. Please just leave." He continued up the stairs, and she followed him. George felt her presence behind him, and it made him want to lash out backward with a fist. The encounter with Donnie had shaken whatever courage George felt he had. He was suddenly grimly aware of his own cowardice and felt that after the shock wore off he was probably going to have a good long cry. He didn't feel good about it, but he also felt lucky to be alive and longed to be back in his apartment alone.

His hand trembled as he put the key into the lock. Liana was right behind him now, her voice pleading. "George, I need a favor. I'm really sorry that I'm asking you, but you are the only one I can ask."

He knew instinctively that turning around was the worst thing to do, but he turned anyway, looking in the general direction of her face, avoiding her eyes that shone wetly under the high sun. Her eyebrows were raised a fraction, her mouth set in a worried half frown. "It's one favor, and it's going to get rid of Donnie Jenks for good, and I promise that it won't be dangerous for you."

He looked at her hairline and felt the muscles in his face contract.

"Please," she said, and the sound of her voice in the echo chamber of his stairwell reminded him so much of the girl she had been, eighteen and unsophisticated, when they had first met.

"If I let you in, and if I think for one moment that one of your friends is going to show up here, I'm calling the police."

"That's fine. They won't come here."

He went through the door and left it open behind him.

She followed, and George heard the oily click of the door

latching shut. They both stepped into the apartment, George's home for over ten years. It had slanted ceilings with heavy beams, and the architect who had converted the space had put in large skylights and a modern kitchen. It was hot in the summer and cold in the winter, but George loved it regardless. He'd lined the largest walls with bookcases and bought a few good pieces of midcentury furniture, all of which had been shredded and scratched by Nora, his fifteen-year-old Maine coon cat.

"You always liked books," Liana said, casting her eyes across the apartment.

George scratched Nora's chin, then went into the bathroom, where he took four ibuprofens and swallowed them down with water directly from the tap. He exited the bathroom to find Liana standing in the middle of his living room, almost dreamily gazing up at the skylights. *Liana Decter is in my apartment,* he thought to himself. *She's real again. She's in my life.*

"Can I get you something?"

"A glass of water. And, George, thank you for letting me in. I know that wasn't easy for you."

George got two waters, then sat in an upholstered chair while Liana perched on the edge of the low couch, her back rigid, her glass of water on the tile-topped coffee table. "I never would have let you go to that place if I'd thought that Donnie might find it. I hope you know that."

"I don't know anything." George took a long sip of his water and wished he'd gotten himself a beer instead. He positioned his body in such a way that he felt the least pain.

"I owe you an explanation. I know that. I'll tell you everything, but I want you to believe me when I tell you that I never intended for you to get hurt. Tell me about Donnie."

George told her about the encounter, all the details, including how scared he had been and the information he had offered up.

"I'm sorry," she said.

"Now you can tell me why he's after you. You owe me that."

She drank the remainder of her water, and George watched her pale throat move. In the clear light of George's apartment, she looked more beautiful than she had the night before. She wore a navy blue pencil skirt with a wide leather belt; her tucked-in blouse had small black polka dots. Her legs, unlike her face, were tanned to a honey brown color. Her hair was pulled back by a clip, and her face looked freshly scrubbed and clean of makeup. The only sign of stress was a dark smudge under each eye. "Can I have more water?" she asked.

George rose. "Do you want a beer instead? I'm going to have one."

"Sure," she said, and George remembered that that was how they'd met. Over a beer. He almost said something, but stopped himself. If anyone was going to get sentimental first, it wasn't going to be him.

He pulled two bottles of Newcastle from the fridge, popped their caps, and returned to the living room. He gave Liana her beer and sat back down. Nora scratched at the leg of his chair, then leapt up and into his lap, purring. She settled in and eyed the guest. She was a cat that had always been skeptical about other females.

Liana took a sip of her beer, licked the foam off her upper lip, leaned back a fraction on the couch. "Can I put my feet up?" she asked.

"Sure," George said and watched as she leaned over to unstrap her sandals. Her blouse fell open, providing a brief glimpse of a pale breast cupped in a simple white bra. She straightened up, pulling her legs up onto the couch, her knees bent, her feet tucked up close to her bottom, and leaned against the arm of the couch. For George, it was like hearing a song he knew every note of but hadn't heard for twenty years. This was the way Liana sat. He'd seen it a hundred times in her dormitory room that freshman year of college. How could something be so familiar and so forgotten at the same time? As though reading his mind, Liana said, "Like old times."

"I guess," George replied.

After another sip of her beer, Liana spoke. "Donnie Jenks has been hired to find me. He was hired by a man named Gerald MacLean. He owns a furniture business called MacLean's, primarily in the South. He's one of those guys who does his own commercials. But it's all a front, at least I'm ninety percent sure it's all a front. He has way too much cash coming and going. I know he operates offshore gambling sites, and I also know that he manages a fairly shady investor group. Anyway, he's worth a lot of money. I was his personal assistant for about a year. In Atlanta, where his corporate headquarters are. I was also his girlfriend."

"And he was married."

"Was married, is married, but his wife is sick. She's young, much younger than him, but she'll probably die, if she hasn't already. She has pancreatic cancer. She's his second wife, and Gerry made it very clear to me that he wasn't going to make me his third. It was a bit of a blow."

"You expected to be?"

"Honestly, I didn't. I just didn't expect to be tossed aside so easily. I didn't harbor illusions that we were some great love, but I also thought I was a little more than a paid mistress. Maybe it was just pride on my part. As you can imagine better than most, I haven't exactly been living a legal life for the past twenty years. When I first met Gerry, all I saw was a rich old man. I wasn't living in America then, and he gave me an opportunity to come back here and live. He didn't ask for proof that I was who he thought I was, and he paid me under the table, and everything was basically copasetic.

"I learned a lot about his business, discovered that he was making the majority of his money operating as a feeder fund for an unregulated outfit in New York. He attracts investors from the Atlanta area and offers some ridiculous rate of return. The money's funneled back to New York, and MacLean makes a commission on every sale. It's an old-school Ponzi scheme, I'm sure of it. The marks think they're investing in the gambling websites that are operated down in the Caribbean. I don't know exactly how it all works, but some of it's legitimate and some of it's not. The gambling sites are real, but I don't know how much money they make. I heard Gerry talking once with someone from New York, about how they needed new money or the house would crash. It's all a pyramid, but it's made MacLean rich. And there's cash around, so I assume that very little of his profits are being reported. He paid me in cash. Obviously I was off the books. But he did get tired of me, and one night he got drunk and started crying about his wife, and that's when he told me that as soon as his wife died he wanted me gone as well. Out of his company and out of his bed. Like I said, it was a blow."

"So what did you do?"

Liana fingered the hem of her skirt. "I stole his money. It

wasn't particularly hard. He was always sending cash down to some bank in the islands. So all I did was wait for a particularly big cash shipment, and I took it. It was half a million dollars."

"You thought you'd get away with it?" George asked.

"I didn't think he wouldn't notice, if that's what you mean. I just thought he wouldn't necessarily care. It seemed a small price to pay to give him what he already wanted—me out of his life. And I figured the money was not quite enough for him to cause a stink, but I guess I was wrong. I guess I pissed him off. He sent Donnie after me. I didn't even know he knew people like that, although that was probably naïveté on my part."

"How did you find out about Donnie?"

"After I took the money, I went to the middle of nowhere in Connecticut, found a motel that would take cash, and just laid low for a while. I have no idea how he found me. I was eating dinner at a casino one night, sitting at the bar, and he sat down two stools away from me, started making small talk. I thought he was just some creepy guy, but I let him buy me a drink, and then in the middle of our casual conversation he began calling me by name."

"Jane, right?"

"That's right. That's been my name for a while actually. What do you think?"

"It fits you."

"Plain Jane."

"I was thinking more of Jane Doe."

She twisted the bottle of beer in her hands. "Where was I? Oh, Donnie Jenks at Mohegan. After he used my name, he moved over and told me that he'd been hired to get the money back, and that he'd been given carte blanche to deal out any punishment he saw fit. He told me he'd decided to kill me, but he thought it would be more fun if he gave me a fighting chance. He kept smiling. It was all I could do not to wet my pants. I don't scare easily, but he's pretty scary."

"He kept smiling at me too today."

"His signature move, I guess." She bit her lower lip. "Again, George, I'm sorry about that."

"He didn't try and shake your hand, did he?"

"He did actually. When he left the bar, he took my hand and kissed the back of it, said how glad he was to have met me and how we'd meet again real soon, and then he left."

"What did you do?"

"I somehow got up enough courage to go back to my motel in my taxi and grab my stuff. He'd been there. Not that anything was disturbed, but I could tell. I'd been smart enough to not leave any money there, which was probably the reason I survived that particular night."

"Where was the money?"

"It sounds hokey, I know, but I'd stashed it at a storage locker at the Hartford train station. Obviously, when Donnie searched my motel room and didn't find the money, he decided to approach me at the bar, try and scare me into making a mistake. I realized he wasn't going to kill me till he knew where the money was, but even knowing that, the five minutes it took for me to pack my bags and check out and get back to the taxi were the longest five minutes of my life. I was so sure he'd come out of the shadows and slit my throat. But he didn't. The cabbie took me all the way to New Haven. I was sure I'd been followed. I walked into a downtown hotel, then walked out the delivery entrance and caught another cab. I did this enough times to finally feel like

I must have shaken him. Then I got a bus to Hartford, got my money, and bought a car with cash. I hoisted a Delaware plate. I don't know how he tracked me to Connecticut, and now I don't really know how he tracked me here to Boston. It's almost like he can smell me or something. I'm actually scared. And I'm tired.

"So I'm going to give up, not something I've done very often in my life. Gerry MacLean has a house near here, just outside Boston—it's where his wife is getting hospice care. I called someone I used to work with, and he said he's here this weekend, that he's been here pretty much full-time now that his wife is hanging by a thread.

"So I'm going to return the money, and I'm going to beg for forgiveness. It's the only way out of this."

"That's why you're here."

"That's why I'm here. I still can't believe Donnie was in New Essex this morning. You didn't see anyone else?"

"Just him. Who's your friend that you're staying with?"

"She's more of an acquaintance than a friend. She let me know about the cottage. I liked it because it was hidden and out of the way. She's also the one who borrowed my car, but when she came back this morning, right after I'd called you, she was pretty sure that she'd been followed. I got scared, tried to call you at the bar, gave up, and drove here to Boston. I thought I was probably being paranoid, but it turns out I wasn't."

"And why did you want to see me?"

Liana finished her beer, then put the bottle down with a hollow clink. "I need a favor."

"You want me to come with you to deliver the money," George said, guessing.

"No, I want you to deliver the money for me. I don't want to see Gerry at all. I don't know how he'd react. But if you brought the money, pleaded my case. . . ."

"And you don't want to give the money to Donnie?"

"No. God, no. He's already told me he plans on killing me. It's not just about the money with him—it's about punishment. That's why I want you to take the money to MacLean, ask him for forgiveness, ask him to call Donnie off."

"What makes you think MacLean would be any more pleased to see me than he would to see you?"

"He doesn't know you. It would be like a business arrangement. Please believe me that I wouldn't ask if I thought it was remotely dangerous. Gerry's an old man. He's not a danger to anyone, but if he saw me, if he saw me coming to him with the money, I don't know what his reaction would be. I clearly got under his skin. It would be so much better coming from someone else."

George hesitated, studied a fingernail.

"I'd pay you," Liana continued. "The money's already short, so what's another ten thousand dollars?"

"If I do this for you, I wouldn't be doing it for any money."

"The last thing in the world you owe me is a favor. If you do this, I'd insist you take the money. Otherwise, I'd feel way too indebted."

"I'm going to need to think about this," George said.

"I understand. And I'll understand if you say no."

"Can I ask you one more thing?"

"You can ask me anything."

"Why me? Am I the only person you know in Boston?"

"There's my friend with the cottage, but I'd rather return the money myself than send her. She's the only person I know, besides you. It's funny. I've never been to Massachusetts before, but it's a place I've been thinking about ever since you and I were together. Freshman year. I've always imagined it as this special place. I guess I built it up, the way I've built up what we had over the years. When I decided to come here, to return the money to MacLean, I knew I had to find you. Somehow I knew you'd still be here."

"I didn't get very far."

"What do you mean?"

"I mean in life. I grew up outside of this city. I've spent almost my entire life here."

"We've led pretty different lives."

"I can imagine."

There was a brief silence. George felt one cold trickle of sweat slide down his ribs. He watched as Liana turned her head, looking around his apartment. He wished it was a little bit cleaner. "You've always lived alone?" she asked. She slid her leg out from under her bottom and placed her bare foot on the hardwood floor.

"Pretty much. I lived with a girlfriend in San Francisco. Right after college. It didn't last long, and I came back here. I'm sure I'll die here too."

"Not too soon, I hope." Liana pinched her blouse at her shoulder blade and pulled it slightly back, then tugged the blouse flat again. It was scoop-necked and low-cut, enough so that George could see the swell of her breasts; there was a faint circular pattern of freckles just under her left collarbone that George remembered. "George, there's one more thing I want to say before you decide. When I'm out of this mess, whether you've helped or not, I would like to spend some time with you. The way we left things . . . it has always bothered me. I can't tell you how much I think about Mather College. It's become a little bit of an obsession with me."

"Okay," George said, his voice sounding a little hoarse. He knew he was going to say yes, that he was going to help Liana return the money. He'd known he was going to say yes to Liana even before he knew what it was that she wanted. He'd known the moment he'd let her into his apartment. He also knew that Liana was as trustworthy as a startled snake, a fact that would have been wildly obvious to any five-year-old, but the thought of what Donnie Jenks would do to her had brought out his protective side. He felt alive, his senses heightened. He did not know what was going to happen next. It was an unusual state to be in. And a welcome one.

Knowing that he was going to say yes, George still felt the need to at least delay his answer. He excused himself and went to his bathroom, where he found he wasn't entirely prepared for the sight of blood in his urine. His knees went weak, and even though he'd read enough pulp novels to know that it was a side effect of getting punched in the kidneys, the sight of the pinkish stream of piss set off another wave of nausea. He nearly threw up again.

"What do you know about kidney ruptures?" he asked Liana when he returned to the living room. His forehead was dotted with sweat.

"Peeing blood?"

"Yeah."

"I have a friend who's a nurse. I can call her if you'd like."

"That would be great, and Liana—"

"Yes?"

"I'll do it. I'll bring the money to MacLean and see if I can get him off your back."

She stood, a wide smile on her face, and George felt for a moment like she was going to come across the room and hug him. She didn't, but she did say, "My hero."

CHAPTER 5

That first night of college, when George went back to his dormitory room to frantically flip through the freshman guide, the name he had been looking for was not Liana Decter, but Audrey Beck. That was the name she had given him when they met at the keg party in McAvoy, that was the name that he found in the orientation guide, that was the name of the girl he fell in love with that fall, and that was the name that had filled his head like a mantra during the longest Christmas break he had ever known.

Audrey.

That January of freshman year, George had taken the train back to school from Massachusetts. His father had dropped him off at South Station, where he'd had just enough time to buy a pack of Camels before racing to catch his train. He hadn't smoked over Christmas break, so as not to upset his parents, and when he finally smoked one—on the platform at New Haven Station during the ten-minute break when the train was switched from diesel to electric—the nicotine had spread through his body like

*wildfire. He felt vaguely ill but was determined to finish the ciga-
rette anyway. The dizzying punch of the smoke reminded him of
his life at college.*

*It was early dusk, and flakes of snow hovered and spun in the
dry air. He'd left his jacket on the train, and the hand that wasn't
cupping his cigarette was jammed into his jeans pocket for warmth.
He looked up and down the platform to see if he recognized anyone;
it was the day before the second semester began, and he assumed
that any train on the Northeast Corridor would be full of fellow
students, other members of his class. But no one looked familiar.
He took one last lungful and ground the butt out under his heel.*

*Back on board he cracked his book—Washington Square—
but couldn't concentrate. He was playing and replaying variations
of what it would be like to see Audrey again. She'd mentioned to
him that maybe she would call him over break, but she hadn't, and
part of him had begun to feel that he'd imagined her, that he'd
imagined his entire first semester of college.*

*To get to his dormitory from the train station he splurged on a
cab, one from a line that idled and spilled plumes of exhaust into
the whipping air. The cab took him the mile and a half down empty
city streets, up Asylum Hill to where Mather College perched, a
steep stronghold of brick and slate, a two-hundred-year-old private
university of just under one thousand students.*

*All the dormitories had combination locks, and as George ap-
proached the double doors of North Hall, the combination he'd
memorized the previous semester went out of him like air from
a balloon. He looked around for passersby to ask but saw no one.
Experimentally, he pressed his index finger to the metal clock-dial
of numbers, and the combination came to him, as if by instinct.
Four, three, one, two.*

His roommate was a six-and-a-half-foot kid from Chicago named Kevin Fitzgerald, whose father was a florid-faced giant of a man who worked in city politics. Kevin's own face, fat and with a chin the size of half a loaf of bread, was destined to be as red as his father's one day, just as his frame was destined to support a basketball-size gut. Kevin, at eighteen, was less interested in politics than in sports, beer, and The Late Show with David Letterman. *George got along with Kevin as well as any two freshmen with no shared interests could get along.*

Swinging open his door, he stepped into his empty dorm room, a charmless square of painted concrete and linoleum floor. Two single beds lined either side of the room, and one window bridged the gap between two pressed-wood desks. Kevin, not there, had clearly gotten back earlier—his bed was stacked with freshly laundered clothes, a basketball still in its box, and a humidifier.

After sliding his bag of clothes to the foot of his bed, George unbuttoned his coat then picked up the phone to dial Audrey's room. After four rings, the machine clicked on: Audrey's voice and the same message from the previous semester. He hung up, lay back on his bed, and lit a cigarette. He heard footsteps from outside in the hallway, then voices—one he recognized as Grant from down the hall. He assumed that this hall's freshmen—there were seven altogether—were gathered in one of two quads at the south end.

Normally, he would have made his way down there, flopped on one of the three cheaply made sofas in the common room, done a bong hit, and shared Christmas war stories. But he desperately wanted to reach Audrey first and make a plan to see her later that night.

"Foss, you in there?" came a yell, accompanied by a pounding on the door.

"No," he yelled back and dialed Audrey's number again.

"Get your ass down to the quad."

There was no answer again.

He shed his jacket, pocketed his cigarettes, and followed the pungent smell of pot to the quad. The door was open, and all four roommates were in there, plus Tommy Tisdale, another freshman from two floors up.

"Foss."

"Fossy."

"Look what Cho got for Christmas." Grant held up a baggie of bright green pot.

Cho was currently taking a long, bubbling pull from Holmes, his two-foot purple bong. The Dead noodled from the stereo.

After a bong hit and a lukewarm can of Stroh's, George returned to his room and called again.

"Hello." It was Audrey's roommate, Emily, her voice clipped and familiar.

"Hey, Emily. It's George. How was your break?"

"Hey, George. It was . . . Where are you calling from?"

"North Hall. What's wrong? You sound weird."

"Did you hear? Have you heard about Audrey?"

George's stomach twisted, and his mind leapt to images of Audrey with a new boyfriend, Audrey fornicating with the entire senior class. "No. What's going on? Is she there with you?"

Emily took a long, audible breath. "I don't think I'm supposed to be talking to you about this."

"About what? You're freaking me out, Em."

"Apparently . . . I just found this out . . . she's dead, George. That's what I heard."

George walked, jacketless, to Audrey's dormitory, Barnard Hall, *and encountered a surreal scene. Barnard was one of the newer dorms, built exclusively for freshman women, and a large common area had been constructed on the first floor so that all the dorm rooms were on the second floor or above. Rounding a short, flyer-plastered hallway, he entered a high-ceilinged fluorescent-lit room, filled with couches and soft chairs, to a hubbub of female voices. The space was crammed with at least two dozen freshman girls, many of whom were crying.*

Their faces turned to George; they were like pale balloons that bobbed, indistinguishable from one another. He scanned them, unable to stop himself from looking for Audrey, trying to pick her features out—hair the color of wet hay, dark eyebrows, long neck, and slim shoulders. One of the balloons floated toward him. It was Emily, preppy, snobbish Emily, mouthing words and putting her arms out as if to hug him.

She gripped his elbow, and he felt like a pinned butterfly, trapped between her terrifying presence and the invisible wall behind him that kept him from bolting back the way he had come. She said, "Join us," and then he knew it was real. Audrey wasn't coming back.

T*he following day George answered his ringing telephone at five minutes past nine.*

"Is this George Foss?"

"Yes."

"Hi, George, it's Marlene Simpson. I'm dean of students."

"I know."

"I'm afraid I have some bad news for you."

"I heard."

"You heard about Audrey Beck?"

"I heard from her roommate, Emily. Plus everyone on campus knows."

After agreeing to join the throng at Barnard Hall the day before, George had spent a disorienting hour among the girls, some of whom seemed genuinely upset and some of whom seemed to be enjoying the dramatics, like vultures jockeying near a fresh kill.

It turned out that Emily had received a call at her home in upstate New York the previous morning. It had been the president of the college, and he had told her that Audrey Beck was dead, apparently by suicide. She had been found in her parents' garage, the car still running, asphyxiated.

Audrey's friends and acquaintances all had the same questions for George. Did you have any idea? Why did she do it? Did you speak with her over break?

He'd answered their questions as best he could, preferring the mechanics of talking to the mechanics of thinking. One of the girls, a rectangular brunette with a long, thin chin, had brought some terrible scrapbook she'd made of her first semester at college. There were pictures in it, but none of Audrey, although some of the girls thought they could pick out her sleeve in a party shot, the back of her head from a shot in a crowded dorm room. George noted the absence of photographs because he didn't have any of her either, and already, four weeks after he'd last seen her, he was starting to worry that he'd forgotten what she looked like.

Later, Emily had walked George back to North Hall. He'd been relieved to enter his room to the beery snores of Kevin, who had been half in love with Audrey himself. George had no intention of waking Kevin up and going over it one more time.

"I'd like to meet with you this morning," the dean of students said. "Would ten o'clock work?"

"Okay."

"Do you know where my office is?"

She told him, and at ten o'clock George was there, having avoided anyone from his hall. He hadn't been able to bear the idea of going to the dining hall, knowing that all conversations would be about Audrey and all eyes would be on him, so he'd bought a cup of coffee at a convenience store just outside of school limits.

He'd also managed to avoid Kevin, who had probably been in the shower when the dean called. He'd learn soon enough.

Dean Simpson's office had windows that faced the main quad of the campus, a slanting frost-bitten lawn split by a line of elms. It was still cold that morning, but there was not a cloud in the sky, and patches of snow and ice glittered from all around the campus. Bundled-up students crossed the quad, mostly in pairs.

"I've asked Jim Feldman to drop by in a little bit. He's one of our counselors, and he'd like to make an appointment to see you. We can't require you to see him, but we'd all be relieved . . . we'd like it if you did. We all know how close you were to Audrey."

George was unclear on who the "we" was, or how the college knew anything at all about his relationship with Audrey, but he simply nodded, then said, "Uh, sure. I'll talk with him."

Dean Simpson was somewhere in her fifties, and just tall enough to not be considered dwarf-size. She wore a purple sweater decorated with silver thread. A cloud of gray hair billowed around her head and shoulders.

"Good. This is such a shock to us all. We're just now receiving details from Florida, and our primary concern is that those who were closest to Audrey remain safe. We'd like you to stay here with *us at Mather for this semester and continue your classes, but we understand if you would find that hard. That's what Jim would like to talk with you about."*

"Okay." He'd barely thought about his immediate plans. The prospect of leaving Mather to mourn was horrific, until it was over-taken by the more horrific thought of staying at Mather without Audrey.

"Also, while I have you here, I was wondering what you could tell me about Audrey's other friends. We've spoken to Emily of course, as you know, and there's been contact made with some of the other girls in Barnard, but we know how traumatizing some-thing like this can be, and we don't want anyone to feel like it's something they have to get through on their own."

George nodded, wondering when Jim Feldman was going to drop by. The bright sun pulsed against the window, and a clock audibly clicked in the office. "I don't know. Sorry," he said, already forgetting what it was he didn't know.

"And you don't have to think about this now, but it would make sense to have some kind of memorial service for her here at Mather. I was hoping you'd agree that that is a good idea."

George shrugged his shoulders and tried to smile.

The dean jutted out her lower lip and tilted her head. "Maybe now would be a good time to call in Jim."

"Okay."

She picked up her phone, and in less than thirty seconds Jim Feldman knocked once on the door and pushed it open. He shook George's hand, placing his free one on his shoulder and squeezing. The dean excused herself from her own office and left them alone.

Two hours later, George was by himself in his room when he heard the unmistakable clop-slap of Kevin's footsteps in the hall

outside. It was early afternoon, and he had yet to see his room-
mate since his return from Boston. The door swung open, and
Kevin swayed in its frame, already drunk; a twelve-pack of Genesee
Cream Ale dangled in one of his ungloved hands.

"Motherfucker," he said. "You have anything to do with this,
I swear . . ." He took two rapid, unsteady strides across the room
and grabbed George by his shirt, pulling upward and ripping out
a button.

"Jesus, Kevin. What the fuck?"

"You break up with her?" Kevin pulled on George's shirt again,
and the collar ripped.

"What are you talking about? No!" George grabbed Kevin's
wrist with both hands in an attempt to pry him loose.

Kevin, his eyes red from alcohol and crying, held on to George's
shirt, and for the first time since he had heard the previous evening,
George began to cry, pledging to Kevin that he'd had nothing to do
with Audrey killing herself.

Kevin settled down and offered George a Genesee. They drank
together, silent through some of the beers and talking through some
of them. It got darker outside, but they didn't turn a light on, and
when people knocked at the door, they didn't answer it.

George hadn't been surprised by Kevin's outburst. He knew that
in his own way Kevin had loved Audrey, but that he would never
have done anything about it. "You were good to her, I think," Kevin
finally said, like a tipsy priest giving absolution. "It wasn't you."

"Thank God for that."

"What are we going to do now?" Kevin said.

"I don't know. My counselor—Jim—wants me to stay in school
for the semester. I don't know if I can."

"Just stay here. Fuck classes. We'll drink beer."

"I don't know if they'll let me do that."

Kevin shrugged.

"I don't know what to do," George said again. In truth, he had formed a plan earlier in the day, when he'd been walking back across campus from his meeting with the dean. The looming towers of brown stone, the brick of the dining hall, the leafless trees, and the huddled students going in and out of the indifferent buildings—all these things were utterly meaningless, almost sickening, with Audrey dead. So he'd decided to pack a small bag and go to Florida. He'd leave early in the morning, walk to the Greyhound bus station, and board the first bus going south. Eventually he'd reach Tampa, and he could visit with Audrey's family and her friends and maybe find out what had happened. Jim the counselor would have called it closure.

"I'm starving," Kevin said.

"Go get food and bring me back some, will ya? The dining hall closes in ten minutes."

Kevin staggered off, and George thought some more about his plan to go to Florida the next day. He wouldn't tell Kevin because he'd want to come too, and this was something George needed to do alone.

Chapter 6

On Sunday, at four in the afternoon, George drove his Saab out of the city for the second time that weekend. Gerald MacLean's house was in Newton, a moneyed suburb just west of Boston. George took Commonwealth Avenue, passing underneath the Citgo sign and past the high walls of Fenway Park. He remembered there was an afternoon game happening against the Rays. If he hadn't run into Liana on Friday night and agreed to this fool's errand, he most likely would have been sitting at his friend Teddy's bar around now, drinking a cold beer and watching the game. He'd be listening to Teddy explain the finer points of why the Red Sox sucked this year, and maybe later he'd call Irene and see what she was doing for dinner, or else he wouldn't call and he'd keep drinking beers and maybe eat Teddy's famous calamari, Rhode Island style, at the bar. But instead, George was driving nearly a half million in cash in a gym bag to a stranger's house.

After George had agreed to help Liana the previous day, she'd called MacLean from George's apartment and set up the transfer of money. He'd tried not to overtly listen as Liana told MacLean she was sending a courier, plus the money, to his house, but it was hard not to overhear everything in an apartment that could fit into half a tennis court. She said something about *most* of the money as opposed to *all* of the money, and George heard her use the word "sorry" at least twice. An agreement was made for the following afternoon. The tone of the dialogue did not sound friendly.

Liana had also called her friend the nurse, who had told her that there was only a small chance that George's kidney was ruptured and that he should keep an eye on the blood in his urine and make sure it was getting better instead of getting worse. George had not felt reassured.

After making her two phone calls, Liana told George that she needed to go get the money and would bring it by his apartment the following morning.

"Where will you sleep tonight?" George had asked, immediately hating himself for raising that question, for sounding like he was coming on to her.

"Not in New Essex. Not with Donnie around. I'll stay in a hotel. I'll figure it out."

"You could stay here. You could stay on the couch."

"I don't think that's a good idea. Donnie knows your name now, which means he knows where you live. In fact, he's probably keeping an eye on this place already."

"Maybe you shouldn't leave here at all."

"No, I'm fine. I've got Donnie all figured out. He's just trying to frighten me into making a mistake, into showing him where the money is. His finder's fee is probably a big chunk of the cash, and there's no way he's going to hurt me till he gets it. When I leave here I can lose him again, go get the money, then lay low till tomorrow. Is there a public place I can meet you tomorrow and hand over the money?"

George had suggested a grocery store on Commonwealth Avenue in Boston, and they'd agreed on a time.

"Is there any way I can reach you if I need to?" George asked.

"There isn't. We'll just have to trust each other. I'll be at the store."

"I'll be there too."

"If I'm not there, then just assume that for whatever reason I thought it was too dangerous. And if you're not there, I'll understand as well. It's a lot to ask."

But George, after another restless night and an aimless, jittery morning, had taken a long shower, shaved, and found something to wear that made him look like a midlevel executive on a casual Friday. He knew it wasn't necessary to dress for his brief role as stolen-money deliverer, but if he was supposed to plead Liana's case, he thought he ought to look presentable. He arrived at the upscale, overpriced grocery store early and wandered the aisles of organic gluten-free products, waiting for Liana. They'd neglected to figure out a specific meeting spot, so when the time came he went to the front of the store, where a number of small booths fronted the tall glass windows that looked out onto a small parking lot. Just as he took a seat he spotted Liana, dressed in the same skirt but a different shirt, casually weaving her way between the parked Priuses toward the entrance. George met her at the automatic doors.

"Come inside with me," she said. She carried a small purse, plus a black gym bag.

"Everything okay?" George asked.

"Fine. I think. If anyone followed me here I didn't notice, and I was looking pretty carefully. Let's sit for a moment."

They sat in one of the booths, and Liana put the gym bag on the laminated table separating them. George felt as though their every move was being scrutinized by everyone within shouting distance.

"There's exactly four hundred and sixty-three thousand dollars in there. Ten thousand of it is on top of the bag wrapped in a newspaper. That's for you to keep. Gerry knows he's only getting four hundred and fifty-three, so don't let him tell you otherwise. You know how to get there?"

"I do. I thought you'd wait to give me money when we met afterward."

"It's up to you, but I trust you."

With one hand on the bag, George hesitated. It was a smaller bag than he'd imagined, but it felt solid, like it was filled with chopped wood instead of paper money. "Why don't you hold on to it? I'd rather not have it in the car when I go to the man's house. It's technically his money."

"That's fine," Liana said, pulling the bag toward her, unzipping it halfway, and pulling out a rolled copy of the *Herald*. George caught a glimpse of stacked green bills and quickly looked around to see if anyone was looking at them. Liana re-zipped the bag and pushed it back toward George.

"Thank you again," she said. "This is a huge relief that you are doing this. I don't think I could bear to see him again."

"And you don't think he'll have the cops there ready to question me?" This thought had been preoccupying George since early morning.

"Not a chance. And if there are police there, then just tell them everything. I don't need you to protect or help me any more than you are already doing. I really don't think anything can go wrong. Just tell the truth and return the money. And if you feel okay about it, then please tell Gerry that I apologize. He won't believe you, but I want him to hear it. In retrospect, I overreacted."

She smiled, and George smiled back. Some of her calmness was rubbing off on George, who'd felt keyed up since morning. "I don't think you overreacted. You're definitely worth half a million dollars."

"You'd think, right?"

Back in the car, George cranked the air conditioner and unbuttoned an extra button on his shirt. He wondered if he'd been foolish about leaving the ten thousand dollars with Liana. It would be so easy for her to take off with it, skip out on their planned rendezvous. But George somehow didn't think so; in fact, he felt the opposite, that holding the money would give Liana an incentive to meet him later. He remembered how she said giving him the money was important to her, that she didn't want to be in his debt.

The four-story brick apartment buildings of Boston slowly transformed into the leafy suburbia and single-family elegance of Newton. MacLean lived up the hill from Nonantum, one of the town's thirteen villages. George took a right on Chestnut Street and wound past the sleepy lawns and faux-Tudor mansions till he found Twitchell. MacLean's was the first gated property he came to. Pulling up to the speaker box, he could see a Georgian mansion squatting on a sloping lawn. George rolled down his window. Somewhere out of sight he could hear the sound of a lawn mower, and he could smell the sharp acidity of cut grass in the thick air.

A tinny female voice from the speaker asked, "Name, please?"

"George Foss."

He waited a moment, and the ornate metal gates began to swing in. He took a deep chest-expanding breath, causing the dull ache in his side to erupt into a sharp twinge. The image of Donnie Jenks rose up in his mind like a shark fin cresting the surface of the sea. Would Donnie be at the house? It seemed possible.

He pulled up next to a landscaping van near the front entrance. He could now see the ride-on mower making a tight circle around a towering maple on the east side of the house. The presence of the gardener made him feel better. If either MacLean or Donnie was planning on burying him in the garden, they wouldn't do it in front of witnesses, would they?

The mansion was brick and trimmed in white, with freshly painted black shutters and a black front door. Before George got a chance to ring the doorbell, the door swung inward soundlessly. A young woman greeted him. She was probably in her midtwenties, wore a tan cotton skirt and a dark blue polo shirt, and had her streaky blond hair tied severely back in a ponytail. George initially wondered if she was MacLean's daughter, but her manner, even the way she opened the door, was the officious clipped style of the professional personal assistant. "Mr. Foss," she said.

"That's me."

"Come in. He's expecting you."

George stepped inside. MacLean's house, from the outside, seemed ostentatious, but it was nothing compared to the opulent

interior. The foyer was easily twice the size of an Olympic swimming pool, an oblong of intricate molding and white marble. A
twisting wooden staircase led to the second-floor balcony. Above
the foyer hung a Chihuly sculpture, twisted tubes of multicol-
ored glass, spreading out like an anemone under the sea. George
had seen one like it at a casino in Vegas. The white walls were
hung with other splashy pieces of art, abstracts in bright neon
colors.

"Chihuly," George said to the assistant and raised his eyes
toward the sculpture. She looked up but didn't seem impressed
by his knowledge of the art world.

"Mr. MacLean will be right down. Wait in here." She led him
to a white doorway a couple of hundred yards of marble away.
"Can I get you anything while you wait?"

"No thanks," he said, and she peeled off silently on espa-
drilles.

George entered the room. It looked like a library, but it had
no books. It was windowless and wood-paneled, with leather furniture and several upright globes, some of which looked genuinely antique. The room was in such a completely different style
from the foyer that George actually turned back to make sure he
hadn't dreamt the previous space. It was unsettling, like walking
through a Miami drug lord's entryway to find yourself in Lord
Wimsey's secret den. Framed maps lined the wall, including one
that was old and yellowed enough to have one of those sea mon-
sters rearing out of the ocean. George was studying it when two
men entered the room.

The first man was older and appeared to be MacLean. He
was a fit-looking man in his sixties with thick white hair that
had recently been given a buzz cut. He wore black pants and

a tucked-in shirt in a red-check pattern. He was a little on the short side, and it was clear that he'd spent his life making up for it by working out. Even at his advanced age, his shoulders looked strong and his stomach was flat. There was nothing distinctive about the way he looked or the way he was dressed except for his belt buckle, which was impossible not to notice—a large glass oval, it held what looked to be a real black scorpion, mounted on yellow felt and framed in silver.

The other man was taller, about George's height but about twice his girth. He was one of those men who, from the waist up, was only marginally overweight, but whose hips spread outward to almost twice George's size. He wore a tent-size pair of khaki pants with a Pawtucket Sox shirt tucked into the elastic waist. His head mirrored his body—thick around the chin and cheeks, then narrowing toward the top. He had black hair parted on the side and wore a perfectly trimmed mustache.

"Money in the bag?" the older man said, jerking his head in the direction of George.

George nodded, held out the bag. The large man came forward, moving in an awkward waddling fashion, and took it from him, then handed it to the older man. "Pat him down, DJ," Mac-Lean said.

The man called DJ turned to George and mimicked stretching out his arms. "Do you mind?" he asked.

George told him he didn't, then held out his arms. DJ quickly patted him along his sides, from his ankles to under his arms. Instead of bending at the waist to reach George's ankles, he went slowly down on one knee, then slowly back up. One of his knees popped audibly, startling George. He wondered if the man was looking for a weapon or a wire. Probably both.

While George was patted down, MacLean placed the gym bag on a side table, unzipped it, and quickly riffled through the stacks of bills. He re-zipped the bag. George thought he heard him sigh.

"He's clean," DJ said to MacLean.

"All right. Thanks. You can leave us alone for a moment."

"Do you want me to take the money?"

"That's okay. I'll deal with it."

DJ left the room and pulled the door closed behind him.

MacLean took a couple of steps toward George, but it was clear that he wasn't going to come all the way forward to shake his hand.

"You're Jane's friend," he said.

"I am."

"That's a precarious position to be in," he said, and one corner of his thin lips went up in a joyless smile. George felt like a tongue-tied child faced with an adult. MacLean sighed again. "Well, have a seat."

George sat on one of the leather chairs. It creaked slightly as he settled in and gave off an acrid smell of floral cleaning product. MacLean sat on the end of a couch, perched very close to its edge, as though he had no intention of staying any longer than he needed to. He placed his hands, palms down, on his knees. His face was pinkish-red under his thatch of white hair, his eyes were slits, and his mouth was virtually lipless. Outside, George could hear the lawn mower shut off, then start again in a high, whining drone.

"I'm sorry, but what is your name again?" MacLean asked.

"It's George Foss. I was briefly in college with Jane, many years ago."

"Okay, George Foss. I'll just assume that's probably not your real name, but I won't nitpick. I'll also assume she's been fucking the living daylights out of you or else you wouldn't be here."

"You can think what you want, but she's an old college friend."

MacLean sniffed, then pinched the bridge of his nose. "Sure. So if you're just an old college friend, what's in it for you?"

"I'm just doing a favor. I figured I was doing you a favor as well. You've got your money back."

"*Some* of my fucking money back."

"Right. And now you'll call off Donnie."

MacLean's thin lips went up again in an involuntary startled smile. "Call off Donnie? Call off Donnie from who? You?"

"No. From Jane. He's been threatening her."

MacLean lowered his brow in confusion. "Who are you talking about? Are you talking about Donnie Jenks? DJ?"

George suddenly felt confused. "The guy you hired to get the money from Jane. I met him yesterday."

"Well, you also met him today. He just patted you down. Donald Jenks. DJ. He's an investigator in my employ. I don't know who the fuck you're talking about."

CHAPTER 7

After a moment, George said, "There's someone else pretending to be Donnie Jenks. I met him yesterday."

"What did he look like?"

George described him.

"He doesn't sound like anyone I know. He's probably just some friend of Jane's, trying to scare you into doing her a favor."

"That doesn't make any sense. It's because of him that she decided to return the money."

MacLean pressed his lips together and squeezed the bridge of his nose again. "Is that what she told you?"

George told him what he knew, about the man's threats to Liana, the way he'd been following her since she'd left Atlanta. "Clearly he knows enough about you to know you hired a man named Donnie Jenks to recover the money, and he's using that name."

MacLean flicked his fingers in a gesture of dismissal. "Either way, it's not my problem. If some gun-for-hire wants to chase down Jane, I'm not going to lose any sleep. Something makes me think Jane's behind it anyhow. I don't know why, but I wouldn't put it past her."

"You got your money back," George said and shifted in his seat. He was ready to go. It had suddenly occurred to him that the miniature assassin going by the name of Donnie Jenks was most likely an employee of MacLean's, an employee MacLean had no intention of owning up to. Someone paid under the table. MacLean was the worst kind of dirty, someone who pretended he wasn't.

MacLean, as though reading George's mind, held up a hand and said, "Look, let me do you a little favor for no good reason. Let me tell you my story about Jane. It probably won't change your mind about her, but I'll feel better." He looked at his watch, a chunky piece of metal that hung loosely on his thin wrist.

George shrugged.

MacLean slid a little farther back into the couch. "As you probably know, I have some money to my name. Not Walmart money, but I've done okay for myself. I've had two wives. The first one died from eclampsia giving birth to my only daughter. That was thirty-seven years ago. My first wife's name was Rebecca, and she had black hair and blue eyes. Raven black hair and eyes that were the palest kind of blue you can imagine. She was like a poem, the most beautiful woman I'd ever seen. I met her on a golf course on a Saturday afternoon in Georgia. She was quite the golfer. Today she would have gone pro and been one of the best lady golfers in the country, but back then she was happy enough to be my wife.

"After she died, I didn't think I would recover, but I did. I met Teresa fifteen years ago at a charity event up here in Boston.

Like my first wife, she has very dark hair and very blue eyes. And like my first wife, she will die before me. She's dying right now in this very house. It's entirely possible that she will die in a matter of days, not weeks. What do you think the probability is that I would have two wives who looked so very much alike and who both met such cruel fates? Don't answer. That's a rhetorical question.

"The answer is that both of them dying young is just another piece of shitty luck, but any psychologist worth his hourly fee would tell you that they looked alike because I am attracted to women with black hair and blue eyes."

He paused, staring at George, challenging him to interrupt his tale. George said nothing.

"Which brings us to Jane Byrne," he continued, then coughed twice after saying her name. "The lady that *you're* interested in. Jane's not her real name of course, but it's all that I have to go on. I met her at the Cockle Bay Resort in Barbados. I was down there on business, and she was working the reception desk. She checked me into my room, and like Rebecca and like Teresa, she had very dark hair, almost black, and very blue eyes. Not only that, but she shared the same haircut that my first wife had. Shoulder length and flipped under a little."

MacLean demonstrated the curve of the hair with his own hand. It was a curiously feminine gesture coming from such a masculine man.

"Now, I know that everything old is new again and old styles come back, but it did remind me of my first wife. Not that I was suspicious at the time. I wasn't of course—why would I be? But I remember thinking that I had just seen the spitting image of my first wife, and no offense to Teresa"—MacLean looked at the ceiling as he said her name—"but I had met the second most beautiful woman I'd ever seen.

"That night I was having a drink in one of the resort's bars with an employee, and Jane came in and sat at the bar and got herself a glass of wine. I assumed it was the end of her shift and she wasn't ready to go home yet. She never looked in my direction, but—and I am to blame for this—I went over and introduced myself. I told myself I just wanted to let her know that she reminded me of my departed wife and that the very sight of her had warmed an old man's heart. I was going to get it off my chest, and then I was going to go back to my table and leave her alone. But she was talkative, asked me questions about my life, about my work. She'd been in Barbados a year and was sick of it, but she loved the weather and she loved the people. We talked till about two or three in the morning. She lived in an apartment building about a quarter mile down the beach, and I walked her home. She was not flirtatious exactly, but she was clearly interested in me. To tell the truth, I thought that she wanted a job in my company, that she saw me as a way out of Barbados.

"I stayed at the resort for about three more days and had a drink with Jane every night. On the last night, I walked her back, I gave her one of my business cards and told her that if she was interested in a position, there might be something for her at my corporate headquarters. I remember she laughed at me, said, 'You think I've been having drinks with you because I thought you could get me a job?' I told her it had crossed my mind and asked her why in fact she was interested in me. Well, she kissed me, and God forgive me, I kissed her back. You won't believe me, but I've had two wives, plus a serious girlfriend in high school and a serious girlfriend in college, and I had never cheated on *any* of them. That's the honest truth."

He stared across at George as though daring him to say otherwise. George scratched an elbow.

"Well, you don't need to hear details about the next part, but I started going down to Barbados every chance I could get, and pretty soon I told Jane that I needed her a lot closer to me than a four-hour flight away, and she agreed to come to Atlanta and work as my personal assistant. This was a couple of years ago. Teresa was seeing a different specialist every week, and each one told us something different, and all the while that was going on I was setting up an apartment for Jane in Atlanta. I felt pretty sordid about it back then, but not as bad as I feel now. I won't say Jane used witchcraft on me, but it was pretty near. I couldn't get enough of her. I'd never felt that way before."

MacLean rubbed the back of his neck, and for a second George thought he might get up and leave the room, but he continued. "It was pretty clear that Teresa was going to die, and there was no doubt in my mind that after a decent period I would ask Jane to become my wife. It seemed like the natural progression of things. Then two things happened." MacLean held up two fingers as though he were giving a presentation. "First, one of the higher-ups at my company came to me and said that he'd been working late one night, and that when he came to see if I was in my office he found Jane going through my file cabinets. He said that he wouldn't have thought twice about it, but that she had one of the drawers completely pulled out and was running her hand along the insides of the cabinet, as though she was looking for something hidden, maybe an envelope, or something stuck to the inside of the cabinet. Here's the rub. I actually did have my office safe's number stuck inside one of my cabinets. I didn't generally use it because I have the numbers up here pretty good"—MacLean tapped his right temple—"but just to be on the safe side, I'd written them out on an envelope label and stuck them inside one of the cabinets. I had no recollection of ever telling Jane anything about hiding away secret stuff like that, but I might have. I didn't know what to make of it. The thing was, if Jane had really wanted the safe combination, I would have gladly given it to her.

"Then came the second part. One night I was staying over at Jane's apartment, and she had to step out for a few things. I won't pretend I wasn't snooping, but I happened to be sitting at her desk, looking at her computer, and I started going through her desk drawer. There wasn't much in it, but there were a few photographs, including a couple of snapshots from Barbados. I knew they were from Barbados because she was right in front of the Cockle Bay. I thought they must be pretty old photographs because (A) they were actual photographs, not something from a computer, and (B) in them Jane had long hair that was kind of a streaky blond. It totally changed her appearance. I flipped the picture over, and it had one of those time stamps on it, with the date, that tells you when the photograph was taken. The picture was from just one month before I'd come down to Barbados, just one month before I'd met Jane.

"And it suddenly all clicked. Jane knew that I had a lot of money and that I was booked to come to the Cockle Bay, and she must have researched me, or Googled me or whatever, and found out I'd had two wives. I'm sure she saw pictures of them, and she changed her hair so that she'd look like my first wife. I could prove none of this, of course, in a court of law, nor did I want to.

But I felt like a fool. I didn't say anything to Jane right away, but I did have her checked out. I hired . . . this person to look into her background, and he found absolutely nothing. And not nothing as in nothing bad, but nothing as in nothing at all. There *was* no Jane Byrne. There were people with that name, of course, but none of them were the woman I knew. There was no past history, nothing to make it seem like she had actually ever existed."

He paused again, and George asked, "What did you do?"

"I didn't go to her with everything I suspected because . . . because I don't know . . . but I did tell her that spending time with Teresa . . . with Teresa dying . . . had changed my mind about my relationship with her and that I needed it to stop. But she knew that I knew, and I saw something go out of her eyes, like she didn't need to pretend anymore. She told me she'd remove herself from my life, and I foolishly decided to not have her escorted from the office that very minute. I told her she could stick around till she figured out what to do next.

"Well, you know the rest. She stole a half million dollars from me and disappeared. I could almost have forgiven her and just let it go—it wasn't that much money—but I kept remembering that black hair and those blue eyes and how much she reminded me of my wife when I first laid eyes on her."

MacLean sucked a rattling breath in through his nose. "Long story short, the cunt played me from the very beginning." A tiny spray of spit flew from his mouth when he swore.

"And that's why you hired Jenks."

MacLean looked up, his slitted eyes bright. "Yes, I asked DJ to look into it, but no, I did not send that little thug after her. I know that's what you're thinking."

"I don't know what to think," George said. "Let's just agree that my returning the money concludes the deal. You'll call off whoever you need to call off and let Jane go on with her life."

MacLean made that rattling sucking sound again, as though he was trying to stop his nose from running. George suddenly wondered if this seemingly confident man was coming apart at the seams. The lean frame and steely eyes suddenly seemed like grief, not health. "I'll tell DJ to stop looking for her, but I want to see Jane herself, just once, face-to-face. She took my money, and now she sends *you* to return *some* of it, and it's just not good enough. I don't want to hurt her, but I do want to see her. Will you tell her that?"

"I'll tell her, but I don't know if she'll do it. I won't make promises for her. She did tell me to tell you she's sorry. I don't know if that helps."

"Just tell her I want to see her, and I want to hear that apology face-to-face. She can't hide forever. I have resources to find out who she really is. She knows that. Now I need for you to leave. I've spent enough time away from my wife today." MacLean stood.

George rose as well and looked across at MacLean. Standing, he seemed smaller, and diminished somehow. George had to stop himself from saying or doing the natural things one says or does with a new acquaintance. He didn't reach across to offer his hand, or tell MacLean he felt bad about his wife. It was an omission that George would think about later, but only because of what would happen to MacLean shortly after he left.

"I can show myself out," George said and walked to the door, letting himself back into the dazzling white of the foyer. Donald Jenks, or DJ, leaned against a wall, looking at his phone. He glanced briefly in George's direction, and George nodded but kept walking, the sound of his shoes echoing as he walked toward the door and pushed his way into the afternoon. His head swam in the sudden harsh light of day, and little blue specks floated in front of his eyes. He felt as if he had just woken from a too-deep afternoon nap.

George stood for a moment before walking to his car, noticing that the landscaping van was no longer parked in front of the house. They must have finished their job, packed up, and left. With the landscapers gone, the world outside of MacLean's house seemed eerily silent. There were no other properties visible through the thick stands of trees. The only sound was the incessant crickety whine of a sweltering August afternoon.

Chapter 8

George and Liana had agreed to meet at the Kowloon, a behemoth of a Chinese restaurant along a gaudy strip of restaurants in Saugus. George took 95 North to Route 1 and pulled into the parking lot a little after six. The asphalt felt soft under his feet, and he was hit by the smell of fryolators and MSG as he walked toward the two-story restaurant. Its front door was between two white Easter Island statues and below an even larger statue, carved in wood. The name of the restaurant shone bright red in the hazy evening, its enormous letters in a faux-Polynesian font.

George walked past the wishing fountain in the lobby, past the old Chinese lady who was trying to hustle him into one of the lesser rooms in the front, and on through into the main dining hall, a space the size of a football field and festooned in Tiki kitsch. It was early on a Sunday evening, but the place was already packed, the buzz of rum-fueled conversation competing with the pumped-in music. George went straight to the bar and sat on one of the low stools that gave him a good view of the main entrance. Liana had told him she'd be at the restaurant between five thirty and six thirty, and they'd agreed to meet at the bar. He'd picked the Kowloon because it was easy to spot along the sprawl of Route 1 and because it was always busy. He also liked their sweet-and-sour shrimp.

He ordered a Zombie from the bartender and waited for Liana. The bar was filling up. Two couples occupied one corner and shared two Scorpion bowls between them. Both of the men had large guts and wore Red Sox caps, and both of the women were leathery and rail-thin with big hair that would have looked cutting-edge in 1985.

His drink came, and the young female bartender, who stood slightly below him in the sunken bar area, said, "You want food too?"

George told her he was waiting for someone and sipped his drink. It wasn't particularly good, but it had a lot of rum in it. He finished half of the concoction with his second sip. He watched the baseball highlights playing out on the suspended television—the Red Sox had blown a three-run lead, then lost in extra innings—but mainly he kept an eye toward the front and wondered if Liana would show at all, and what he would say to her when she did.

He intended to tell her about the two Donnie Jenkses, and how the small man with the gray grin was not in the employ of Gerald MacLean, or at least not according to MacLean. It had occurred to George during his drive from Newton to Saugus that either Liana or MacLean could be pulling the wool over his eyes and that he had no real reason to trust either of them. Did Liana need him for some other reason than just returning the money?

He caught himself chewing on the inside of his cheek and made himself stop. He had done what he said he would do. The money had been delivered, and now he had to deliver MacLean's message to Liana, if she even showed up.

What George wasn't sure about was whether he should tell her the full story as MacLean had related it. He didn't necessarily need, or want, to hear her repudiate MacLean's version of events. Liana was capable of bad things. He knew this not because of any kind of intuition, but because of facts. He knew what she had done twenty years earlier, and would always wonder just how premeditated her actions had been. But if MacLean was telling the truth—and there was little reason to think he wasn't—what Liana had done to MacLean *was* entirely premeditated. She'd gone after a man with money and a sick wife. And he'd fallen for her. It was clear from MacLean's story that part of his downfall came from pure sexual obsession. George empathized. Ever since seeing Liana again two days earlier, he'd been swarmed with memories of their brief relationship. She had been his first sexual partner, and she had also been his best. They had learned everything together. It was as though they had been explorers who came upon undiscovered ruins in a jungle, their eyes the first to see a hidden city. Over the years he'd been back, with other explorers, with tourists, but it had never been the same. Nothing could match the feeling of discovery and compatibility that he had felt with Liana.

George finished his Zombie and ordered a Fog Cutter. He watched the bartender make it. Except for a different glass and some different fruit, it looked pretty much like the Zombie. He checked his watch, and as he did Liana came into the room, spotted him at the bar, and headed his way. She wore a green sleeveless dress, and she swung a small purse at her side as though it were a riding crop.

"How'd it go?" she asked, settling onto her stool and catching the bartender's eye.

"Order your drink first, and I'll tell you all about it."

She ordered a vodka on the rocks. Her cheeks were flushed, as though she'd been racing to meet him. Her forehead shone.

"You want the good news or the bad news first?"

"Good news of course."

"The good news is that I met Donnie Jenks again, and he's not going to hurt you. He looks like he wouldn't hurt a fly. The bad news is that he's not the same guy who threatened me in New Essex."

"What do you mean?" Liana plucked the lemon wedge from the glass's rim, discarded it on the cocktail napkin, and took a swallow of her drink.

"When I arrived at the house, MacLean had me patted down by a very fat man with a small mustache. His name was Donnie Jenks. Whoever threatened you in Connecticut and followed you here is someone else."

George studied Liana for her reaction. She swirled her drink, watching the ice cubes spin. There was a genuine look of confusion in her expression. "You think that Donnie Jenks, the little Donnie Jenks, is not working for MacLean?"

"I don't know what to think. Could he be someone working independently? He found out about the money, pretended he was this Jenks in order to try and wrangle it out of you. You obviously foiled his plan by delivering the money directly back to MacLean."

"It's possible, but I think it's much more likely that he actually is working for MacLean. It sounds just like something he'd do."

"What do you mean?" George asked.

"I mean that he'd never be open about hiring someone like the thug who threatened both of us. So he hired a legitimate private eye to look like he was working within the law, and then secretly hired a genuine money collector. That's the way he operates. He wants to look like a good guy."

"It still doesn't make a lot of sense. Why would this guy use the same name?"

"I don't know." She sipped her drink. "God, I'm tired of this. Did he agree at least to leave me alone?"

"That's the other bad news. MacLean says he's going to keep having Donald Jenks investigate you, that he's going to discover who you really are—his words—unless you agree to meet him face-to-face."

"Okay. Why?"

"I don't know. He didn't really go into it, but as you said, you got under his skin. He doesn't want to let you off the hook."

"But he took the money back?"

"He did."

Liana sighed. "What else did MacLean say? Tell me everything."

George told her the story from the beginning. He described the house and the young woman who let him in the front door, and more about DJ the private detective and how MacLean had him wait in a wood-paneled room that looked like something out of a Sherlock Holmes story. Then George retold MacLean's story about his wives, even telling Liana the part about another employee spotting her looking through his file cabinets.

"Philip Chung," she said. "No surprise there. Thing was, I actually *was* looking for the combination to the safe, but only because I wanted to put some files in there. Gerry would have given me that combination if I'd asked."

"He said the same thing."

George told her the rest of it, pretty much as it happened, except that he left out the part about the dyed hair and how MacLean had begun to believe he had been set up from the beginning. He knew Liana would deny it, and he didn't want to hear the denial. He was worried he wouldn't believe it.

"What did you think of him?" she asked.

"He seemed okay. Clearly not a man to mess with, but he didn't seem like someone who would purposefully do harm to someone else. I think you should trust him, go see him and apologize. Then hopefully he'll just let you continue to live your life."

"What life is that?"

"Could you go back to Barbados?"

"I could, probably, but I'm not sure I want to."

"There must be other places you could return to, other places where you established a life since . . . since I last saw you."

She had been looking down at the dregs of her drink but lifted her eyes to meet his, and he saw a little flash of anger in them that quickly changed into something else. Sadness maybe, or regret.

"I'm so tired of restarting my life every three years. I'm not looking for pity, because I know that everything that has happened to me I caused, but I don't even feel related anymore to the girl I was when we first met. I was trapped, and I did some awful things to get out of that trap, and now I have to be punished for the rest of my life." She laughed a little, her eyes crinkling at the edges. "Okay, obviously I *am* looking for pity. Waah, waah. Poor me. You're seeing me at my absolutely most maudlin, I promise. I'm just so fucking sick of being on the run. These days I constantly wonder what my life would have been like if I'd just turned myself in and gone to prison. Maybe I'd be out now, and my name would be mine."

"You could turn yourself in now," George said.

"I've thought about it. It's just that I can't stomach the thought of returning to Florida, and that is where the trial would be. I've never been back there, you know."

"I wouldn't think you had."

They were quiet for a moment. George wanted to ask questions, wanted to find out exactly how much of what had happened in Florida was intentional and how much was a terrible accident. But he couldn't bring himself to do it. He watched as Liana tipped her glass back and slid an ice cube into her mouth.

"What do you want to do now?" he asked. "I mean, tonight, right now. Do you want to order some food?"

"I'm strangely hungry," she said. "Can we just sit here for a while and drink and order ridiculous appetizers and talk about something other than Gerry MacLean?"

"Sure."

"Maybe you could tell me about your life."

"It's pretty dull stuff."

"You could tell me about that pretty woman you were with at the bar last night. She looked interesting."

"Irene."

"She your girlfriend?"

"On and off. It's complicated." George eyed the bartender over and ordered another round plus one of the combo platters of grease-laden appetizers. While he ordered, Liana pushed her empty glass toward the back of the bar, straightened her back, and pushed her hair behind both ears. She turned and smiled.

They stayed for several hours, switching to Tsingtao beer and ordering only dishes that arrived lit on fire. George told her about the years since college, the work he did at the magazine, the starts and stops of his romantic life. He also told her about the final three years he'd spent at Mather. She remembered everyone. He told her what he knew about Emily and what had happened to all the guys on his floor from freshman year. He was surprised by how much he was able to remember about the minutiae of college life, and he was doubly surprised by how interested in it all Liana seemed to be. He supposed, for her, it was like hearing the story of the life she could have had if things had turned out differently.

When they finally left the windowless restaurant, it was dark and a steady summer rain was battering the outside world. Thunder stirred in the distance. "Where's your car?" George asked.

"About a mile away. That direction."

They ran across the parking lot, now half-empty, and Liana found her Volkswagen. George stood by while she unlocked her door, but before she opened it, she spun and threw herself into his arms and their mouths met. George emptied his mind of all earlier doubts and just concentrated on the feel of her, the wetness of their kisses, the rain soaking his head and his back, while his front, pressed against Liana, stayed warm and dry. He placed a hand on her cheek, and she pulled herself even closer, kissed his neck, and said, "Can we go back to your place?"

"Okay," he said, because there was nothing else he could have said.

"I'm not starting anything."

"I know," George said.

She pulled away and got into the front seat of her car. "I'm soaked," she said, pushing tangles of wet hair away from her face. "Do you need to follow me in the car?"

"I can figure it out, I think. How long should it take?"

"Half an hour," he said. "I'll see you there."

George walked back to his car. The rain had picked up, sparking whitely off the parked cars and turning the parking lot into a dark shallow lake. Women stood under the Kowloon's awning waiting for their husbands to pick them up.

George tried not to think too much on the drive back toward his apartment. The rain continued its assault, and the Boston drivers, in deference to its power, kept to the speed limits. He fiddled with the radio, found a station on the far left of the dial that was playing Solomon Burke. He shifted wetly in his bucket seat and felt a painful twinge on his right side where he'd been hit in the kidney—when was it? It seemed months ago. Cars moved around the Saab, painting tunnels of light into the deluge, and one of them might have been Liana's, on her way to his apartment. He wasn't convinced she would really show up, but he wasn't convinced she wouldn't either. He wasn't convinced of anything. Maybe MacLean had misread her, maybe all along she'd just wanted a new lease on life and the dyed hair had been a coincidence. She'd stolen his money, but only after he'd betrayed her, only after he'd stopped believing her. And after all, she'd given the money back. George suddenly remembered the money, the ten thousand that Liana had tried to give him earlier in the day. Did she still have it with her? It was a lot of money, and it would make a huge difference in George's life, but thoughts of the money quickly dissolved into thoughts of Liana, the way they had just been kissing and the fact that she was coming back to his place.

One thing gnawed at him, though, and he was trying hard not to think about it. At the Kowloon, Liana had asked him about Irene, about the pretty woman he'd been with Friday night at the bar. She'd said she looked interesting, and for the life of him George couldn't think when Liana would have even seen Irene. Had Liana been watching them the whole night? And if so, why hadn't she approached him? She'd already told him that she came to the bar in hopes of seeing him. Had she wanted him to see her first? Was it all calculated? And if so, why was it so important to have George return the money?

All these thoughts disappeared after he'd parked his car and walked down his alleyway to find Liana waiting for him under the dripping back awning. Without saying a word, they began kissing again. She squeezed both her arms around his lower back, causing a spasm of pain, which he ignored, to rocket through his body. "Upstairs," he said in a hoarse voice.

In the small foyer, with Nora nudging at his ankles, George stripped Liana of all her clothes. Despite the heat of the night, her damp skin was cool and shivery. They moved to the couch. Liana stretched out while he tried to quickly shuck his clothes, their wetness squelching against his skin. Nora had followed them and was now meowing plaintively. George scooped her up, put her in his bedroom, and shut the door. He'd suffer her wrath later, but there were certain things that possessive female house cats should not have to witness.

George came back to the couch. Liana was so much as he had remembered her—her high round breasts tipped by large pink nipples, the shallow dimple of her navel, the extra swell at her hips, an almost imperceptible strawberry birthmark on her right thigh—that he was transported into the mind of the eighteen-year-old virgin who had first seen her naked. Nervous, he stood by her side for a moment, naked and trembling. She met his eye and with her left hand reached up and stroked him while sliding her other hand down between her own legs. Her dark pubic hair was cut shorter than he remembered. She pulled him on top of her and gently bit his ear. A nerve fluttered in his neck. George entered her in one deep slide that caused them both to gasp and arch their backs.

CHAPTER 9

The second time the doorbell chimed, George rolled over across his empty bed and sat up, bleary and confused. There was no sign of Liana. The only evidence that she had spent the night was the knotted disarray of the sheets and the humid smell of sex that still permeated the room. George's watch said it was nine in the morning, and a brief stab of anxiety shot through him. It was a Monday and he needed to be at work. Was that someone from the office calling him? But it wasn't a phone that was sounding. It was the doorbell.

George stood. Maybe Liana had risen early and gone to get breakfast. She must not have taken a key.

Pulling on his robe, he noticed a stack of bills on the center of his bureau. He instinctively touched them with his index finger—the top bill was a fifty—but left them where they were. The subject of the ten-thousand-dollar payment had not come up the previous evening, and George had not thought of it since Liana and he had arrived back at the apartment and their clothes had come off. The doorbell chimed again, and George's stomach flipped a little in fear. The money on the bureau meant that Liana had left. Who was at the door? He walked across the living room, put his hand on the knob, and asked who was there.

"Police" came the muffled answer. A female voice.

George opened the door to a man and a woman. The woman quickly showed a badge that was clipped to her belt. It seemed a redundant gesture since these two, both in suit bottoms and button-up shirts, could only have been cops.

"George Foss?" the woman asked.

"Uh-huh."

"I'm Detective Sergeant Roberta James, and this is my partner Detective John O'Clair. Can we speak with you for a moment? Do you mind if we come in?"

Detective James was as tall as George, somewhere in her late thirties, with light brown skin and short, tightly curled hair. Her face was long with sharp cheekbones. Her partner, O'Clair, was younger but had graying hair. His face was a well-shaved rectangle, his neck overwhelmed by thyroid cartilage. He was bouncing slightly on the balls of his feet.

"I'm sorry. Can I ask you what this is about?"

"I had some questions about your visit to see Mr. Gerald MacLean yesterday afternoon. You did visit Mr. MacLean yesterday afternoon?"

George hesitated half a second, considering the possibility of playing dumb, but it seemed both unnecessary and possibly foolish. "I did, but I don't—"

"We'd just like to ask you some questions."

"I'm confused. I barely know Gerry MacLean. I met him yesterday. . . . Did he ask you to talk to me?"

"Why would he have asked us to talk with you?" Detective James asked the question with the expectant look of a child asking when she could open up a present.

"I'm sorry. No reason. I guess I'm just confused as to why you're here," George said, knowing while he was saying it that he should just shut up and invite the officers in.

"We're here because Gerald MacLean was murdered last night."

She said nothing more, and George knew from the countless episodes of *Law & Order* he'd watched that both of the detectives were studying him for his immediate response to that information. He felt like an actor on the stage who had forgotten his lines. He half-smiled, a wave of inexplicable guilt passing through him. "Where?" he asked.

"Do you mind if we come into your house, Mr. Foss? Or, if you'd be more comfortable, we can go back to the station."

"No, come on in," he said and stepped aside, pulling his robe tighter around his naked frame. He felt exposed all of a sudden, and confused. As the two detectives moved into his living room he glanced through the half-open door into the bathroom, looking for signs of Liana.

The female detective named Roberta James saw him look around. She asked: "Is there someone else in here with you?"

"No," George said, suddenly sure that that was the truth. Liana was long gone. Again.

CHAPTER 10

The bus terminal smelled of bacon grease and stale piss. When he reached the ticket seller, George was told there was a bus in an hour that would take him to DC, and from there he could board another bus that would go directly to Tampa. Audrey lived in Sweetgum, Florida, about an hour south of Tampa.

He sat toward the back, which turned out to be a mistake because the door to the toilet was partially busted and kept flying open and smacking closed again.

His head pulsed from an afternoon and evening spent drinking beer. He'd gotten up early and packed quietly, although there was little chance of waking Kevin, who was snoring like a bear hit with a tranquilizer dart. He'd left a note that said:

Taking off. Don't worry.
I'll call my parents this afternoon.

George pulled a sweater from his bag, folded it several times to use as a pillow, then drifted in and out of troubled sleep all the way to Washington. There was a twenty-minute wait before he had to catch the bus that would go all the way to Florida. He ate half a cheeseburger at McDonald's, then went to a line of pay phones to call his parents, using the calling card they had given him back in September. His dad would be at work, and he was hoping his mom would be having lunch with one of her friends. No such luck—she picked up.

"George, what's wrong? What do you need?"

His was not a family that checked in with one another very often. "Mom, remember I told you about that girl named Audrey Beck?"

"I don't, but I'll take your word for it."

He explained what had happened, eliciting a series of sighs from his mother. "What a waste," she said, as though she had personally known Audrey and her prospects. "But what I'm most concerned about is you, darling. I don't want this to affect your time at college. This should be a happy time for you."

"Don't worry, Mom," he said. He couldn't tell her that he was about to board an overnight bus to Tampa. If the school caught wind of his absence, they would have to notify his parents, but he'd deal with that if it happened.

"Mom, I'll call you in a week. I'll be fine."

"I know you will, George."

For the second leg of his journey, he sat toward the middle of the bus, eating his way through a bag of apples and watching the grim highways of the South go by. He hunted his memory for any signs that Audrey had been suicidal and could find none. He had gotten the sense that she was not entirely happy with her home situation, that it was a part of her life she chose not to speak of, but George hadn't felt that she was deeply unhappy. What could possibly have happened to turn a well-adjusted college freshman into someone desperate enough to take her own life?

He tried to remember every detail of their final moments together. They had taken their last exams on a spit-sleety Thursday morning when half the school had already decamped to their parents' homes. The dining hall that night was not even a quarter full. George and Audrey had eaten together, alone at a table for ten. What had they spoken of? George remembered that they had analyzed the beef Stroganoff on their plates, wondering if it was made up solely of leftovers before the kitchen closed up for over a month. He also remembered annoying Audrey a little by continuing to express his concern that she was planning on driving the entirety of the trip from New England to Florida in two twelve-hour days of driving. George was convinced that it was a dangerous idea, but Audrey insisted that she had done it on her way up and could do it again on her return. Plus, she didn't have enough money for two nights at a motel. George had offered to pay and had even offered to help her with the driving down to Florida, knowing she would say no. In the end, after arguing for a while, Audrey ended the argument the way she always did, by saying, "You can worry all you want, but I'm going to do it." And George had let it go.

They had packed that night, separately in their own rooms, then spent the night in Audrey's, before getting up and parting ways just after dawn. George remembered the damp, frigid air of early morning, the black ice on the sidewalk as he walked Audrey to her silver Ford Escort with the duct-taped bumper. She'd started the car and put the unreliable heater up to maximum, then come out to give him a final hug good-bye. "Be careful," he'd told her, then,

*without meaning to, he'd added, "I love you." The first time he had
spoken those words.*

*"I love you, George," she'd said without hesitating. "We'll see
each other soon."*

*She had looked—George remembered—full of hope. Excited,
almost as though her life had just gotten better and there was much
more of it to come. Or was that simply what George had felt and
he was transposing his own feelings onto Audrey? He kept picking
away at the memories till he felt he couldn't trust them anymore.*

*The bus continued its monotonous journey south. The bright
blue skies and frigid temperatures of New England had turned into
low cloud-cover and bursts of icy rain. Night came. George turned
on his reading light and opened* Washington Square, *but the look
of it, the feel of it, nauseated him. It would always be the book he
was reading when he heard that Audrey was dead. He slid it into
the netting on the back of the seat and never touched it again.*

*Somehow, despite his inability to either read or sleep, morn-
ing arrived, the bus driver announcing that they were still on 95
and had crossed over into Georgia. The hazy fields that bordered
the highway were free of snow, and dull green leaves adorned the
trees. George pressed the palm of his hand to the bus window: it
was cool to the touch, not cold, and the spiderwebs of frost that had
feathered the window the night before had turned to pinpricks of
condensation.*

*At a rest stop, he bought a large coffee in a Styrofoam cup
and two honey-glazed doughnuts. He was actually hungry for the
first time since he'd heard the news about Audrey. Leaning against
the bus and eating the doughnuts, watching a pale sun spread its
warmth across the acre of asphalt that was nearly devoid of cars, he
wondered what he would do when he reached Tampa. He was not*

old enough to rent a car, but he'd extracted a wad of cash from the machine at school, enough to hire a taxi to drive him to the cheapest motel in Sweetgum. From there he'd figure out what to do next. He could call Audrey's parents, ask to meet them. Find out if there was going to be a funeral. Find her friends and talk to them. What had happened to Audrey since she'd left school that would cause her to kill herself? Had she left a note? Was there a reason?

The bus driver flicked her Virginia Slim into a gutter, announced that their break was up. George followed her onto the bus.

T ampa was warm, somewhere in the high sixties under a low white sky. The air smelled like tar and tidal water. One rust-eaten cab was parked outside of the bus station. The driver, a short-looking Latino man, had his elbow out the open window, his head resting on his arm. He looked half-asleep.

"How much to go to Sweetgum?" George asked.

"Why you want to go there?"

"How much would it cost?"

"I don't know. Eighty bucks."

"I'll pay you a flat fee of sixty if you take me to a motel in Sweetgum."

The cab driver looked at his watch. "Okay," he said, and George got into the backseat with his bag. A slow trickle of sweat had begun high up between his shoulder blades. The cab crossed a terrifying bridge that rose high above Tampa Bay. There was cloud break in the distance, and the sun dotted the gray water with a pool of light. Once out of Tampa, the ocean disappeared, and the highway was edged by motel signs higher than the grand palms, pockets of chain restaurants, gas stations, and topless clubs.

Audrey had rarely talked of her life prior to college, but she had spoken about the town she grew up in.

"I'd like to visit," George had said once.

She laughed. "There's nothing to see. We've got a Waffle House and a pawnshop."

"What did you like about it?"

"I liked leaving it. Small-town life and me. Like this." She held her two index fingers three inches apart.

The cab driver took the first exit for Sweetgum and pulled into a motor court that advertised rooms for $29.99 a night. It was between a restaurant called Shoney's and a used-car dealership. Above it loomed a billboard that advertised a place called Billy's that was selling fireworks and oranges a quarter mile down the road.

"You wait here while I make sure they have rooms?"

The driver peered out the passenger-side window at the row of empty parking spaces in front of the vinyl-sided motel. "I think they'll have a room," he said. George paid his sixty dollars and walked across the lot to the front office. It was late afternoon, but still warm, and he realized he'd forgotten to pack a pair of shorts.

The motel took cash up front for two nights. He filled out the card, leaving the information for the car blank.

"No car?" asked the desk clerk, a yellow-skinned old lady with a black tooth.

"No car," George said. "What's the best way to get around Sweetgum?"

"With a car."

"You think I might be able to rent one? I'm not twenty-five."

"That how old you have to be to rent a car?" She laughed. "Try Dan next door. He might lend you one of his tin cans for cash. How old are you anyway?"

"I'm eighteen," he said.

"Well, that's about how old you look too."

His room had beige carpet, a shiny floral bedspread, and poorly papered walls. The front window that overlooked the parking lot and exit ramp was darkened by a grimy venetian blind; the back window was propped open and fitted with an air conditioner, currently turned off. George threw his bag onto the bed, stripped, and showered.

I'm in Audrey's town, *he thought as the water battered at the back of his neck.* Maybe it's all been a mistake, and she is here, still alive, recovering in a hospital. *That thought had been hiding at the back of his mind, a secret hope. As he toweled off, the steam fading from the mirror, he took a look at himself, at the plain brown hair that curled out like wings when it got too long, an unexceptional face, a nose maybe a little too big, a dimple in the chin that made up for it. His eyes were a light brown, the color of grocery bags. It was a face that Audrey had stared into as recently as a few weeks ago. What had she been thinking? And where were those thoughts now? He tried to feel her presence, but could not.*

He dressed in a pair of Levis and a dark green polo shirt with horizontal yellow stripes. The top drawer of the bedside table contained a Gideon Bible and a telephone book. There were two Becks listed in Sweetgum: a C. Beck, and a Sam and Patricia Beck. He guessed Sam and Patricia, lit a cigarette, and dialed their number. A man answered.

"Mr. Beck?"

"Who's this?"

"Hi, it's George Foss. I was a close friend of your daughter's. At Mather. I don't know if she mentioned me . . . ?"

"Maybe to my wife. . . . I don't really know."

"I was so sorry to hear what happened."

"Yep."

"I was wondering . . . I've come down to Florida. . . . I was wondering if I could come and talk with you and your wife?"

"Jesus Christ. Hold on a moment."

He heard Audrey's father yell out, "It's some boyfriend. He wants to come here."

George took a deep breath through his nostrils, then nervously yawned.

"Honey, who's this?" It was a woman's voice, on the line after a click.

"George Foss. I knew your daughter at Mather."

He heard another click, probably Mr. Beck hanging up his end. He pictured Mrs. Beck in her bedroom, a framed picture of Audrey in her lap.

"George, honey, did you come all the way from Connecticut? That's so sweet." She sounded drunk, slurring a little bit on the word "sweet."

"I was wondering if there was going to be a funeral of some kind? Unless I'm too late. . . ."

He heard a sigh from the other end of the line, or else it was the sound of cigarette smoke being exhaled. "There'll be a funeral. There will be. But we want to bury our little girl, and right now they tell us they can't do that. . . . Oh God." Her voice had started to quiver a little on "funeral" and had snapped outright on "little girl."

"I'm sorry," George said. "I probably shouldn't have called."

There was no immediate answer, and he was considering simply hanging up the telephone when Mr. Beck's voice came back on:

"Who's there?"

"It's still me. George Foss."

"Goddammit. What was it you wanted?"

"I'm sorry, sir, I don't really know. I was hoping to attend her funeral, maybe to see someone who might have some insight into what happened, to try and understand." His words were making sounds but not much else, so he changed tack. "I've brought flowers. I was hoping I could bring them by?"

"Sometime tomorrow maybe," Mr. Beck said, after another pause.

"Thank you, sir. I'll come by."

George ended the call and fell back on the bed, exhausted, temples pulsing, shoulders bunched and knotted. He was also hungry, having eaten nothing since two apples at lunchtime. He considered going next door to Shoney's, eating a hamburger, drinking a glass of milk. But the more he considered the effort that would take, the more tired he got. Exhaustion trumped hunger, and he slid beneath the prickly sheets, pulled the spare pillow against his chest, and fell into a long hole of dreamless sleep.

The following morning, after a breakfast of scrambled eggs and grits at Shoney's, George walked across the already glaring asphalt to Dan's Pre-Owned Automobile Emporium.

"What can I do for you this morning?" said a heavyset, pink-cheeked man wearing a tan suit.

Having internally rehearsed his approach over breakfast, George cleared his throat and said, "I'm in a predicament, and I was hoping you might be able to help me."

A thin smile pressed itself onto the man's lips, taking all the blood out of them. "All right, son, I'll hear you out." He wore a shiny purple tie that exactly matched the handkerchief that flopped out of a front suit pocket.

"I'm only eighteen, but I need a car for a couple of days. I'll take any car you have and leave you my parents' credit card. I'm a very good driver. And I can pay you in cash."

The man laughed. "That's a first." He tilted his head back, exhaled sharply through nostrils that were filled with dark hair. "Tell you what. I'll do you one better: my employee took his eleventh sick day of the year today, so I'm in a bind." He spit out the word "employee" as though he were spitting out a piece of gristly steak. "I need to deliver papers and get two sets of signatures, and I need it by noon. If you do that for me, I'll let you have free rein on one of my cars, provided it stays in Manatee County."

"All right," George said. "I don't know my way around here, though."

"Can you read a map, son?"

The car was a vinyl-wood-paneled Buick LeSabre with a steering wheel that pulled to the left. With a map and some written instructions from Dan Thompson, George drove past the cow pastures and subdevelopments of Sweetgum and over the Dahoon River into Chinkapin, a town that at least had what appeared to be a center—several five-story cinder-block buildings stuck in close proximity. He brought papers to an insurance broker whose office was between a pawnshop and a thrift store, and then to a couple in the Seavue Trailer Court for Residents 55 and Over who were purchasing a $575 Dodge for their grandson. Back in Sweetgum, he spotted a florist in a strip mall and bought a $10 bouquet of flowers that he was told would be appropriate for a funeral.

Driving back to the used-car lot with procured signatures in duplicate and fiddling with an air conditioner that made a lot of noise but produced no cold air, George imagined Thompson offering him full-time employment. He'd take it and become a world-class car salesman, the best in the county. He'd live in the motor court and eat every meal at Shoney's, and every day he would deliver flowers to Audrey's grave. His home in Massachusetts, his semester at Mather, would fade into memory as the days and years passed away. George grinned and lit a cigarette off the car lighter, blackly caked with the residue of a thousand lit cigarettes.

Thompson was with a customer, so George placed the paperwork on his desk, then drove the hundred yards to his motel room to change his damp shirt for the last clean item of clothing he had, a short-sleeved pin-striped Oxford.

He took his flowers, already wilting in the heat, and returned to the Buick. He'd studied the map and knew exactly how to get to Audrey's parents' house. He drove about two miles, then spotted the pair of painted coral pillars that welcomed visitors onto Deep Creek Road, a stretch of asphalt recently patched with squirrelly lines of a blacker tar. The houses on Deep Creek Road were mostly two-story dwellings with flowery yards; they looked as though one tiny, shuttered house had been dropped onto another, then painted some tropical color: pink, or aqua, or an occasional neon green.

Number 352 Deep Creek was aqua; its scrubby yard and roof-high palm tree looked like everyone else's. But 352 had a police cruiser parked on its curb.

George pulled behind the cruiser and killed the engine. Walking toward the door, gripping the flowers, he tried hard not to focus on the two-car garage where Audrey spent her final minutes, breathing carbon monoxide.

The door was answered by a policeman in uniform. "You the kid from Mather?" he asked.

"I am."

The policeman, who had blotchy skin and a wispy mustache

and was probably less than five years older than George, jerked his head to the right. "Come in."

George followed him into a living room that was located at the back of the house. An L-shaped couch and two leatherette recliners surrounded an entertainment center with a television the size of a large bureau. The closest recliner was occupied by a tall, skinny man wearing a denim shirt tucked into a pair of jeans. He had pocked skin and the kind of blond hair that was almost white. Mr. Beck. His wife, Audrey's mother, was on the couch. She wore jeans as well, with a black silk blouse tucked into them. A roll of fat, pushed up by the too-tight jeans, was visible under her shirt. Her hair was blond as well, but looked like the color came from a bottle. She was drinking a glass of pink wine.

Next to her was an older man in a nice gray suit. He had silver hair cut short over a scalp that was rubber-ball red. His face looked like it had been punched flat, then squeezed back into normal proportions in a vise. George thought that he might be Audrey's grandfather.

As he stepped into the room, passing the young skinny cop, George held the flowers toward Mrs. Beck, who regarded him with puffy eyes. "Mrs. Beck, I'm so sorry. These are for you."

The man in the suit stood, hoisting himself upright by pushing his right hand against the armrest. He held a mug of coffee in his left. "This him, Robbie?" He was speaking to the uniformed cop.

"Yep."

"You the boyfriend from Mather College?"

With the eyes of the room on him, George felt as though a gesture was needed: a speech about the love he felt for Audrey, or a burst of emotion. Instead, he nodded. Why were the police at the house?

"What's your name?"

"George Foss."

"Uh-huh. I'm Detective Chalfant. This is Officer Wilson. Have a seat. We have some questions."

George sat on the edge of the available recliner. "I'm a little—" he began.

"Don't worry about it," said the plainclothes detective. "I'll explain it all in just one minute. How'd you get down here, son?"

"I took the bus."

"You didn't take the bus all the way from Connecticut to Sweetgum."

"I took the bus to Tampa, then I got a taxi to here, and then I borrowed a car. That's how I got here today."

"So you know some folks in this town? You've been here before?"

"No. Never," George said. "I borrowed the car from Mr. Thompson at Dan's Emporium. I did him some favors, and he let me borrow it. Am I in some kind of trouble?"

"Not at all, George. We're just trying to find out everything we can about what might have happened with Audrey."

George flicked his eyes toward the giant television, the top of which was clustered with framed photographs. Front and center was a picture of Audrey, what looked like a graduation photo. He realized he had never seen a photograph of Audrey before, and without asking, he stood and walked toward the television. As he neared the picture he realized it wasn't Audrey after all, just a girl who looked a little bit like her, a girl with dark blond hair piled up high on top of her head. She was probably about eighteen and might have been pretty after washing off some of the green eye shadow. She had bunched-up lips and dark eyebrows.

George cast his eyes over the other photographs on top of the television. There were several school portraits of the same girl, but there were no photographs of Audrey.

"You can look, George." It was Audrey's mom.

George turned, confused. Detective Chalfant came up behind him and said quietly, "Can you identify that girl in the picture?"

"No. I'm sorry. Should I?"

"Are you sure?" The detective turned back and looked at the family. George's mind raced. Had he come to the wrong house?

Mrs. Beck said, "Oh God," then rocked forward a little and began talking to herself, saying something indiscernible. Mr. Beck stood up and walked across the room with three great strides, then stopped and turned.

"Goddammit," he said.

"I'm sorry," George said. "I'm confused. Who is this a picture of?"

"That's Audrey Beck," the detective said.

CHAPTER 11

A nd what was her name?" Detective Roberta James asked, a ballpoint pen poised over her unfolded notebook.

She had accepted the offer of a seat and was settled on George's couch. Her partner, O'Clair, had chosen to stand. He was still bouncing almost imperceptibly on the balls of his feet, glancing around George's apartment as though looking for rodents.

George had bought some time after inviting them inside by going into his bedroom to pull on a pair of jeans and a T-shirt. While he was there, he took the stack of money that Liana had left behind and tucked it toward the back of his sock drawer. His mind was still scrambled from lack of sleep, from the sudden disappearance of Liana, and from the news that MacLean had been murdered. It was all connected; he knew that much. Either he'd been set up or MacLean had been set up, and Liana had left in the early dawn because she knew that detectives would soon be arriving here, or at least she suspected. Still, as he slowly pulled the T-shirt over his head, he was wondering if, once the questions began, there was a way to protect her while at the same time protecting himself. He knew that he was being foolish, that the only logical move was to squarely face the two detectives and tell them everything he knew, but he couldn't shake the image of Liana's face, only hours earlier, a few inches away from his own in the colorless predawn light, her eyes damp, telling him that her biggest regret in life was having to let him go, having to let that one semester of normalcy go, and, George, despite knowing better, had believed her.

So after he'd told Detective James that he'd been to see MacLean to hand over money as a favor for a friend and she asked him for that friend's name, he looked her in the eye and said:

"Audrey Beck. I knew her from my freshman year of college, but hadn't seen her since." It was a lie with some truth in it. They could check it. They probably would check it. And they'd find out that Audrey Beck was a dead girl from Sweetgum, Florida. But if George was questioned again, he could always claim that that was the name he remembered. He had known her for three months. Her name was Audrey. It was a long time ago.

"So help me get this straight," Detective James said. "This Audrey Beck, whom you hadn't seen in about twenty years, approaches you at a bar and asks you for a favor?"

"I recognized her at the bar, and I approached her. We made plans to meet the following day. She came to my place, here"—George had decided to leave out the situation with the two Donnie Jenkses and the cottage in New Essex—"and that's when she asked me to do her this favor. She had worked for Gerry MacLean, and she had taken some money from him—"

"She'd stolen money from him?"

"That's what she said. It was a complicated story, but she'd worked for him, and they'd been romantically involved, and I guess he dumped her. That's why she took the money. But she'd had second thoughts and wanted to return it. That's why she was in Boston."

"How much money had she stolen?"

"About five hundred thousand dollars."

Detective O'Clair turned in George's direction and sniffed loudly. Detective James raised a single eyebrow. "That's a lot of money," she said. "Did you see it?"

"As I said, I brought it in a gym bag to MacLean. I looked at it briefly but didn't count it. MacLean did."

"And this . . . Audrey Beck . . . came up from *where* to deliver all this money?"

"I'm guessing she came up from Atlanta. That's where Mac-Lean's company is located. I really didn't get a whole lot of personal information from her."

"Well, it sounds to me like you *did* get a whole lot of personal information." The detective smiled, and it changed the contours of her face. Without the smile, her face was a downward-sloping mask, almost wooden in appearance. The wide smile lit up her golden brown eyes, and it had the immediate effect of making George feel bad that he was lying to her. She continued:

"She told you about her affair with a married man and that she was jilted and stole money from him. Why didn't she simply drive out to MacLean's house in Newton and drop the money off? Why did she need you to do it?"

"She said she was scared. She said he had hired someone to get the money back."

"Did she tell you who that someone was?"

"She didn't, but she seemed genuinely scared. I think she also didn't want to face up to MacLean again."

"The way you're telling it, you didn't seem to think it was at all strange that someone you hadn't seen for twenty years shows up out of the blue and asks you to deliver stolen money for her?" She smiled again. It was her weapon of choice. O'Clair stopped bouncing on his feet for a moment and waited for George's answer.

"Sure, I thought it was strange. It's not the type of thing that happens to me every day."

"But you agreed to do it."

"It's been a boring summer."

Detective James made a throaty sound that could have been a cough and could have been a laugh. "Fair enough. Had you been involved, romantically, with Audrey Beck back when you first knew her?"

"Yes," George said.

"Okay. So I wouldn't be too far off in assuming that part of your willingness to perform this errand for someone you barely knew was that you hoped it might lead to more romantic entanglement? Or am I being too coy about this? Was it a quid pro quo?"

"What do you mean?" George asked.

"Audrey Beck spent the night here last night, didn't she?"

George hesitated, just long enough that it would have made no sense to deny it. "She did."

"I thought so. You have the look of a man who didn't get too much sleep last night. You know, I think my partner and I might have actually seen Ms. Beck." She looked up at O'Clair, who shrugged and frowned. "We had to drive around in a couple of circles to find your place this morning, and we passed a woman walking down toward Charles Street. She had a green dress on, dark hair about shoulder length?"

"That sounds like her."

"I thought so. Didn't look like the type of dress one wears early on a Monday morning. So we just missed her." She made a frustrated clicking sound. "Did she tell you where she was going?"

"She left before I woke up. I was surprised she wasn't here."

"And what about my earlier question? Was it a deal? You return the money and she returns the favor? Or did she give you some of the money? I'm assuming that not all of it was returned."

"No, that wasn't it at all. There was no mention of sex. Obviously, the fact that she was an ex-girlfriend and that I was still attracted to her . . . it crossed my mind. Or maybe the better way to put it is that I was hoping."

"You were hoping that by returning the money she would agree to sleep with you."

"No, I was hoping to sleep with her, period. I returned the money as a favor."

"Uh-huh." She looked skeptically at her notebook. As far as George could tell, the only words she had written were Audrey Beck's name. "So I'd like you to tell me about going to see MacLean. Ms. Boyd said you arrived at the house at a quarter to four in the afternoon."

"Is Ms. Boyd the assistant who let me in?"

"Yes. Karin Boyd is also MacLean's niece. She's the one who found the body."

"Where was he killed? What happened?"

"We're trying to find out what happened. That's why we're here to ask you questions. So you arrived at quarter to four?"

"That sounds about right."

"And how long were you there at his house?"

"If I had to guess, I would say I was there about forty-five minutes."

Detective James glanced at her partner, then back at George. "That's close enough to what Ms. Boyd said. Why were you there for that long? I thought you just had to pass over the money."

George told them how MacLean had invited him in, how he'd been patted down, how he'd been left alone with MacLean, who told him his side of the story. He left out the part where MacLean had said that he suspected that Liana had set him up all along, that she had dyed her hair to look like his dead wife, and that she had pursued him from the start down in Barbados. But George did tell them that he had seemed to have a lot of anger toward Liana.

"And he kept the money?" the detective asked.

"Yes. Then he asked me to leave. He mentioned returning to his wife's side. She's sick."

"They think she'll die this afternoon. Apparently they're not telling her what happened to her husband."

"Oh."

"What was your impression of MacLean? Did he seem scared at all?"

"Scared? No. He seemed irritated that he even had to be in the position of accepting his own money back, and he seemed sad about his wife. And I also thought that he seemed like he needed someone to talk with. I was surprised by how much he opened up to me. Can I ask you how he was killed? Was it shortly after I left?"

"Did you notice anyone else around the house? It was Ms. Boyd who let you in, right?"

"There was Ms. Boyd. And the man who patted me down. MacLean called him DJ, I think."

"Donald Jenks. He works for Mr. MacLean. Are you sure those are the only people you saw at the house?"

George thought for a moment, pressing his fingertips against his closed eyes. A delayed hangover from all the rum and beer he'd drunk the night before was beginning to set in, and he was also acutely aware of just how much lying he was doing to the police officers. He had initially planned on telling the truth, except for Liana's real name, and suddenly he had found himself omitting big details, like the fake Donnie Jenks. "There were gardeners," he finally said.

"We know about them."

"But they finished their job and left before I did."

Detective James flipped backward through her notebook. "You sure of that?"

"Yes, I remember coming out of the house, and the van wasn't there anymore."

"The gardeners' van?"

"Right."

Detective James wrote in her notebook. George glanced at her partner, who was still standing, and wondered for a moment if he was a deaf-mute. George hadn't heard him utter a word. "Do you mind if I get myself a glass of water?" he asked into the space between the two police officers.

Detective James told him he could.

"Can I get either of you anything? Water? Orange juice?"

Both declined, Detective James in words and Detective O'Clair with his Zen-like mastery of silence.

George walked unsteadily to his alcove kitchen and poured himself a tall glass of water. He drank it down, refilled it. Before he sat back down, Detective James said, "I just have a couple more questions. Can you tell us what the bag of money looked like, and how much *exactly* was in there?"

"I didn't count it myself, but Audrey said it was four hundred and fifty-three thousand. As I said, MacLean counted it. It was in a black gym bag."

"When you were alone in the car with this money driving out to MacLean's house, you didn't decide to take a look at it?"

"I know what money looks like."

"Or take any of it for yourself?"

"I was trying to do my friend a favor, not get her into any more trouble."

Detective James tilted her head to the side a fraction, as though trying to straighten out a kink in her neck. "Where do you work, George?"

He mentioned the name of the literary magazine, and recognition flickered across her face, as though maybe she'd heard of it sometime far away in the distant past.

"I don't suppose you have contact information for Audrey Beck? An address? A cell-phone number?"

"No, I don't."

Detective James didn't immediately speak, and George drank his water, willing himself to not chug it down. Nora had settled herself on a nearby windowsill next to a neglected spider plant.

"One last thing: do you know someone named Jane Byrne?"

George almost denied it, but caught himself just in time. Of course he would know that Jane Byrne was the name that Liana was going by. It was the only name MacLean would have known, and it was the name that the assistant/niece would have given to the police.

"That was the name MacLean knew her by. I guess she was using a different name when he worked with her."

Detective James smiled and glanced at her partner. "You didn't think to mention that to us?"

"Sorry. I knew her as Audrey Beck, and that's how I think of her."

"And you have a lot of friends who go around changing their names at a whim?"

"No, I don't. Just Audrey. Look, to tell the truth, Audrey might not even be her real name. She was only at Mather College for half a year and never came back. I remember hearing that she got into some trouble down in Florida, that maybe she'd faked her way into college." George didn't know how far the detectives would check into the Audrey Beck/Liana Decter story, if at all, but he figured he should cover himself, if only a little. Obviously, if they decided to go so far as to read the original case reports, his name would come up, and they'd know he'd been lying. He'd deal with that if it happened.

"You'll let us know if you see her again, or if you think of anything that might be helpful."

"Of course," he said.

Before standing up, Detective James slid a card out of her notebook and placed it on the coffee table. George walked both the detectives to the door. James had turned her back to him and was leaving when her partner said, "One more thing, Foss. Don't leave town." His voice was high and nasal, and hearing it for the first time almost made George jump.

"Oh," he said. "Am I a suspect?"

"Yeah, you're a fucking suspect," Detective O'Clair said and smirked from one side of his face.

CHAPTER 12

George called his supervisor at the office to let her know he was running late, then showered and shaved. It seemed surreal to him that it was a workday, a Monday, when he was expected to be at his desk, despite his sudden status as a murder suspect.

It was even more surreal to him when he arrived at his office on the third floor of a converted factory building halfway between the Back Bay and the North End. Darlene, at the front desk, greeted him by uttering a prolonged "Ughhh, huh?" It took George a few perplexing seconds to realize that she was referring to the Red Sox, who had dropped three in a row since Friday.

"Good thing it's a long season," George said as he made his way toward his office.

"Thank God," she said to his retreating back.

The magazine had been shedding jobs for several years but hadn't yet relocated to a smaller office, probably because the landlord, scared of the downtrending market, kept lowering rents and offering incentives for the magazine to stay. For this reason, George's long amble to his south-facing office, passing bare desks and empty meeting rooms, had become increasingly bleak. He had begun work at the magazine less than a year after graduating from Mather College. It was his second postgraduate job; he'd worked at a chain bookstore during the stint in San Francisco when he was living with Rachel, his senior-year girlfriend. That arrangement had lasted only six months, ending when George came home early from work and found Rachel in bed with one of the bartenders from their favorite neighborhood dive.

He'd moved home. His mother had never been a particularly happy woman, but over the years she had become more and more verbal about the disappointments of her life; she felt as though she'd given up a career in the arts for a life as a wife and mother, and now she was left with nothing but an empty nest and a near-silent workaholic husband. She'd joined a potters' group, and George wondered if she was having an affair with one of its members. George's father, unlike his mother, had become noticeably quieter in his later years. He still worked hard, coming home exhausted and red-faced on a nightly basis, settling into his predictable nightly routine of one large drink, dinner, then reading in his study. Despite his father's quiet, unreachable nature, George felt more at ease with him than with his mother. His father was a man who seemed comfortable in his own shoes.

During George's two-month stay, his father had told him, after a rare second scotch and water, that he believed the key to happiness was to find one job and do it as well as possible. He said that his own father had told him the same thing. Be a builder and learn to hit a nail straight and you will never lack for happiness. George's father also confessed that he feared and dreaded his retirement years. It was the most revealing conversation George ever had with his father, and it was a conversation he thought of often, especially after his father had a massive heart attack and died at the age of sixty-five just a few years later.

While home, George scoured the newspapers for job listings, then applied for, and accepted, a position as an administrative assistant in the accounts department of Boston's most prestigious publication. "You were always excellent with numbers," his father opined. His mother was impressed with the magazine's stature in the literary world.

George moved to the city and found an apartment, one floor of a cheap triple-decker in Charlestown, to share with a pair of acquaintances from Mather College. George excelled at his job and was taken under the wing of the magazine's business manager, Arthur Skoot, a man who had never married and who was, at the time of George's arrival, the most senior member of the magazine's staff. Arthur showed George how to do everything, quickly promoted him, and took him out for long semi-boozy lunches. George found the job both satisfying—putting out a magazine on time and on budget was akin to hitting that nail as straight as possible—and also stimulating; he enjoyed the idea of being part of a grand literary and intellectual tradition, even if his job was just to balance the ledger sheets.

The magazine paid for George to take night classes, and in a few years he received his CPA degree. The bump in salary allowed him to move out of Charleston and into the rent-controlled attic apartment he still occupied. It was the first time he had lived alone, and he found that he loved it. He kept the apartment exactly as he wanted, book-lined and dust-free. He began to date Irene, an assistant editor who seemed in no rush to either move in with George or get engaged. And in this way, George swam merrily through his twenties and into his early thirties. Although he thought less and less about Liana, he still kept an eye out for her, catching himself scanning crowds for her face or her walk, and he still had powerful and disquieting erotic dreams in which she loomed large and inescapable.

About a year after Arthur's forced retirement, George was promoted to business manager. It was during a tumultuous time at the magazine: The Internet was exploding, and ownership had recently changed. The staff was downsized, and the magazine's bent shifted dramatically from the literary to the political. Short stories were jettisoned from the monthly issues and ghettoized into a summer fiction issue. Poetry was eliminated. A feeling of doom swept the office. Irene got a plum job in the website division of the *Boston Globe,* but George stayed put, knowing that as long as the magazine stayed in business he'd have a job. He always kept the nails straight. Plus, George knew that the new ownership group, overseer of many profitable enterprises, was happy for the magazine to take a monthly loss, which it did in a staggering way.

Now at his desk, George scanned his in-box for any looming emergencies, and when he didn't find any, he went online to hunt for information about Gerald MacLean's death. There wasn't much, just a few stories reporting that MacLean had been found dead in his home in Newton and that the cause of death had not been disclosed. Anyone reading it would assume that the elderly MacLean had succumbed to a heart attack.

One of the stories ran with a photograph, a corporate shot of MacLean in a light blue suit that was at least fifteen years old. The common description of MacLean, phrased almost identically in both stories, read, "Gerald MacLean, founder and president of MacLean's Furniture, a wholesale outlet operation headquartered in Atlanta, had recently partnered with Paul Hull to form the Hull Foundation, a charitable organization devoted to cancer research. Mr. MacLean leaves behind a wife, Teresa MacLean née Rivera."

No mention of murder. No mention of feeder funds and Ponzi schemes. No mention of offshore accounts. And no mention of gym bags full of cash.

George attempted to work. The magazine was hosting a summer conference—really more of a fund-raiser at which paying customers could come and hobnob with some of the magazine's more famous writers—at a college in western Massachusetts. The college required that a certificate of insurance be added as a rider onto the magazine's insurance for the duration of the conference, and George had become the go-between for a very fickle college administrator and a very lazy insurance agent. He began an email to the agent, explaining the exact phrasing that was needed in the certificate, but he couldn't bring himself to finish it. His mind kept returning to the events of the weekend and how he might have fit into them. He could only assume that MacLean had been murdered for the money that had been returned. And if that was the case, then Liana would not have been involved in the murder. She'd had the money to start with; then she'd returned it. It was one mildly comforting thought.

Midmorning, George's desk phone rang. It was Irene.

"Did you forget?" she asked.

"Apparently."

"We're supposed to be having lunch."

"Right," he said. George vaguely remembered making plans with Irene for a Monday lunch. "Where again?"

"That new place on Stuart Street. It's got sort of a Mexican name."

George waited for Irene outside the restaurant. The temperature had climbed back into the nineties, and no sign remained of the biblical deluge of rain that had pounded Boston the previous night. He read the menu framed outside the door. It was standard Tex-Mex mixed in with entrées such as pork belly tacos and cilantro margaritas. He felt starved all of a sudden; the hangover from the previous night of beers and bad Chinese food had been lurking at the edges of his consciousness all morning. He decided on the shredded-beef burrito and a large Diet Coke, maybe with some rum in it.

George spotted Irene from three blocks away. She was walking slowly and with her head down, her arms clamped tight to her sides. He'd joked with her that twenty years of Boston winters had permanently altered her physicality so that she always looked as though she were moving through subzero temperatures. She claimed that she always *was* cold, even in Boston's humid summers, that the terrible winters had crept into her bones and stayed there all through the year. Watching her walk toward him made the bizarre events of the previous two and a half days seem even more unreal. *She is my real life,* George thought, *like it or not,* and she was coming toward him in all her average glory. Irene was only Irene. Bookish, sarcastic, hardworking, but so loyal that she wouldn't even give up on an on-again off-again disappointment of a boyfriend. With Irene still a block away, George decided that he wouldn't tell her the story of his weekend. Not today anyway. He wanted an hour of his previous life, to drink and eat with Irene and feel normal again.

But when Irene came up to George in the bright swimming air and raised her face to his, he could see a strip of white bandaging from the outside of her left eyebrow that went down about two inches along her face. The skin around her left eye was a pale bluish white, and the eye itself, a sliver of which was visible between her swollen lids, was completely red.

"What the fuck?" George said.

"I'll tell you about it inside. It's not as bad as it looks."

"No, tell me now. What happened?"

She shrugged and said, "I kind of got mugged."

"What do you mean 'kind of'?"

"Well, he didn't take anything. Long story short, I was coming home last night at about eleven, and this man asked me for the time in front of my building. I looked at my watch, and when I looked up he punched me in the face."

"Jesus," George said.

"I know. That's what I thought. I hit the pavement and thought I was a goner, but then he just took off. He didn't even take my purse."

"Did you call the cops?"

"I almost didn't. It just didn't seem real, but I thought better of it, and since he'd given me his name—"

"What do you mean he'd given you his name?"

"I don't know if it was a real name, but after he punched me in the face and before he walked away, he very politely introduced himself." Irene smiled, then winced a little when her bandage moved.

"What do you mean he introduced himself to you?"

"I was on the ground, expecting to get raped or shot in the head, and he looked down at me and said, 'Nice to meet you. My name's Donnie Jenks.' And then he walked away."

CHAPTER 13

Over the next ten minutes, George was shown several other photographs by Detective Chalfant. He studied them all. The Audrey Beck he was shown was not the Audrey Beck whom he had known at Mather College. Both girls had dark blond hair, blue eyes, fair skin. On the wide spectrum of human differentiation they would have been close to each other, but they were indisputably different girls. The nose of the girl in the picture—the real Audrey?—had a slight bump, the type of thing a richer girl might have eradicated with plastic surgery. Also, the pouty mouth was wrong, and the eyes were too close together.

"I don't suppose you have a picture of your girlfriend? Not with you, I know, but back at your motel, or at college?" Chalfant asked.

"I don't have any pictures of her at all. I thought of that already, after I heard she'd died."

"And you're sure this isn't her?"

"I'm sure. Positive." Still baffled by what had transpired in the course of a quarter of an hour, George kept registering little bursts

*of comprehension and hope. If his girlfriend wasn't Audrey Beck,
then she was still alive. He wanted to ask this of the detective, to
confirm what seemed to be happening, but he was acutely aware of
the grieving family of the real Audrey Beck around him. The father
continued to pace, shaking his head and sighing to himself.*

*"What's going on?" The voice, a new one, came from the front
door. All the heads in the room swiveled. A teenage boy had entered the living room, a tallish blond kid with braces, wearing a
Florida Gators T-shirt and a pair of basketball shorts.*

"Nothing, Billy," said Mr. Beck.

George thought to himself: This is the brother, but she never
mentioned she had one. She said she was an only child. *He
turned to look at Detective Chalfant, who said, to the room in
general, "Let's wrap up here. George, if you don't mind, I'd like
you to come down to the station so we can get an official statement
from you. There's no reason to bother the Becks any longer. George,
you'll follow us in your car, unless you'd prefer to ride with Officer
Wilson and myself."*

George stood. "Either way is fine—"

*"So what you're saying is, Audrey never went to college at all?"
This was from Mrs. Beck, her voice shrill, her wine slopping a
little over the lip of the glass she still held. She directed the statement into the middle of the room so that it fell somewhere between
George and the two policemen.*

*Chalfant held a hand up. "Now, Pat. Let's not jump to any rash
conclusions—"*

"Rash conclusions?"

*"—but, yes, it seems that there's some confusion as to who
was going to college under your daughter's name. We're going to
clear this up and get to the bottom of whatever happened here.*

*I'll let you folks know as soon as I find out anything at all. That's
a promise."*

*"Where would she have been if she hadn't been going to
college?"*

"That's what we're going to try and find out."

George followed the cruiser to a beige stucco police station. He
smoked a cigarette along the way and tried to concentrate on driving. The palms of his hands were damp with sweat.

The detective led him to his own office, one of several that
lined a long, nondescript hallway that reminded George of the al-
lergist's office he'd had to visit frequently as a kid.

Chalfant's office was homey, with cluttered shelves of knick-
knacks and a wall crammed with tilted pictures, mostly of kids.
George was offered a high-backed swivel chair, while Chalfant
walked around his desk and perched on a wooden stool. "Keeps me
from falling asleep on the job," he said and winked at George. "The
stool," he added, then picked up the phone on his desk.

George said: "Did you know about this? Did you know about
Audrey not being Audrey? I don't mean to be pushy, but—"

Chalfant held up a finger and said into the phone: "Denise,
honey, do me a favor, will ya? I'm going to need all the Sweetgum
High School yearbooks for the past three years. . . . Yep. . . . No,
starting with last year's and then backward. . . . We have them
here, right? . . . Might as well go four years back, then. Bring them
here, will ya. ASAP. . . . Thanks, hon."

Chalfant hung up the phone and placed the heels of his shoes
on the lowest support of the stool. He looked less like a detective
and more like a dyspeptic baseball manager in the middle of a losing
season. "Let me tell you what we already know. I always find it easiest to disclose all the relevant facts. We know that the real Audrey

Beck, the daughter of Sam and Patricia Beck, whom you just met, spent part, if not all, of last semester in West Palm Beach. She told her parents and most of her friends that she was going to school at Mather College. She packed her car full of sweaters and jeans and took off, heading north, but apparently at some point she turned around and headed east. According to Ian King—have you heard of him? No, I didn't think so. According to Ian King, she spent the majority of the fall with him and other members of his band in a rented house. He's in a group called Gator Bait, I don't suppose . . ."

George shook his head.

". . . No, of course you haven't. I know all this because Ian King showed up here yesterday. He came to me because he thought Audrey Beck had been killed by a drug dealer named Sam Paris. Apparently, Gator Bait and Audrey Beck owe money for drugs. We weren't surprised that Audrey Beck was a drug user because that showed up pretty clearly in the coroner's report. We were surprised to hear she hadn't spent the semester at school. We were getting all set to call Mather—oh hello, Denise, right on the desk, please."

A pear-shaped, heavily made-up woman of at least fifty placed a stack of high school yearbooks on the desk.

"We were getting all set to call Mather, and then the Becks hear from you, a college boyfriend. You can imagine that we were very interested to hear your story."

"You think someone else went in her place?"

"Seems that way, son, unless you think she was in two places at the same time."

"The pictures I saw earlier, they were definitely not the Audrey Beck I knew."

"Right, so what I was hoping you could do for me is flip through that stack of yearbooks. If someone went in Audrey's place, pretend-

ing to be her, it makes sense that maybe it's someone she knew from high school."

"Okay." George placed a hand on the padded fake-leather cover of the top yearbook. "I'll do anything I can to help you, but you have to help me find the girl I'm looking for. She must still be alive, don't you think?"

"I don't want to speculate, son, but it's one and the same what you said about the help. You help us, and we'll help you. I have some things to do here in my office for a while. Here okay, or would you prefer I get you another room?"

"Here's fine."

George flipped through page after page of Sweetgum High School yearbooks to look for a girl with no name. He scanned portrait shot after portrait shot: girls with teased hair and shiny lips, girls in three-quarter profile looking back over a shoulder, girls with acne covered by thick makeup, girls who wore crosses around their necks and over their blouses, girls who were told by the photographer to lift their chins just a little bit higher, girls who looked like they were going places, and girls who looked like all the good times had already happened. All these girls were interspersed with dazed-looking senior boys, some handsome, most not, almost all with jock haircuts and expressionless eyes. George also studied the other photos, the black-and-whites of the clubs, the teams, the societies, the prom, all the group shots that might give him a glimpse of his own Audrey. He flipped through page after page till the tip of his finger felt dry and raw. He found many elements of her—her haircut on a girl named Mary Stephanopolis, her profile on a brunette doing a layout for the school newspaper, her curved hips and tapering legs on a member of the swim team—but none of them were her.

"Are there more for me to look at?" George asked a now-standing Detective Chalfant, who peered through bifocals at an opened manila folder in one hand.

"No. Quit. I'm worried about your eyes." He came up behind George and unexpectedly placed a large hand on George's left shoulder and squeezed. George, descended from a long line of unaffectionate men, found the gesture both disconcerting and almost unbearably comforting. "Tell me about this girl you knew. What was she like?"

George told his story and as he spoke he became aware of how ordinary and uninteresting their courtship and relationship had been. They had met at a party. He liked her. She liked him. It was a ritualized dance enacted by a million matriculating students across the globe. "I never suspected she wasn't who she said she was," he said. "She was cagey about her past, a little, but I thought she just didn't like to talk about it. Not everyone does."

"What did she like to talk about?"

"She asked me questions about me, my town, my parents. We talked about movies and books. We analyzed friends we had in common. She didn't like Florida. She said it was ugly and provincial."

"And your town wasn't?"

"Apparently not. I come from a small, pretty wealthy place. I never thought much of it, but she liked to hear me tell stories."

"What else was she interested in?"

"She was smart. She said she wanted to major in political science and minor in English lit. She planned to go to law school."

"She got good grades?"

"All As."

Detective Chalfant, who had worked his way back around his

desk, placed one foot on his stool and began to tighten his shoe-
laces. "How long are you here for? In Sweetgum."

"A while, I guess, now. Till I find out what happened."

"Okay." Chalfant slid a business card into George's hand. "You're
at the motor court, right? We'll be in touch."

O utside, the blue sky had been checkerboarded by thin pat-
terns of clouds, cotton balls pulled apart. There was a note
under George's windshield wiper—a piece of lined paper torn
out of a notebook. All that was written on the sheet was a phone
number, seven digits, scrawled in lavender ink.

He carefully folded the note and put it in his pocket. It didn't
look like Audrey's handwriting, but he couldn't be sure.

Driving back to the motel, slowed by the rush-hour traffic from
an emptying tomato processing plant, he felt a sense of elation, not
just because the girl he'd known was probably still alive, but also
because he had become embroiled in something far more mysteri-
ous than he'd ever hoped to be involved in. The dull realities of
Mather College and his suburban home were receding into a pedestrian, grayish past.

He pulled the Buick into the car dealership's lot and left the car
with Dan Thompson, who offered him, in succession, a cold beer
and a similar deal the following day. George told Thompson that
he'd more than likely be by again in the morning, and he declined
the beer, not because he didn't want it, but because he didn't want
to hang around the office that smelled of cigar smoke and Lysol any
longer than he had to. He had a phone call to make.

George fiddled momentarily with the lock of his motel room
door. It jammed a little, and he muttered a curse to himself, loud

enough so that he didn't immediately register the sound of the car door opening and shutting behind him. He did register something, the sense of an impending threat, but that was only in the quarter second or so before he was violently shoved forward onto the floor of his motel room.

CHAPTER 14

Lunch with Irene was interminable.

In the time it took to enter the restaurant, give his name to the hostess, and be seated by the disorienting glare of a window table, George had decided that there was no way he could tell Irene that the man who punched her in the face was actually sending a message to him. It would only alarm her, and he would be forced to tell her the whole story, which would only make it more dangerous for her. His plan was to survive a pleasant, run-of-the-mill meal, take the rest of the day off from work . . . and then what? If he could somehow find either Liana or the man who was pretending to be Donnie Jenks, maybe go back to the cottage in New Essex, then he could make sure that Irene was left out of it, whatever *it* was.

Despite a sudden loss of appetite, George ordered the shredded-beef burrito as he'd planned. Plus a rum and Coke. He managed to get about half his food down even though his stomach felt like it had shrunk to the size of a shriveled lemon.

George asked questions, wanting to make sure that her assailant who had identified himself as Donnie Jenks was the small
skinny man with the grayish teeth and not the portly employee
of Gerald MacLean. Her description left no doubt. She had been
assaulted by the same man George had met in New Essex. Irene
seemed strangely calm, as though she had finally seen the dark
side of city life and it wasn't so bad after all. It was clear that
the incident had already become a humorous anecdote that she
would be telling at cocktail parties and in the office kitchen. The
more she talked about it, the more George could feel pinpricks
of sweat breaking out along his hairline.

"You don't look so hot," she said.

"I'm just worried about you."

"Honestly, I don't think I'll ever see him again. My guess is
that he did to me exactly what he wanted to do. Punch me and
introduce himself. I was lying there on the pavement, and my
first thought was that I hoped he would just kill me and not rape
me first, then kill me. Isn't that terrible? And it wasn't a panicky
thought; it felt commonsensical. *Let it be straight-up murder, because I don't think I can handle being raped.* I thought of you too.
My mother first, of course, and then you, second. I just wondered what you would do when you heard that I was dead. Isn't it
strange? I had all these thoughts in about five seconds, and then
he just ups and leaves. I feel like I've been granted extra time.
What's that you're drinking? A rum and Coke? Maybe I'll have
a margarita."

George looked around for their elusive waitress.

"Seriously, you don't look so hot. When was the last time you
went to see a doctor?"

"For a hangover? Never," George said.

"Hungover on a Monday. I haven't asked you anything about your weekend."

"It's all a blur. Hey, I actually don't feel well. I think I ate some bad calamari at Teddy's last night. Do you mind if we cut this lunch short?"

Back on the pavement, George was able to talk Irene out of walking with him back to his office. They hugged good-bye, and George held on a little longer than he normally did. Irene pulled back and looked at him quizzically. He kissed her gently on the side of her head, just above the dark blond fuzz of her eyebrow. "You're beautiful," he said. "Even with the one eye."

"Now I know you're not feeling well."

"No, I mean it. It's scary what happened to you."

"Call me later if you start to feel better. Okay? And call me if you don't. Call me either way."

He watched her walk away and felt a complicated surge of love and protectiveness. He knew that if he saw Donnie Jenks at that very moment he wouldn't be scared of him, he would just be angry. When it had just been him on the chopping block, it was terrifying, but now that Irene had been brought into it, some vestige of gallantry was coursing through his veins.

George drove to New Essex. He didn't know what else to do. There was no way to get in touch with Liana, and there was no way to track down Donnie Jenks. The only real information he had about either of them was that they were somehow connected to that run-down cottage along the shore. Donnie Jenks had been there, and Liana had at least claimed to be there, although George now took anything she had said with a very large grain of salt.

He called the office and said he felt lousy and had gone home. He put the air conditioner on high and sports radio on low. It felt good to drive, the mindless routine allowing him time to think. It was obvious that the money George had returned to MacLean was somehow directly or indirectly connected to his murder. But none of it made any sense. It was possible that little Donnie Jenks had somehow found out that George was returning the money and that he went to the house and killed MacLean to get it. But he'd had opportunities to take the money before. From Liana. According to her, he'd come right up to her at Mohegan Sun. He could have taken it then. George considered the possibility that Liana and Donnie had been working together, but that made even less sense. If they had been, then they could have just split the money. Why go to the trouble of returning it to MacLean and then killing him for it? There could be a third party involved, someone he didn't even know, maybe someone who was working at the house and saw the suitcase full of money and decided to take it. The real Donnie Jenks? A murderous nurse in charge of the ailing wife? The niece who had let him into the house?

He cruised slowly through downtown New Essex. Tourists were out in full force, mostly retirees ambling from gift shop to ice cream stand to gift shop. George saw several men slumped on sidewalk benches, waiting for their wives to finish shopping. They had the sagging, unmoving quality of men who expected nothing momentous to ever happen to them again.

Beach Road was quiet till he reached the old stone church, where cars were double-parked along the already narrow road. He eased by, caught a glimpse of a gleaming black hearse and dark-suited men standing at the church's entrance.

He found Captain Sawyer Lane and turned onto it. The ruts in the dirt road seemed deeper, and some were still half-filled with the previous night's rain. Shafts of light penetrated the pine canopy, and in them George could see swirling clouds of the tiny bugs that pollute New England's marshland in summertime. There were no cars in front of the cottage when he pulled up, but everything else looked the same. He parked his car and went up the front steps, knocked on a rotting door, its paint long worn away. He peered through a grimy side window, the inside of which was thickly covered with a spiderweb. It took a moment for his eyes to adjust, but when they did, he could see that the cottage was essentially an abandoned property. The walls were blackened by mold, and the only piece of furniture he could make out was an upholstered couch with yellow stuffing oozing from its seams. He heard a sound behind him and quickly turned, but it was just the click of his car engine cooling down.

George went around to the back of the cottage, where the rotted pier listed in the marshy water. Roped to the sturdiest section of the pier was a fiberglass boat with an outboard motor. The boat, no more than twelve or fourteen feet long, didn't look particularly new or expensive, but it still stood out in its neglected surroundings. He tried to remember if he'd seen it the first time he'd been to the house. He remembered seeing the pier but couldn't recall a boat.

He turned back toward the house. There had once been a screened-in porch, but half of the screen had been pulled off, and one side of the porch had sunk down to the ground. White bloated mushrooms sprouted on the two-by-fours.

The porch door was latched, but he pushed on it, and the latch gave way in its rotted wood. The door from the porch to the cottage's interior was open but harder to move. It had come off its top hinge, and its bottom corner had dug into the floor. He kicked it, and it swung inward, ripping wood away from its frame. The smell of acrid dust billowed into George's face. He took a step inside but decided to go no further. The floor was covered with Styrofoam ceiling tiles that over time had molded and dropped onto the cracked and blistered linoleum. The couch that he had seen from the other window looked even worse from this new angle. It was clear that it had been hollowed out by wild animals. Yellow curds of stuffing were scattered everywhere.

He turned around and went back out to his car. He might not know a lot of things about Liana Decter, but he did know that she would never have spent a night in this cottage.

He drove to the end of the lane, passing the only other property, a brown deckhouse that was almost invisible in the piney darkness. He was about to pull back onto Beach Road when he shifted the Saab into reverse instead and backed up to the driveway of the deckhouse. A recently painted mailbox had the number 22 on it, and above the mailbox was a plastic box for the *Boston Herald,* its lettering faded to the point of being almost unreadable. He drove the short distance down the driveway, scrubby weeds scraping at the underside of his car, and pulled up in front of a garage. The house was bigger than it had looked from the lane. It had a stone foundation, a barely sloping shingled roof, and boxy floor-to-ceiling windows that were as dark as the stained siding. It was impossible to tell if anyone was home, but the low hedges around the front steps had been trimmed recently, and as George got out of the car he thought he could detect movement in one of the narrow windows that ran the length of the front door.

He rang the bell and heard a deep gong from within the house. About ten seconds passed before he heard the sound of a security chain sliding into its groove. The door cracked open about three inches. Above the taut chain were two of the largest, spookiest eyes George had ever seen, so pale blue that they were almost the color of skim milk.

"Sorry to bother you," he said. "I was looking for someone down the lane, at the cottage by the water, and I was wondering if you had any information about whether anyone's living there."

The woman took a half step back, and George could see her better. She could have been twenty-five or forty-five or somewhere in between. She had long, stringy hair, parted in the middle. She wore a patterned housedress, the kind that zips up the front, but it was too large for her and slid down off one shoulder. Her skin was so white, it was almost transparent. You could tell that she had once been beautiful; she had elfin features and prominent cheekbones. Her lips were wide and flat, but they were deeply dried out, lined with tiny cracks and fissures, and one side of her mouth had a white crusty appearance.

She grasped her housedress with one hand and bunched it together at her chest. "I don't really live here," she said. "It's a family house," she added.

"No worries. I was just wondering about that cottage. My friend told me she had been staying there, but I just went and looked at it, and it seems pretty unlivable. You don't know anything about it?"

She leaned her large head forward and shifted her eyes in the direction of the cottage as though she could possibly see it from inside the house. Her head was so close to George's that he could smell her breath, sour like wet grain. "No one lives there. At least no one that I've ever known has lived there."

"Do you know who owns it?"

"No."

"Who owns this house?" he asked and watched her lean back fractionally from the door, her puffy eyelids lowering. George knew he had asked too much.

"Do you have a cigarette?" she asked.

"No, sorry, I don't."

"Okay. Well, I should go." She shut the door. A cloud had passed over the sun, and it suddenly felt like dusk under the spread of trees. In the stillness, George could hear two gulls squawking at each other over the marsh. It seemed an odd sound in the dark shadows of the pines. He returned to his car and drove back to Boston.

After parking in his garage, George walked slowly back to his apartment. He planned to sleep. To ignore doorbells and raps on the door. To ignore ringing phones. He didn't know what he planned on doing after he'd slept, but he'd worry about that then. The ride back from New Essex had been sludgy and surreal, the tiredness catching up with him.

George had lived in his neighborhood long enough to be able to instantly detect an unfamiliar car. In front of his building was a white Suzuki Samurai, its removable hard top still on. It had racing stripes on its boxy sides in black and red and the word SAMURAI was still stenciled in white across the top of the windshield. There were two occupants, one large and one small, behind the shielding glare of its front windshield. George slowed down, knowing with all certainty that they were there for him, and as he slowed both doors opened. From the driver's side emerged the large, pear-shaped man George had met at MacLean's house in Newton. The other Donald Jenks, or DJ, as MacLean had referred to him. He looked toward George, held up a hand in what seemed a gesture of friendliness, and turned toward his companion, the woman getting out of the passenger side. She was familiar to George as well. He recognized her as the young woman who had let him into MacLean's house. The police detectives had mentioned a name, but he'd forgotten it.

"George Foss," she said in a querulous manner.

George nodded and came forward. She moved around the Suzuki to stand by the man. "I'm sorry . . . your name?" George said.

"I'm Karin Boyd. We met yesterday in Newton. I let you into Gerry MacLean's house."

"Right. Of course."

She looked less officious than she had before. She wore black capri pants and a white sleeveless shirt with a scoop neck. Her blond hair was down and slightly frizzy in the humidity. Her eyes looked smudged and red, as though she'd been crying, and George remembered that the detectives had told him that she was MacLean's niece.

"Do you mind if we talk with you for a moment?"

The driver of the vehicle stepped forward. "We met as well. It's Donald Jenks. DJ." He produced an ID from his wallet, identifying himself as a private investigator. Close up, he was a handsome man, his face tanned and poreless, and with a trimmed dark mustache above his upper lip. "I'm a private detective who was employed by the deceased. You are aware that Gerald Mac-Lean is now deceased?"

George said that he was.

"We'd like to speak with you."

George, hesitant to invite them into his apartment, suggested a nearby coffee shop. They found a back corner table as far as possible from the counter. George bought himself a large iced coffee, but neither Karin Boyd nor DJ ordered anything. When George sat down at the table, the pint glass of coffee already slick with condensation, DJ said, "We're leaving the murder investigation up to the police, Mr. Foss, but we'd like your help in possibly recovering what was stolen. There's a lot of money involved."

George, in the time it took to buy himself a coffee, had decided to tell them just as much as he'd told the police. He would leave out the part about someone impersonating Jenks. He knew he might eventually have to tell everything, but for now he still felt like there were things better left unsaid until he understood them better himself. A part of him was worried about Liana, and a bigger part was now worried about Irene.

"The police didn't tell me much," George said. "What happened?"

DJ and Karin glanced at one another, and Karin said, "Just tell us how you became involved first. Why were you sent by Jane Byrne to return the money she stole?"

"I'll tell you what I told the police. Jane was someone I knew in college, although I knew her by a different name—"

"What name was that?" DJ asked and pulled out a cell phone with a keyboard. George told him, "Audrey Beck," the same name he had given the police, and DJ typed it in with his thumbs as quickly and smoothly as a texting teenager.

"I hadn't seen her in twenty years. We met at a bar . . . it was near here . . . and she asked me to do her this favor. It seemed strange, but she explained that she wanted to return the money without having to come face-to-face with MacLean—with your uncle," he said to Karin. "It made sense to me at the time."

"Where did you go after you left the house?"

"I drove to Saugus and met . . . Jane at the Kowloon. I told her how it went. She seemed relieved. We had dinner. Can one of you please tell me how MacLean was killed? I think it would help me in trying to help you. Did it happen right after I left?"

Again they glanced at each other, and Karin almost imperceptibly nodded at DJ. It was clear that he was now in her employ.

"He was hit on the back of the head with a hammer." DJ tapped the back of his head with a hand that was small for his size. He wore a wedding band, and his fingernails looked as though they were professionally manicured. "It was in his bedroom, and it was probably just moments after you left the house. You're very lucky that Karin saw you leave the house, Mr. Foss, or I think the police would have you in custody right now."

"You saw me leave?" he asked Karin. George didn't remember seeing her on his way out of MacLean's house.

"I have an office on the second floor. My uncle popped in after his meeting with you, and before he went to his room, just to let me know that everything had gone okay. I stepped out of my office, and I could see you from the balcony. There are windows above the front door. You were getting into your car and leaving. You understand that this doesn't mean I don't think you're involved with my uncle's death." Her eyes had the flat impassive look of a trained interrogator.

"I promise you that all I thought I was doing was returning

money for a friend. I knew nothing about a murder until the police showed up at my place this morning."

Karin looked at him with her unchanging expression. She had pale, slightly freckled skin and was not wearing makeup. A pinkish blotch had spread at the base of her throat, caused by either the humidity of the day or the stress of the situation.

"We believe you, Mr. Foss," DJ said with the calm tone of a lawyer about to reveal his surprise witness to win the case. "What we're really after is some kind of lead to finding out where Jane Byrne is, or to finding out who she really is."

"So I take it that the money is gone?"

"The money that you brought in the suitcase?"

"Yes."

"Well, yes, that money is gone, but that's not entirely the issue at hand. The reason Mr. MacLean went to his bedroom after seeing you was to put that money in his safe. We're assuming that whoever killed him was waiting in that room for him. A second-floor window was open at the back of the house, and we think that's how they got in. There were gardeners around, and they usually bring ladders, because of the wisteria. None of this is an excuse. We should have had better security. Anyway, the safe had been opened, and everything but his papers was gone. Mr. MacLean didn't trust in currency, not completely anyway, and for several years he'd been buying up uncut diamonds. Expensive ones, with rare colors. It became almost a hobby with him, wouldn't you say, Karin? He had significant assets in that safe. Worth a lot of money, a *lot* more money than five hundred thousand dollars. We can only assume that the money was returned in order to get him to open up the safe; then he was attacked, and the safe was looted. I am positive that it was the diamonds they were after. Your friend clearly knew about them. This is a very serious situation."

As soon as DJ mentioned the safe, the air inside the coffee shop began to swim a little in front of George's eyes. Not because he was confused, or overtired, or confounded by too much information, but because it was suddenly so clear to him, the final piece falling into place. All along he'd been thinking that what was at stake was a gym bag full of money, more cash than he'd ever see in his lifetime, but that was just bait, a device used to get MacLean to open his safe at a specific time.

"You okay?"

"Sorry," George said. "I didn't know about the safe. How much were the diamonds worth?"

DJ and Karin looked at each other. DJ spoke: "I'm not at liberty to say exactly how much, but it was significant. At least five million dollars, we think. We are not accusing you of taking the diamonds, I hope you understand. . . ."

"No, no, I understand completely. Sorry. This is a new development to me. Obviously." George looked helplessly at his half-filled iced coffee. A cube of ice shifted in the glass.

"As I said," DJ continued, "we were wondering if you had any idea how to contact Jane Byrne, or where she might have been staying while she was up here. Anything would help."

George barely heard the words. His mind was racing to keep up with the new information he was getting. And it was all bad news. Unwittingly or not, George knew he'd been involved in getting a man killed. He took a sip of his coffee to buy time, but his stomach churned and saliva squirted into his mouth. Breathing deeply through his nose, he said, "I'm sorry. I'm just trying to keep up with what you're telling me, and it's a little upsetting.

I need to go to the bathroom." He said these words while pushing back his chair, rising, and walking away from the table. He
was now convinced he was going to be sick. The men's room
door, toward the back of the coffee shop, swung open, and he
pulled and latched it. Its fluorescent light fluttered in an irregular pattern. The floor was wet, as though recently mopped, but it
still looked dirty, dark hairs clinging to the tiles. George kneeled
down in front of the toilet. The smell of ancient pipes reached
his nostrils, and he buckled, now willing himself to be sick despite the shooting pains in his side. Nothing else happened. The
churning nausea disappeared and was replaced by dizziness. He
pushed himself back onto his feet by gripping the edges of the
toilet bowl. He ran cold water from the tap and washed his hands
several times, then splashed water onto his face and the back of
his neck. He breathed deeply again through his nose and stood,
leaning against the sink.

He looked at himself in the mirror. The paleness of his skin
shocked him. His hair was wet with sweat. *I've been a fucking
fool,* George thought, staring at his reflection for another minute,
waiting for the dizziness to pass.

Chapter 15

George rolled his body so that he was on his back. Two men entered the room and shut the door behind them. One of them, the smaller and skinnier of the two, tried to stomp on George's knee and missed. The other one, taller and fatter, said:

"Get up, asshole. I'll fucking kill you."

George slid back toward the middle of the room, his eyes adjusting to the lack of light. The men were his age, or younger, still in their teens. They looked like a couple of high school linebackers dressed to go to a Burger King on a Saturday night. They each wore stonewashed jeans and tucked-in Ocean Pacific T-shirts.

"Maybe I'll stay down here," George said.

"Fucking faggot," said the one who hadn't spoken before. "If we say get up, then you get up."

"Let me think about that for a moment."

The littler one, the stomper, reached down and grabbed the front of George's last clean shirt. George tried to punch him in the nose, missed, and hit him in the Adam's apple instead. He made a ragged sucking noise and jumped back, his hand at his neck, his mouth wide open in an "O."

"Asshole," the kid managed to croak.

George stood up. He knew he should feel scared, but his instinct for survival kept him calm. He held both hands palms out. "I don't know what you two want—" he began.

The larger kid charged him. George tried to throw a punch, but before his fist even got all the way back he was tackled and dropped to the top of the freshly made bed. His assailant twisted George's limbs so that he was pinned facedown, the back of his neck held by a forearm, the small of his back speared by a knee.

"How do you like that, asshole? How do you like that?"

Assuming it was a rhetorical question, George said nothing in return. The kid he'd punched in the neck walked over to the edge of the bed, stepping into the slivered light that came through the pulled blinds. He was breathing easier and gingerly fingering his neck. He had a narrow chin, red with acne, and a crew cut that showed a white scalp speckled with moles.

"I oughta fucking kill you," he said, his voice raspy.

"Just tell me what I did," George said.

"You know what you did," the big guy said as he leaned all his weight onto the knee that pushed against George's spine. A spring broke inside the bed.

"Honestly, I don't. Has this got something to do with Audrey Beck?"

"No duh," said Skinny, who was now moving his jaw in a circular motion, like an airline passenger trying to pop his ears.

"Seriously, I don't know anything more than you probably know. I don't even know if I really knew her."

"You get her into drugs?"

"Look, I don't think we're talking about the same person. Audrey Beck didn't go to college. Someone went in her place. Audrey went down to West Palm Beach with someone named Ian King. I swear to God."

"What the fuck are you talking about?"

"Let me up a moment. I'll tell you."

"Yeah, right," said Skinny, while the kid holding George performed another complicated set of wrestling moves and turned him so that he was on his back, the knee now in his solar plexus. George got a look at his primary assailant. He was wide and tall with a fat chin and a forehead bigger than the rest of his face. His blond hair was short on the top and sides and long at the back.

"Will you just listen to me for a moment? I'm not lying. I don't think I ever met Audrey Beck."

Forehead shook his head, like a parent being lied to by a young child. "If we find out you had anything to do with what happened to her, I will hunt you down like a deer and shoot you. You understand?"

"Yeah, b—"

"You understand, asshole?"

"Yeah."

"Scott, let me punch him in the throat like he punched me."

"I'll do it," said Scott and reared a doughy fist back. George scrunched his shoulders up and tucked his chin down to his chest so that when he got punched it was partly on the upper lip and partly on the nose. Blood sprang from both places, and tears streamed from his eyes.

The boys took off as fast as they had come.

George stumbled to the bathroom and put his face into a thin towel that smelled of bleach. The worst pain was in his nose;

second place was a tie between his cheekbones and eye sockets. He held the towel against his face for about five minutes, then realized that the door wasn't locked. He walked across the room, locked the door, then sat down on the bed and dialed the phone number from the note he'd found on his car. His heart was pulsing in his chest, and he wondered if he'd have trouble speaking when it came time to speak.

"Hello?" It was a girl's voice, worried-sounding, and with a slight Southern hitch to it, but other than that, not very much like Audrey's voice.

"You left me a note, with this phone number." George sounded as though he had a bad cold.

"Are you the one here from Mather College?"

"Yeah. Who are you?"

"I was friends with Audrey."

George shook his pack of cigarettes until one filtered end appeared. "So was I, I thought, but I guess I wasn't."

"She didn't go to college," the girl said.

"Well, someone did. What's your name?"

"It's Cassie Zawinsky."

"So you knew that Audrey didn't go to Mather?"

"Yeah, I did."

"Do you know who went in her place?"

"I don't know her name, but I know that someone did. She was from Chinkapin High, I think. You met her, you knew her, right? What was she like?"

"She was my girlfriend. She was nice." George lit the cigarette. The first drag unclogged his nose a little, and he could smell blood.

"But you don't really know anything about her?" Cassie asked.

"Look, I have lots of questions for you too. I don't even know how you know I'm here or what you're trying to figure out. Maybe we could meet?"

"I could do that."

"Do you know the Shoney's off the highway?"

"Sure."

Two hours later, showered, dressed, with a bruised nose and a cracked and sticky lip, George waited in a back booth, an extra large Coke in front of him.

Shoney's was filled with couples, old ones who were alone and young ones with boisterous kids. Cassie was easy to spot when she walked in—alone, George's age, wearing a man's vintage suit vest over a Crowded House T-shirt and a pair of tight, ripped jeans. George waved in her direction, and she came over, slid in across from him.

"What happened to you?" she asked.

"Two guys met me at my motel and wanted to know what I'd done to Audrey. Maybe you know something about it."

"What kind of guys?" She had short reddish hair, small blue-green eyes, a button nose with a snub tip, and a huge mouth with big white teeth. It didn't help her looks that she was wearing about a quarter-inch of bright red lipstick and some of it had come off on one of her canines.

"I don't know. Jocks. One of the names was Scott."

"Oh jeez. Scotty's my brother. Was the other one skinny with Frisbee ears?"

"Yeah."

"That's Kevin Lineback, my brother's sidekick. Ah jeez, I'm

sorry about that. They had no . . . They wouldn't've even known you were here if it wasn't for me."

"I still don't understand how you knew."

A waitress appeared, and Cassie ordered a Dr. Pepper.

"So you were at the Becks' today, right?" she said. "Did ya see Billy Beck, Audrey's brother? Yeah, well, he was the one who called me and told me, probably about a minute after you left the house. Thing is, he was like the only other person besides me who knew that Audrey wasn't planning on actually going to college, and he knew I knew, so he called me right away. My brother, the a-hole, must have overheard me talking on the phone with Billy. That's what I figure anyway. Scott went out with Audrey for about five minutes last summer, and he's all hung up on her still."

"How did you know to leave a note on my car?"

"Billy told me that you followed the policemen to the station. And he told me what your car looked like. I figured that I'd leave just a phone number. That way if anyone else saw it, it wouldn't give anything away." Keeping her hands down by her sides, Cassie leaned forward and sipped at her Dr. Pepper through her straw. She looked pleased with herself.

"So how did Scott and his friend know where to find me?"

"Billy. He told me over the phone, and I must've repeated it out loud or something, because Scott heard. Or else he listened in. I have a phone in my room, but it's not my own line, so anyone can pick up anywhere else in the house. Anyways, that's how Scott found out where you were staying. I guess he beat me to you."

"So what I don't understand is why Audrey didn't want to go to school. She must've applied."

"She had to. Her parents made her do it. She's like one of the few kids from Sweetgum who could even afford to go to a four-year college, let alone get into one. Anyways, her parents told her she had to go. She picked Mather, I think, because it was so far away. But she didn't want to go. At all. She was into this guy Ian King—"

"From Gator Bait."

"Oh my gosh, you've actually heard of them."

"No, not really. The detective told me about them today. He said Audrey went off with this guy Ian."

"That was her plan—what she told me anyways. She was telling her parents she was going to go to school, and then she was just going to skip town. She figured, what could they do to her if they couldn't find her?"

"But then she found someone to go in her place?"

"Yeah. The thing is, Audrey didn't tell me so much about it. We were friends, Audrey and me, but not like best friends forever or anything. We all kind of grew up together. My dad knows her dad. My mom knows her mom. That's how come Billy and I know each other, and Scotty and Audrey. It's like a family thing. So when Audrey told me she wasn't going to go to school, I was like . . . I don't know. But then she told me that she met this girl from Chinkapin who kind of looked like her, and she was totally smart but came from a bad family with no money, and she wanted to go to college real bad."

"How did they meet?"

"Forensics, I think."

"What's that?"

"Competitions for the debate club. I don't know so much about it."

"But she never told you this girl's name?"

"I think she got spooked that she told me so much as it was. As I said, we weren't best friends or anything. She told me I better not rat her out, and I promised that I wouldn't. I guess now I feel a little guilty. Maybe I should've said something."

"Refills, guys?" The waitress had materialized.

They both nodded.

"Have you two figured out what you want to eat?"

George said, "I'm actually not that hungry."

"You wanna split a plate of fries?" Cassie asked. "They're good here."

The fries, crinkle cut, arrived in ten minutes on a big oval platter. Cassie had a lot more to say, but the crucial information had already been spoken. The girl George was looking for was from Chinkapin, and she was on the debate team. The following day he could find her name by going through yearbooks again. What he hadn't decided was whether he would try to do that on his own or enlist the help of Detective Chalfant.

George walked Cassie to her car. She looked up at the star-flecked sky. "Look, it's the Big Dipper," she said, pointing.

"You don't think this other girl had anything to do with what happened to Audrey, do you?" George asked.

"Sure, I thought about it. But Audrey was pretty into drugs, so who knows, you know?"

"Will you call me if you find out anything more?"

"I promise. And don't worry—I'll tell Scotty you had nothing to do with this, and he won't bother you again."

"I'll be ready for him next time."

"He's kind of mean."

"I noticed."

Sporadic bursts of rain came in the night as George lay awake, his face still aching, on his broken mattress. The joints of the weathered motel clicked and whistled. Cars on the highway cast shadows that wheeled through the room, long to short to long again. George filled the ashtray with butts and turned the television on and off several times. At dawn, when the wind had died and the rising sun bathed everything in the same thin light, he fell asleep, lips stinging, mouth thick with the taste of cigarettes.

He called Chalfant in the morning, told the detective that he thought the girl they were looking for might come from a neighboring town; maybe he could look at more yearbooks. George told Chalfant he thought Chinkapin was a possibility. Chalfant told him to come by the station after lunch.

Dan Thompson lent George the car again. "You speak Mexican?"

"Sorry, no."

"That's okay, but it would help. I do need one favor from you. There's a Mexican joint—Abelito's—you know it?" He wore the same light tan suit again, but with a different matching set of tie and handkerchief. Today they were a shiny neon blue.

"No, but I can find it."

Thompson gave him the avenue and the cross street, and the paperwork that needed signatures.

George timed his errand to coincide with lunch and ate at the busy Mexican place. The food was good, but he barely had an appetite. He knew with what felt like certainty that in a few hours he would find out the true identity of the girl he'd known as Audrey. How soon after that would he be able to see her again? He paid for his meal and drove to the police station.

Chalfant was out, but Denise had left a stack of yearbooks, including Chinkapin High's, in his office. Left alone with the books, George started with the most recent. Instead of looking at the individual photographs first, he flipped toward the back, where there were group shots of clubs and teams. He found "Speech and

Debate," a half page with a black-and-white shot of about seven students in two rows, and nervously scanned the faces.

There she was. Her hair was not the same in the photo—it was longer and feathered and somehow looked blonder—but the rest was the same, the face, the posture, the half smile.

He read the names printed along the bottom. She was in the second row, third from left: L. Decter. He flipped the pages back to the early section of the senior portraits and found her: Liana Decter. She wore a black, scoop-necked dress and a string of pearls. He stared at the picture for a long time, her eyes staring back at him. They told him nothing new.

He closed the book but kept it on his lap. Ever since Denise had ushered him into the office, he hadn't heard any activity at all in the hallway. He made his mind up. Leaving the yearbook behind and casually walking out of Chalfant's office, George passed through the reception area when Denise had her back turned and a file cabinet was open. He swung through the glass doors and into the warm gusty day.

There were six Decters listed in the Chinkapin area. He started with the first and dialed the number, deciding to simply ask for Liana, no matter who answered. Two of the numbers rang and rang—no answer, no machine—and one produced an unpromising message. Twice he was told that he had the wrong number. But on the final try a man's voice, in response to his question, said, "Who's asking?"

"I'm a friend of hers, sir."

"You gonna tell me your name, or do you want me to guess?" The voice was old and wavery, with a thick, phlegmy sound to it.

"My name's George Foss."

"All right, George. I'll let her know you called. Can't promise you she'll call back, but that's your goddamn problem."

"Thank you, sir." George rarely referred to anyone as a *"sir,"* but he realized he'd taken up the habit since arriving in Florida. *"Can I give you my number?"*

"What, she don't have it already?"

"No, sir."

"Then fuck you, boy. You think I'm my daughter's dating service?" He hung up.

George looked down at the phone book, spread open across his thighs. His index finger, white at the tip, was pressed against the number he'd just called. There was also an address.

K. Decter lived on Eighth Street, and after driving for half an hour, George found it. It was in one of the more run-down sections he'd seen so far. Boxy houses with paved-over yards, most with two or three junky cars in front of them. A drainage ditch filled with greenish water lined the road instead of a sidewalk. Behind the houses ran a fence, and behind the fence was a stagnant-looking artificial lake. Even the palms along the street seemed old and tired. Yellowed fronds littered the ground.

George drove slowly, looking for number 401. He had to turn around once but found the place, not because it was marked, but because the house next to it—397—was. The house at 401 was sided in faded vinyl. Parked in its carport was a battered-looking pickup. In the small patch of dirt was an oak tree, dripping with dirty gray beards of Spanish moss. George, assuming that only the father was at home, decided to watch the house. He pulled his car onto the side of the road under the oak, hoping its shade would keep the car both cooler and less conspicuous.

After half an hour, George realized it did neither. The inside of the Buick heated up like an attic in July, and the few cars that had passed him had all slowed down, their inhabitants craning their necks to get a better look at their neighborhood's intruder, the perv in the paneled car. He realized it was only a matter of time before one of them stopped or someone emerged from a nearby house to ask him just what the fuck he thought he was doing.

Those worries competed with a riot of thoughts. His proximity to the home of Liana Decter—also known as Audrey Beck—was conjuring a whole reassessment of her character, her upbringing. He wondered if she had taken the opportunity to switch identities with Audrey as a way to escape some calamitous fate on this very street. And what had been her long-term plan? Could she have gone on being Audrey Beck indefinitely? Maybe she could have at Mather College, all those miles and states and realities away, but eventually the truth would have come out. And in fact it had. Audrey's death had ensured that. George grappled with all he had learned in the past twenty-four hours while also trying to work out the logistics of what exactly he was doing, staked out in a car. It was Liana he was hoping to see, emerging from her home or returning to it. He wanted to get to her first, to hear her side of the story, to warn her of what was coming, to tell her that the police were aware that Audrey Beck had never been to college.

A car pulled up across the street, some sort of unidentifiable muscle car bubbling black exhaust smoke. George slid in his seat, an unlit cigarette between his lips.

The car door swung open, and a gangly, denim-clad man unfolded himself from it. He looked to be in his late twenties, with long black hair pulled back into a tight ponytail and a face that, from a distance, looked pale and small-featured. He was wearing Ray-Bans.

George watched him cross the street with a long, swinging gait and idle up to the Decter residence. Because of the position of the

Buick, under and slightly behind the oak, there was no clear sight line to the front door, but after two minutes the man reemerged into view and casually strolled toward George in his car. Before he arrived, George quickly lit his cigarette, the filter of which had become wet between his lips.

The man placed one hand on the roof of the car, the other on the window frame, then dropped down a considerable distance to place his plate-size face almost into the car. His eyes, an almost pretty blue, scanned the interior of the vehicle. George wanted to speak first but could not think of what to say.

"How ya doing?" the man said, his voice casual, friendly enough to be on radio. George noticed that he had a pencil-thin mustache right over his colorless lip. He had high cheekbones for a man.

"Not bad."

"I won't ask ya what you're doing out here because I know. Liana told me all about you. She said you were a good kid from a good family."

"I just want to see her."

"Oh, I know you do. That's totally understandable. I think, under different circumstances, she would want to see you too. But you have to understand that right now is not a good time. She told me to ask you to leave town and go back to college."

In what he hoped was a reasonable tone of voice, George said, "So what will happen to me if I don't go back to college?"

There must have been some calculable time that it took for the man with the ponytail to move his hand from the roof of the car to the base of George's throat, but George could never have measured it. One second he was finishing his question, and the next he was struggling for breath, the man's large-knuckled hand simultaneously constricting his throat and pushing him back against the headrest.

"It looks like someone already hit you recently, so you're probably thinking that taking a punch isn't so bad. Let's see what we got here. . . ." The man explored George's face with his free hand, turning it delicately one way and then the next, like a plastic surgeon examining a woman with crow's feet. "This must've hurt when you took one in the nose." The man pressed against George's tender nose with a thumb as wide and flat as a coffee spoon. George reflexively lifted an arm to protect himself.

"Don't fucking move." The man squeezed tighter around George's throat and pressed harder with his thumb against his nose. Fresh blood trickled down George's upper lip and into his mouth, and he could hear the sound of cartilage grinding together. "If I hit you in the nose, you wouldn't be up and about the next day. It would be permanent damage. You'd have nothing left but a flap of skin in the middle of your face. You understand what I'm saying to you?" The man moved George's head up and down like he was a ventriloquist with a dummy. "Good." A car drove slowly by but didn't stop. The ponytailed man was unfazed.

"All right, George, I'm going to take off now, and I suggest you do the same. If you see me again, it means that you are about to endure some terrible pain, so you better hope you don't ever see me again."

The man released George's face and stood. George wiped the fresh tears away from his cheek and took a deep, painful breath. He knew he was going to cry at some point, not just tears but sobs and snot, but he thought he could hold off until the man was out of sight. Outside of the car, the man adjusted his tight black jeans—they were topped by an enormous belt buckle with the Jack Daniels logo. Then he strolled, as casually as he had arrived, back to his low, dark car, folded himself into it, and drove away.

Back at the motel, George did cry, but not as long and hard as he thought he would. The worst had passed—the terrible fear that the man with the ponytail was going to really, truly hurt him. Permanent damage, *he had said, and the phrase had stuck in George's head.*

It was time to leave Florida. He would take a bus back to college, and from there he'd call Detective Chalfant, tell him everything he knew, let him sort it out. Liana was in some kind of trouble that was too much for him to deal with.

The phone rang, and he almost didn't answer it.

"Hi, George," she said.

Chapter 16

George stood in the bathroom of the coffee shop, the nausea passing but the panic still there. He needed to decide what to tell Donald Jenks and Karin Boyd. He owed it to them to tell them everything, but still wanted to be careful. Not to protect Liana, but to protect himself. In his interview with the police, he hadn't mentioned meeting the other Donnie Jenks, or going to the house in New Essex, or even knowing Jane Byrne's real name. But at that time he also hadn't known the extent to which he had been conned and used by Liana; he hadn't known that his participation had led to a murder. It had been a brilliant and simple plan. How do you get someone to open a safe? You give him something that will cause him to open it and then just wait and watch. George was the perfect actor for the situation because he didn't know he was acting. Just a good guy trying to do the right thing. Return money to its owner. Keep a woman from being terrorized. Return the world to order. And while he was doing his part, someone—probably the man who pretended to be Donnie Jenks—was waiting upstairs by the safe, holding a hammer. How did he get in there? Had he arrived with the gardeners?

There was still some part of George that wanted to believe that Liana was innocent, that she was not behind the robbery and the murder. He wanted to believe this not because he thought she wasn't capable of such crimes, but because he hoped she wasn't capable of using him for those purposes. Just as George had always stayed a little bit in love with Liana, he hoped that she had always stayed a little bit in love with him. But protecting Liana was not enough of a reason for not going to the police with everything he knew. If she was innocent, then she would be in danger as well.

No, what was really stopping George from telling everything he knew immediately to Karin Boyd and DJ, as well as to the police, was that Irene had been approached by the fake Donnie the night before. It had been a warning, specifically for him, that his actions affected not just his welfare but hers as well. But why? Surely, after killing MacLean and taking the diamonds, all that was left to do was to meet up with Liana and skip town. Neither of them could be traced. He knew Liana's real name, but she hadn't used it for years, and he had no idea who her accomplice really was. So why had they threatened Irene? And how had they even known who Irene was and how to find her? George suddenly realized that whatever had occurred over the weekend must have been planned far in advance.

He returned to the table more composed and with a plan for what he was going to say. Karin and DJ were talking to each other in low voices but stopped when he pulled his chair back and sat down.

"You okay?" Karin asked.

"I've been better. Until right now, I don't think I realized exactly how planned out everything was. It's a little bit of a shock to find out that I unwittingly assisted in a murder."

DJ's eyes brightened, and his thin mustache twitched a little under his nose. "You want to tell us everything that happened?"

"I will," George said. "Everything. But I can't do it right now. I need a few hours to straighten a couple of things out."

"I don't like the sound of that," DJ said, sounding like a professor being asked for an extension on a paper.

"It's the best I can do. Trust me, when I tell you all I know, you'll be disappointed. I don't know where Jane is, or where the diamonds are. If I had to guess, I'd say they're long gone from here. But I'm going to have to call you later."

DJ suddenly looked resigned, but Karin was turning red, the flush from her chest spreading up her neck. She twisted a ring on her finger. "If you know something, you have to tell us," she said, looking back and forth between George and DJ. "Right? We'll call the police. You're withholding information in a murder investigation."

"Karin, it's okay," DJ said, holding out his soft-looking hand. Karin's voice had escalated in volume, and the barista behind the counter had looked up.

"I'll tell the police everything I know too," George said. "I just need a couple of hours. I promise."

"We can't let him go," Karin said.

"It's okay. We don't have a choice. Mr. Foss, you'll call me?"

"I will."

"You understand I'll have to let the investigating officers know that you have information you are withholding."

"I understand."

Karin's cell phone was ringing in her purse. As George stood she spoke quickly into it, informing whoever was calling her that she'd phone right back.

"You have my card," DJ said, and George touched his shirt-front pocket, where he had put it.

"I'll call you," he said and turned and left.

George walked, fatigued and sweaty, down the alley that led to his back stairs. He fully expected someone to be waiting in front of his entrance. Liana with tears rolling dramatically down her cheeks, or the fake Donnie Jenks wielding a hammer, or a team of detectives with search warrants and questions. But there was no one there, and no one in his apartment either. Just Nora, asleep on a shirt he'd left on the floor. He picked her up, cradling her in his arms. She purred, happy that it was just George back in the apartment. He agreed with her, wondering suddenly how he had ever disparaged his uneventful life.

He put Nora down and turned the window air conditioner to high in his bedroom. One advantage of his ancient unit was that it made so much noise that he would never hear his phone or someone knocking at his door. He stripped out of his clothes and crawled under the bunched sheets of his bed, expecting to still smell Liana but somehow he couldn't. She'd faded already. Or maybe this had all been a feverish dream. It was his last rational thought before falling into a deep, empty sleep.

He woke in the early evening with that fuzzy unreal feeling that comes from sleeping through an afternoon. The air conditioner, rattling at a symphonic pitch, had chilled the room to midwinter temperatures. His skin was sticky where the sweat

had dried, his mouth still had the bitter taste of coffee, and his
teeth were furred. Lying still, he looked at the diminished light
that struck his ceiling and tried to guess the time, when all he
had to do was turn his head to look at his bedside clock.

Beneath the air conditioner's hum, he could hear the faint
rhythms of a frantic scratching, Nora protesting at his locked
door. It must be her dinnertime, probably six.

He closed his eyes again and felt the heavy blanket of sleep
descend. Maybe he'd just sleep through till morning. What
day was today? Did he have work tomorrow? As soon as those
thoughts entered his consciousness, other thoughts did as well.
He remembered his promise to Karin Boyd and Donald Jenks
that he would tell them what he knew. He remembered what
he had decided about Irene, how she needed to know everything that was going on. His eyes opened again, and this time he
turned to look at the clock. It was just past seven.

He fed Nora, then checked his answering machine. He remembered hearing the distant sounds of a phone ringing somewhere in his deep afternoon sleep, but there was no message.
Maybe he'd dreamt it. He showered and dressed, then went to
his tiny alcove of a kitchen to search for food. He toasted an English muffin, ate it dry with a glass of milk. The shower and food,
instead of reviving him, made him even more tired. He longed
to lie down on his couch, see if there was a baseball game on, or
an old movie, but he had woken with a plan and he needed to
follow through.

Irene lived just over the river in Cambridge. She owned a loft-
style condo in a three-story brick building that had once been

a shoe factory. It had been converted to airy, eco-friendly lofts in the 1990s, right before the real estate boom in the greater Boston area. At the time, Irene had paid what seemed an outrageous price for her 1,200 square feet, but it now seemed an incredible bargain. The purchase of her loft had precipitated the first of many minor crises in George and Irene's early relationship. They'd been together just under two years, both living in cruddy postcollege apartments, when she'd mentioned the possibility of purchasing a condo and asked him if he'd want to go in on it with her. They'd visited the empty space together with a big-haired real estate agent who treated them like they were a young married couple as she pointed out the reclaimed timber, the stainless steel, the built-in skylights. All George had seen was a mortgage he couldn't afford at the time and a space with no interior doors, a grown-up's apartment where he and Irene would be spending every waking minute in each other's company. Over beers in Allston that evening, he told her it was too much, too fast. She'd been disappointed but determined to purchase the condo on her own. It was the first of many small detonations that year that eroded their relationship.

He parked a couple of blocks from Irene's building. There had been no need to call first; it was a Monday evening, and he knew that Irene would be home for the night. She was a believer in routine, and one of those routines was never going out on a Monday evening, which was reserved for simple dinners and imported English dramas on public television. He walked through Irene's dense neighborhood, the narrow streets crammed with triple-deckers. The converted factory she lived in took up nearly half a block on its own; it was like a yacht moored among a hundred sailboats. The stairwell to her top-floor condo was reached by walking through an open-air central archway, then gaining entry through a locked door. George pressed the button adjacent to her name (I. DIMAS) on the burnished metal panel next to the heavy door. As he waited he looked up through the fire escapes at the darkening sky. Despite the lingering heat, summer was nearing its end and the days were getting shorter. "Hello?" came her hollow voice through the intercom.

She met him at her door wearing short pajama bottoms and a faded Red Sox jersey; he knew without looking that it had Tim Wakefield's name and number on the back. Her hair was held back with a cloth headband, and her face was shiny, as though she'd recently washed it and put on some sort of overnight moisturizing agent. She'd applied a fresh bandage to the side of her face where Donnie Jenks had punched her, and even just since he'd seen her that morning the skin around the bandage had puffed and yellowed.

"You okay?" she asked.

"Sorry for dropping by, but I need to talk with you. Can I come in?"

The inside of her loft was darker than outside, and before they sat together on her sofa she turned on a tall lamp. It cast a pool of soft light in an irregular circle. Despite the cold geometry of Irene's spacious loft, she'd designed it beautifully so that pockets of it were as cozy as small warm rooms. George didn't spend a whole lot of time at Irene's place—it was a constant reminder of their failure as a couple, a museum exhibit that demonstrated his absence, his inability to commit. He didn't believe Irene thought that way about the place that had been her home for over a decade, but when he came there it was impossible not to think that it might have been his home as well.

He turned down a drink, settling onto one end of Irene's enormous couch. She sat across from him.

"Remember on Friday night when I talked about that woman at Jack Crow's?" he began.

Irene nodded.

"She *was* that girl I'd told you about from college. Liana Decter."

"I thought she might've been. You were a little too spooked to see her. Did you go back and see her? Is that why you told me you weren't feeling well?"

"Yes."

"So you've spent the weekend with her, I take it?"

"I did, but that's not why I'm here. It's a bigger story than that, and it has to do with what happened to you on Sunday night."

He told her everything, exactly as it had happened. Irene barely spoke through the whole tale until he got to the part about Gerry MacLean, and she mentioned that she'd just been reading about the suspected murder in that day's *Globe*.

When he'd finished, she said, "Georgie, Jesus," and wiped at an eye with the corner of her jersey.

"You're upset?"

"No, I'm scared. For you. What the fuck were you thinking? She killed people."

"I know. I'm scared too. You can't imagine what it was like to have you tell me your story about being punched, knowing the whole time that it was my fault and feeling like I couldn't tell you that."

"I don't know why you thought you couldn't tell me. I'm a big girl. I would've handled it, and it would have saved you having to make this trip."

"I know. I'm sorry about everything. It's been a confusing day, and I've just now figured out what I need to do."

"So what are you going to do?"

"I'm going to tell the whole story to the police, and to Mac-Lean's detective, and to anyone else who wants to know. I'm not going to protect Liana or her identity. Right now I feel like I owe her nothing. And that's why I came here first, to you. I needed you to hear the whole story, and another thing . . . I think you should leave Boston for a while."

"What do you mean?"

"For whatever reason, on the night that Donnie Jenks took the diamonds from MacLean's safe, he went and visited you, showed that he could hurt you, and left his name. He knew I would hear about it, so it was a direct message to me. To do what, I don't know, but it was probably a message telling me to keep my mouth shut. I can't think of what else it could be. So now that I've decided to not keep my mouth shut, you need to leave town, go visit Alex in San Francisco or something. I'd feel much better."

"I have work. I have a meeting first thing tomorrow."

"This is non-negotiable."

She laughed. "Are you serious? What does that even mean?"

"It means that my stupidity has put you in danger, and that you've already been hurt"—he gestured vaguely in the direction of her beat-up face—"and I need you to do me this one small favor so that I don't have to worry about you anymore. I'll pay for your trip."

"It's not the money. . . ."

"I know that. It's just . . . I couldn't live with myself if something happened to you. If I'm overreacting, then that's the reason."

Irene's mouth pursed. He knew she was gently biting the

inside of her lip, thinking about what he'd told her. Her eyelids, usually darkly made-up, always looked vulnerable when they were scrubbed free of makeup. She sighed, shifted on the couch, moving her right leg up onto the cushion. Her cotton pajama bottoms stretched thinly across her dimpled thigh. George turned his eyes away; he knew she was self-conscious about the thickening of her legs. She pulled her other leg up onto the couch, pressed them both together. George was suddenly flushed with an almost unbearable desire for her, a feeling he knew had more to do with comfort and safety than sex.

"I can go," she said. "I wouldn't mind seeing my nieces. And there's something a little bit exciting about suddenly having to leave town because your life's in danger."

"Thank you, thank you, thank you," George said.

"But what about you?"

"I can handle myself," he said in a mock baritone.

"Clearly not."

"No, clearly not. But I'm going to put myself in the hands of the police. It's the only thing to do, and it's the right thing to do. Honestly, I can't even imagine that either Liana or Jenks is still in Boston. It doesn't make any sense. They got what they came for."

"How do you know that one of them didn't screw over the other? Maybe Donnie Jenks took the diamonds, or maybe Liana did and that's why Donnie is still around."

"I thought of that. It's a possibility. There are lots of possibilities, really. That's why I want you to leave town. I have no idea what's going on."

"Agreed. I'm leaving town. I can't help feeling I'm going to miss out a little. On everything that's going on here." She smiled.

"It's not funny. All I can see is your horrible eye."

She brought her hand up to the bandage. "I keep forgetting about this somehow. You have to promise to call me every day and let me know what's happening. I'm worried about you too."

"I will," George said, but remained on the couch.

"You're not leaving," Irene said.

George leaned across the couch and kissed her. He didn't know what to expect, but Irene returned the kiss with a hungry intensity, pushing back against George so that she was on top of him. He unbuttoned her Wakefield jersey and cupped her breasts, her small dark nipples already hard. "Bedroom?" George asked, his voice hoarse and low. She shook her head no as she unzipped his shorts. He slid his fingers under the waistband of her pajama shorts to shuck them off. She stopped him, pulled the stretchy fabric to the side, and guided him inside of her, her shorts still on. He bit his lip to stop himself from immediately coming, and she bore down hard on him, bucking her hips back and forth with a singular ferocity. She took hold of his hand, folded it into a fist, and pressed it against her, rubbing against his knuckles. They came together in just under a minute.

Irene walked him to the door. "You should nearly get me killed more often," she said as they hugged good-bye.

"No kidding."

They pulled apart. Irene's cheeks were deeply flushed, and she was not meeting his eye. "I *am* sorry about this mess," George said.

Irene flicked her hand, saying, "Psssh. You didn't mean to sic a murderer on me."

"It's not just that. . . ."

"All right, you're getting maudlin. You look exhausted. You can stay here if you want, you know."

"I have to go to the police."

"Be careful out there. I'll call you when I know my travel plans."

George stood for a moment after the door had shut, confused but also settled in his intention.

CHAPTER 17

Outside Irene's building the sky was an electric blue, but the archway was in total darkness. A wind chime that hung from one of the fire escapes chimed tunelessly. Two mounted lights cast thick intersecting shadows across the brick courtyard, and in one of the shadows George thought he saw the silhouetted figure of a man. He stood still for a moment, allowing his eyes to adjust to the night. A Prius zipped silently by on the street, its headlights briefly illuminating the courtyard, enough so that George could tell he was alone.

He started toward his car, alternately telling himself he was being too cautious and not cautious enough. If the fake Donnie Jenks was still around, then why wouldn't he be here? He'd been here the night before, when he knocked Irene to the ground. If he wanted to get to George, he'd know that this was a likely place for George to show up. George walked a little faster, passing a house with wide-open windows, *America's Funniest Home Videos* blaring from a monstrous flat-screen TV. When the sound faded, he thought he heard an echo of his footsteps behind him. He sped up a little, tilted his head, and felt rather than saw someone behind him. His heart rate seemed to double. The street he'd parked on was coming up on the right; turning onto it would give him a chance to look back and see if there really was someone behind him. He sped up a little more to make the turn, and as he did he looked back as casually as he could. There was someone, about half a block back, who was walking almost listlessly and was partly obscured by the row of trees planted along the sidewalk.

He considered his options. His car was a couple of hundred yards down the street. He could run to it, in the hope that whoever was following him was in even worse shape than he was, or he could keep walking, hoping that it all was just paranoia, that the person behind him was on an evening stroll. But nothing about George's recent life suggested that he was being overly paranoid about anything. Coming up on his right was a minivan sitting in a driveway in front of a single-family home. Without thinking, he darted behind it and crouched down, hoping he'd done so before his follower reached the corner.

Willing himself to breathe quietly, George listened. The footsteps, loud and with a slight drag on one side, grew louder. He thought he heard a hesitation, as though his follower was suddenly confused about where he'd gone, but the footsteps kept coming. It was dark where George was crouched, but he'd worn a light blue shirt and the minivan was painted a dark metallic gray. He pressed himself into the driver's-side door, and as his head grazed the door handle a piercing siren erupted from the vehicle, its front and back lights flashing on and off.

Despite the impulse, George neither screamed out loud nor

pissed himself. Instead, he lurched from the van as though it were suddenly on fire and careened into the sharp branches of a hedge that lined the driveway. Gritting his teeth, he turned toward the man on the sidewalk, who had turned toward him. George knew instantly from his bowling-pin shape that it wasn't the Donnie Jenks he was scared to see. It was DJ, the private investigator. He held a flat hand above his heart and looked as scared as George did. He was still partly in shadow, but what George could see seemed deathly white and sweaty. DJ put both his hands on his knees and breathed heavily. "You okay?" George asked, coming out onto the sidewalk. The siren pealed across the neighborhood. "Let's get away from this van."

They walked together toward his car, DJ breathing like a linebacker who had just run a forty. "You followed me here?" George asked.

"Yeah. That siren nearly gave me a heart attack."

"You're not really having one, are you?"

"I don't think so. I actually had one once, so I know what it feels like. It doesn't feel like this."

George didn't know what to say, so he asked, "Where'd you follow me from? Boston?"

"Yeah. Kind of hoping you might lead me to Jane Byrne."

"How do you know I didn't?"

"Because you went to visit Irene Dimas, and unless she's somehow harboring Jane . . ."

"How do you know about Irene?"

"I'm a detective. I detect. Were you somehow trying to hide your fifteen-year relationship with an ex-co-worker?"

"I guess not. You've been outside this whole time?"

"I have. I missed my dinner."

They reached George's car. The siren still screamed in the background. They stood awkwardly together for a moment, as if they were wondering whether to continue the date or call it a night. "I don't know where Jane is," George said.

"I believe you. Ms. Boyd does not. We also know there are things you haven't told us yet."

"That's true. I've thought about it. I'm ready to tell you anything you want to know. The police too."

"Okay." The siren stopped. As far as George could tell, no one, including the owners of the minivan, had come out onto the street to determine if a crime was happening.

"I'd rather not tell you everything here on the street. Is there somewhere else we can go? Where's your Suzuki?"

DJ laughed. "Next street over."

"I wouldn't think that's the best vehicle for remaining undetected."

"I followed you, didn't I?"

"What do you do if someone gets onto a highway? Can it go over sixty?"

"All right now, you're talking about my baby. Let's just say that in my line of work I don't actually do a lot of tailing of suspects on highways or otherwise. I spend more of my time in an office."

"So where should we talk?" George asked. "We could go back to my neighborhood in Boston. There's a comfortable bar."

"Fine with me. I can meet you in front of your building. I think I'll manage to keep up."

George moved around to the driver's-side door, and DJ prepared to cross the street. He looked both ways down the darkened, quiet street, and George smiled to himself at such overcaution, but as DJ began to cross a white car came barreling down the street, its lights off. George yelled to DJ to look out, but DJ was already halfway across. DJ hesitated a moment, deciding whether to keep going or turn back; in that moment the car's brakes screamed like a girl in a horror movie, and DJ managed one step toward the curb before being upended over the still-moving car's hood. George watched his enormous hips float up into the air as though he were weightless. DJ got a forearm out in front of his head, and that was what hit the windshield, splintering it. DJ pirouetted out of sight, and as the car halted, the brakes' scream abruptly ceasing, George heard the sick, heavy thud as DJ hit the pavement.

George moved toward DJ, casting an eye toward the driver of the vehicle, but stopped short. The window of the car—it was a white Dodge—was rolled down, and its driver held a sawed-off shotgun, its twin barrels resting casually out the lip of the window. George stopped, hands instinctively rising, and his feet beginning to reverse direction. His heel hit the curb he'd just stepped off, and he fell backward onto the sidewalk. He heard what he supposed was the pump of the shotgun and half rolled/half slid himself behind his car just as the explosion of the shotgun shook the air. George's Saab rocked on its wheels. One of its windows disintegrated. In the quiet aftermath, he heard the Dodge leave with another short scream of tires. The smell of burning rubber and hot metal filled the air.

"DJ," George called out into the night, but he heard nothing back, just the hiss of a ruptured tire and, from somewhere else, the sound of a screen door slapping open, voices coming toward him.

George had been in the interrogation room of the Boston police station for over an hour, left alone on a plastic chair under fluorescent lights. He'd finished his coffee, then steadily torn pieces from the rim of the Styrofoam cup till it was half its original size. It was just before midnight when the door swung inward and Detective Roberta James entered. She wore jeans, a short-sleeved button-up blouse, and a green Boston Celtics cap.

"Hi, George," she said, placing a mug and a folder on the table and sitting down.

"Detective," George said.

"You had a scare tonight, I heard?"

"What can you tell me about Donald Jenks? I've asked just about everyone here."

"Broken elbow. Dislocated shoulder. Concussion symptoms. They're keeping him overnight in the hospital."

George exhaled. After being shot at, he had willed his rubbery legs to move and had gone to the other side of the street. DJ was half on the sidewalk, twisted onto his side, his hair soaked and sticky with blood. He'd been conscious, but when George asked him how he was, he'd only looked up with confused eyes, then looked back toward the pavement as though the question had shamed him.

"What happened?" a voice had said from behind them. It was a woman in her thirties with a blond buzz cut. She hovered a few yards away, a worried frown on her face.

"He was hit," George said. "By a car. The car drove off." His voice sounded both formal and shaky, and he thought that he was probably in some kind of shock. The woman took a hesitant step toward them. There was suddenly a man next to her, speaking into his cell phone. He was whispering, as though he didn't want anyone else to hear. A patrol car arrived moments before the ambulance. More neighbors emerged onto the street, forming a low-talking semicircle. While the EMTs dealt with DJ, George spoke with a police officer, showing him the skid marks on the asphalt and the side of his Saab that had been peppered with shotgun spray. The officer, clearly another car lover, studied the damage with a grim solemnity. George told the story as it had happened, omitting the far more complicated larger picture, but he did produce Detective James's card and tell them that what had happened was connected with a case she was investigating. After the ambulance had left, he was taken to the station and told to wait in an interrogation room.

"You want to tell me what happened?" Detective James asked. He wondered about her partner, O'Clair, and whether he was watching and listening on a monitor somewhere.

"Sure," George said.

"Do you know who shot at you tonight?"

"I know who it was, but I don't know his real name. The name he gave me was Donnie Jenks."

"Donald Jenks who's in the hospital right now?"

"No, that's the real Donald Jenks. The man who ran him over with his car, and the man who shot at me, is calling himself Donnie Jenks, but it's obviously not his real name, or else it's a *very* big coincidence."

"I'm confused."

"Okay," George said. "I'll back up and tell you everything I know."

And he did. It was the second time he'd told the story that night, the first time to Irene, and retelling it only made him feel increasingly naïve and incompetent. He told Detective James everything that had happened since Friday night without going into specifics about his past, twenty years earlier, with Liana. He did, however, give up her real name. "There'll be a file on her. She's wanted in Florida for homicide."

"How does she spell her last name?"

"D-E-C-T-E-R."

"Why didn't you give us this information this morning?"

George shrugged. "I didn't know at that time that she'd . . . that I'd been implicated in a murder. I still thought it was possible that what she'd told me had been the truth, that she was in Boston to return money and to try and get back a semblance of safety in her life. Obviously, I was wrong."

"And you don't know where she might be?"

"No idea. I doubt very much that she's still in the area. I would say it's a certainty that she's long gone except for the fact that, clearly, her partner is still around."

Detective James opened the folder in front of her, removed a black-and-white mug shot, and spun it so that it faced George. "Is this the man who called himself Donnie Jenks?"

The man in the picture had long, swept-back hair and was at least a decade younger than "Donnie Jenks," but the features seemed right, small and clustered on a head that seemed larger toward the top. George looked at the nose; it was hard to make out in the grainy shot, but it looked like the same nose, snub and with a flattened bridge. "It looks like him," he said. "Who is he?"

"His name is Bernie MacDonald. That name mean anything to you?"

George told her it didn't.

"But you're sure it's the man you met in New Essex, the man who punched you in the kidney?"

George looked again. The face in the mug shot was calm, almost cocky, as though he was not particularly worried about whatever had led him to be in that situation and whatever was going to happen next. It was that calmness that told George this was definitely the man calling himself Donnie Jenks. "Yeah, I'm sure. Is he connected to Liana Decter, or Jane Byrne?"

"We have nothing concrete, but until recently he lived in Atlanta. He was a bartender at a place near where Liana worked and lived. His prints showed up on a stolen vehicle outside of the city. That's how we pulled his file."

"What was he arrested for?"

"Nothing too serious. Aggravated assault. Petty theft. No murder, or attempted murder. Not yet anyway."

"Good to know."

"Do you think that Bernie MacDonald and Liana might be holed up at that place in New Essex?"

"I don't. It's a total dump, not even habitable. For whatever reason, one of them knew about this place, and it's where they decided to stage my meeting with this guy . . . this Bernie. The plan was obviously that he would scare me enough so that I would feel the need to do this favor for Liana."

"What about somewhere near the place? Why do you think they picked New Essex?"

"There's another house on the lane. I knocked actually, to see what I could find out. The woman there was pretty strung out."

"Did you get her name?"

"No. I just asked her if she knew anything about who might live in the old cottage. She wasn't too helpful."

"Okay." The detective slid Bernie MacDonald's mug shot back into her folder and closed it. She arched her shoulders back, and George heard an audible pop. "Am I free to go?" he asked. His entire body ached. Despite his nap earlier in the day, he felt as though he could fall asleep by simply closing his eyes.

"Unless you can think of anything else you're not telling us." Detective James said and leaned back, putting both her hands on the arms of her chair. George noticed, for the first time, how sculpted and smooth her arms were. "I really don't want to find out you're still holding out on us. We won't be so charitable."

"I'm not. If I've forgotten something, it's because I can barely think straight. I just want to go home and go to sleep."

The detective stared at him with a look that managed to be both threatening and bored, then pushed herself up into a standing position. "Come with me. You're free to go."

A patrol officer drove George home, since his Saab was sitting in a body shop on the other side of the river.

He sat in back, the cracked vinyl smelling of Pine-Sol and public bathrooms. The officer driving talked on his cell phone the entire time, arguing with his wife about whether his teenage daughter could go unchaperoned to some event. He couldn't quite tell what side the officer was on, but he seemed to be losing the fight. *The world goes on,* George thought, *despite murders and million-dollar heists and idiots like me who get involved.*

The officer pulled up to George's building, told his wife to hold on a moment, and turned. "This okay? You want me to walk you in?"

George peered down his dark alleyway, wondering for a

moment whether it was populated by the Bernie MacDonalds of the world. "I'm all right," he said, and the officer released the security lock on the door. George thanked him and got out, too tired to care about who might be waiting for him on his back steps. There was no one. And there was no one in his apartment either, except for a very verbal and hungry cat. He fed Nora, drank several glasses of water, and climbed back into bed. His body felt inordinately heavy on the mattress, and his muscles ached. He imagined that when the shotgun blast blew a hole in the Saab, his entire body had violently tensed.

He shut his eyes but did not immediately fall asleep. Questions buzzed in his mind. He couldn't figure out how he was still involved in what was happening. It was clear to him how he'd been initially used, but clearly something had transpired between Liana Decter and Bernie MacDonald to cause a rift. Otherwise, why was MacDonald still around? Did he think George had the diamonds?

George heard the barely perceptible meow as Nora leapt onto the foot of the bed. He could feel her start to settle herself into her usual position. He turned onto his stomach and began the slow descent into sleep. He thought of Liana, replaying moments from twenty-four hours earlier when she had been naked in this very bed. He could still recall her face, the way it had been reduced to a mask by the dawn light. The foggy notion of a pair of eyes, a nose, a mouth. He cringed, remembering what he had asked her as they lay together, limbs entwined. "It was real, wasn't it?" he asked. "What we had in college?"

The unreadable mask that was her face gave nothing away. "Shhh," she had said, pulling him closer so that her lips were by his ear. She had run the tip of her tongue along the side of his neck.

Then he thought of Irene earlier that evening, how after they had both come she buried her head in his neck and they lay still, George inside of her, her breath warm against his collarbone.

The images fought against each other, then merged and intertwined as George tumbled into a disturbed and restless sleep.

CHAPTER 18

H i, Audrey," George said to Liana Decter on the phone. He was sitting in the motel room, still reeling from his encounter with the man from the muscle car, and he was sure that his voice must be trembling.

"So you thought I was dead?"

"What did you think I would think?"

"I'm sorry about that."

George didn't say anything, so she continued. "I guess Dale scared you pretty bad this afternoon. I'm sorry about that too."

"He was pretty scary."

"Yeah, that's what he does. That's his job. He's gone back to Tampa, though, so I was thinking we could meet tonight. I'd like to explain."

George let a second pass, then said, "Okay."

"There's a place called Palm's Lounge, in Chinkapin." She gave him the street address. "Do you think you could find it?"

They agreed to meet at 9:00 P.M., and before George could ask

*more questions she hung up. He sat for a moment on the edge of
the bed. He could still follow through with his plan. Leave Florida.
Call Detective Chalfant from the road and tell him everything.
Never see Audrey, or whatever her name might be, again. But the
phone call had changed all that. She wanted to see him, and there
was no way that he was not going to go. He had come to Florida to
look for the truth, and he was about to get it.*

*He showered, even though he had no clean clothes to dress in,
then visited Dan Thompson and asked him for the car overnight.
He was told he could keep it overnight so long as he checked back
in at 8:00 A.M. the following day.*

*It was early evening and still light, and because he was too anx-
ious to remain in his motel room, he drove. He crossed the Dahoon
River into Chinkapin, then took Cortez Avenue all the way to St.
Anna's Island. He parked by the beach. The Gulf was a deep metallic blue, and the lowering sun reddened the sky and spread dazzling white light across the sea. George walked down the beach and
found an old wooden pier with a structure at the end. He walked
the length of the pier, passing fishermen and elderly tourists. There
was an outside bar at the end, with three empty weather-stripped
stools. He ordered a bottle of Budweiser and was given it. He'd
drunk in bars before—a few dives near his college were notorious
for never carding local students—but he had never been served in
a bar outside of that area. He drank the first beer fast, then ordered
another, lit a cigarette, and drank the second one slowly, watching
boats drift in and out of the receding light.*

*An hour and a half later, but still an hour and a half before
his scheduled meeting with Liana, George parked the Buick in the
gravel lot of Palm's Lounge. It was at the intersection of two flat
empty roads, an old farmhouse with a painted palm tree fading on*

its side and a neon beer sign above its door. He'd bought a cheeseburger to go from a fast-food joint and eaten it in the car. There
were only two other vehicles in the lot besides his, both trucks. He
was relieved to note the absence of muscle cars.

The inside of Palm's Lounge was the size of a train car, harshly
lit toward the front with a hanging fluorescent light and barely lit
toward the back. There was one employee and one customer, each
drinking a mixed cocktail at the dark end of the bar. The employee
was a fifty-year-old man with a thick mustache and thinning hair
on top; his customer was a woman about the same age wearing a
short-brimmed straw cowboy hat.

George walked to the middle of the bar and rested an elbow on
it. As the bartender made his way toward him he asked for a Bud.

The bartender got the beer and took George's two dollars. "The
jukebox is busted. If you want to play a song, it don't cost nothing,"
the bartender said.

George walked with his beer to an old jukebox in the back,
with its line of forty-fives stacked horizontally behind the curving
glass. The names of the songs were on little cards, some typed and
some handwritten, and most were country songs. George selected
a bunch, randomly picking them, based on little more than name
recognition. Hank Williams, for instance, rang a bell. So did Patsy
Cline.

He brought his beer to a table in the far back corner and waited.

She came through the door at one minute past nine. Since
he'd been waiting, a short man in a vinyl jacket had come in,
sat next to the woman with the straw cowboy hat, and ordered a
Jack and Coke. One other couple had entered, an obese man with

a skinny tattooed wife. They'd ordered two whiskey sours, brought them to a table near the front, drunk them wordlessly, and left.

Audrey/Liana stepped through the front door, letting it swing closed behind her. She was in the full blaze of the overhead lighting, and George watched her gaze unseeing for a moment toward the back of the bar. She wore a pair of black cotton pants, the kind waiters and waitresses sometimes wear, and a short-sleeved blouse in green, her favorite color. She looked as he'd remembered her: small-shouldered, a little wide at the hips, exotic-eyed, startling. She spotted him.

He remained seated as she walked out of the glare of the doorway lighting and into the dim interior, taking a quick sideways glance toward the bar, then putting a hand on his shoulder, leaning in slightly. She smelled the same—like cinnamon gum—and he realized it was something about her he'd forgotten in just a few weeks.

"Did he card you for that?" she asked, indicating the beer.

"No. I don't think you need to worry about it."

"You want another?"

"I'll get it," George said. "You sit. You want a beer, or something else?"

"A beer'll be fine."

She sat at the table while he went to the bartender for two more beers.

When he returned, she had placed her hands flat on the table surface, expectantly, like a child waiting to be fed. George had seen her do such a thing before. Despite her forged identity, Liana was the Audrey he had known. Half-drunk, he wanted to reach across to her and clasp his hands around her shoulders. He wanted to kiss her.

"I can't believe you came all the way down here," she said after sipping the rising foam off the neck of the bottle.

"I don't think you're allowed to start a sentence with 'I can't believe' in it before I do."

She smiled. "That's fair."

"I thought you were dead. Do you have any—"

"Look, stop. I feel terrible about that. Let me take a moment to explain and maybe you'll understand. You saw where I live today, so you know I don't come from much money, not enough to go to college with. I don't really want to go into all the details, but I live with just my father. He's old for a dad, nearly seventy. He wrote for television about thirty years ago, in California. He says he wrote a Twilight Zone, but I don't know about that. Now all he likes to do is drink beer, smoke pot, and gamble. God, this sounds like . . . poor me, eh? Anyway, long story short, no mother around forever, old horrible father who's constantly in debt, and plain me, who thinks maybe she can go to MCC for a two-year degree after high school. If she's lucky."

"Then you met Audrey Beck. Because of speech and debate."

She took a chest-filling breath. "Right. You figured all this out, Detective Foss. I became friends with Audrey, acquaintances really. We would talk to each other at forensics meets. She told me she liked my earrings. I told her I liked her jeans, et cetera. She also told me how her parents were making her go to college, though all she wanted to do was go to this beach house her boyfriend and his band were renting. I told her I'd kill to go to college, but there wasn't any money. And I told her how my dad probably wouldn't notice if I moved my boyfriend into my own bedroom at home. And then we hatched a plan. No, that's not true exactly. We hatched a fantasy, both saying how great it would be if we could just switch places. If I had her parents, I could go to college and everyone would be happy. If she had my dad, then she could go live with *her boyfriend on the beach. This was back in May. Then we both graduated from high school, and I didn't hear from her till August."*

"What were you doing all summer? What were your plans?"

"I was working as a hostess at a restaurant called the River-view, like I'd done the past two years. I'd signed up for classes at community college. It sucked, but what could I do? Then Audrey called me. She told me she'd decided not to go to college. She was going to West Palm Beach instead, and when she didn't show up at school her parents would find out everything. And then she said that I should go in her place. I had my own car. I could tell my dad I had decided to take off—he wouldn't care anyway—and I could drive all the way up to Connecticut, matriculate as Audrey Beck, and no one would know. She'd arrange a time to call her parents every week, pretend like she was in school. If I got a call from her parents, I'd pretend to be a roommate and take a message and then relay it back to Audrey in Florida. It seemed plausible. . . . I mean, it was plausible. We did it, and it worked." Liana clenched her teeth and looked directly at George. "And I think it would've gone on working—"

"But Audrey died."

"Right. Audrey died. So I died." One of Liana's eyes glittered in the light from the jukebox. Patsy Cline sang something about walking after midnight.

"What happened?"

"You mean with Audrey?"

"Yeah."

"She called me when I got back to Florida. She was back in Sweetgum. We met. Here actually. She was a mess. No surprise, her boyfriend turned out to be an asshole. She said that all he was into was drugs and getting laid. She said he tried to talk her into

having sex with the whole band. I guess the final straw was that there were drug dealers after them for money. It sounded like a nightmare. She asked me about Mather College, and I told her what it was like. I didn't lie, I told her I'd had this great semester, and I told her about you. I could tell she thought she'd made this giant mistake, which I guess she had. I think she was still doing drugs that night—she seemed like she was on something when she came here to meet me—and then she got drunk. Anyway, she told me she wanted to switch back our lives. She wanted to go to college for the second semester."

"Did she think no one would notice?"

"I know, but she wasn't thinking. I told her that it wasn't possible, that she couldn't just show up there, telling people she was the real Audrey Beck. I told her that I would stop going in her place if that was what she really wanted and that she could transfer to another school. That's how we left it. She was upset. I think she actually thought she could just jump back into the life she had traded away. It's not like we looked exactly alike or anything."

"You don't."

"And that was it. She drove home, and so did I. That was the night she died."

"So you think she killed herself?"

"She was real drunk, so I think she might've just pulled into her garage and passed out. I didn't hear about it till two days later. Obviously, I'd already decided not to go back to Mather. I was planning on calling you and Emily. Then she died, and I didn't know what to do."

"Jesus," George said and lit a cigarette. His beer was already gone and his head was swimming a little, but something about her story was not making sense. "How did you feel when she told you

she wanted her name back? You must've been planning on coming back to school."

"Well, I was, but still, I always knew it was temporary. Being Audrey was temporary. I had become this different person, this person I'd rather have been—you know, in school, doing well, with a boyfriend, a boyfriend like you—but it was like I had a secret disease, or there was this clock inside of me, ticking like a heart, and at any moment an alarm would go off and Audrey Beck would no longer exist. She'd die and I'd have to go back to being Liana Decter. God, it's like a dream now, that whole semester."

"It must have been strange."

"And good. It was a good time, wasn't it?"

"Maybe you could come back somehow. As yourself. You were doing really well there."

Liana laughed. "You think they'd just forgive me for faking my identity? You think Audrey's parents would forgive me? They paid for a stranger to go to college."

"Her parents know now that Audrey didn't actually go to Mather. I mean, everyone knows, the police as well."

"Yeah, I heard that. I thought that would probably come out. I wasn't positive—"

"But thanks to me—"

"But thanks to you, and your unswerving devotion." She reached out and put a hand on his cheek. They were silent for a moment. The beer and her closeness had dissolved any sense of reality from where George was, and from what they had been talking about.

"I miss you. I missed you," George said.

"I miss you too."

"Can I kiss you?"

"Okay."

"My lips are kind of beat-up."

"Yeah, I noticed that. It's okay."

They kissed, gently, in the dark corner of the bar, an up-tempo rockabilly song replacing the Patsy Cline number.

Y ou haven't told me the whole story," George said.

"I know. But first tell me what it was like at school. How did people react?"

He told her about the two days he'd spent at Mather, about finding out from Emily, about the makeshift wake at Barnard Hall, about his meeting with the dean, about how Kevin nearly kicked his ass. Liana listened intently, her lips slightly parted, eyes wider than usual. "It's like being allowed to see your own funeral," she said. "It's kind of fascinating in a morbid way."

Then he told her about his trip down to Florida and what had happened during the past two days. When he got to the part about staking out Liana's house, George said: "Now you need to tell me about that guy who was there."

"Dale."

"Right, Dale."

"Okay. I suppose you've earned this, but you're not going to like it much."

"He's a friend of yours?"

"Sort of."

"He's a boyfriend?"

"Not really, but in a way. Just let me tell it. First off, as I said, my dad gambles. Majorly. He used to go to the races, but then he started betting on sports through a bookie in Tampa. Honestly, I don't even know the name of the guy he calls, but he used to be on *the phone all the time, more than me when I was in middle school. He owed a lot of money, and when he wouldn't pay it, scary guys would show up. And one of those guys—"*

"—was Dale."

"Right. He was a collector, and he used to come by pretty frequently. He's very good at inflicting pain and not leaving any marks apparently—"

"That's not what he told me. He told me there'd be marks."

Liana gripped his forearm. "I'm sorry you had to deal with him. I'm sure that was less than pleasant. He'd been away for a while. He wasn't around the summer before school started 'cause my dad had started going to Gamblers Anonymous. That's partly why I felt I could leave and go to Mather. I told my dad I was driving cross-country with a friend, and that I'd call him and check in. He said he'd be fine. I made him promise he would keep going to Gamblers Anonymous, but he didn't make it."

"That's why Dale was back."

"Partly, but he was also back looking for me. Can I have one of those? I'm out." George lit a cigarette for her. "This is the hard part to talk about," she continued. "Things got really bad for a time, and we owed a lot of money. Dad owed it, really, but I felt it was my problem as well. Dale was talking about severely disabling him, maybe even killing him. Dale knew me 'cause he would come to the house. And he liked me. So, eventually, an arrangement got worked out."

"What kind of arrangement?"

"What do you think?"

"Jesus."

"Yeah."

"How old were you?"

"When it started, sixteen, but then I got my dad to quit gambling, pretty much my whole senior year, so Dale wasn't around so much."

"Jesus."

"You think I'm sick?"

"No . . . yeah, I think it's sick. I think Dale is sick and your dad. It's awful. Jesus, I'm so sorry. For you."

"Well, it wasn't Little House on the Prairie, but it's over now. My dad's going to quit gambling—he already has. Dale'll stop sniffing around—"

"Did you and he, this Christmas . . ."

"Yeah, that's why he showed up, but no, nothing happened. It's weird, even though it was coercion, in a strange way he really does think of me as his girlfriend. He protects me. That's why he went after you this afternoon. My dad spotted you in the car out the window, and he called Dale, and Dale did his thing. I wasn't even at the house today."

"There must be something you can do about it."

"Don't worry. It's over with. Let's talk about something else, or let's get out of here. This place is depressing."

They stood outside in the dark parking lot, a spill of yellow stars above them. Liana had parked her car next to George's, and they stood between them, hugging and kissing. George felt like he was a million miles and a million years from any other part of his life.

"I'll only say good-night tonight if I know I can see you tomorrow," he said.

"Okay. But you need to go back to Mather eventually."

"I don't know. Maybe I could stay here with you."

"I won't let you stay here. I don't care how much you like me, this is not a place for anyone."

"What? Florida? Or with you?"

"Both."

"Florida's not so bad. Where else can you buy fireworks and oranges at the same place?"

"Ah, fireworks and oranges. The perfect definition of my state. Let me tell you: oranges are not all they're cracked up to be. I used to have to drive past a juice factory, and do you know how bad they smell, those places? Made me never want to see another orange, let alone drink a glass of orange juice. And don't let me get started on fireworks."

"What have you got against fireworks?"

"They're meaningless. A bunch of people ooh and aah at some stupid explosions in the sky. A few flashy lights and everyone's IQ drops twenty points."

"I don't remember you being so cynical."

"Now you see the real me."

He hugged her tighter, and she kissed his collarbone. "Will you come and see me tomorrow at the motel I'm at?" George asked.

"I promise. What time do you want me to come?"

"As soon as you can."

"I'll be there at noon. We can have lunch."

"Okay. And we can talk about options."

"Okay. Options. I like options."

"We could move somewhere together, but not right away. I think the police are going to want to know what happened between you and Audrey."

"I know. I'll deal with that later," she said.

"No, we'll deal with it."

"Right. We."

Liana got in her car first. She rolled down her window, and

George leaned in to kiss her good-night. "You haven't called me by my name yet."

"Good-night, Liana," he said before she drove away. "It sounds strange."

"Well, it's my real name. Truth is, I prefer Audrey. You can still call me Audrey if you want."

"No, I want to call you by your real name."

He watched her taillights bounce their way out of the gravel driveway, then cut a steadily dimming swath down the pasture-lined road. He wondered later if she had just kept driving all through that night, all the way to wherever she went, or if she had stopped in one more time at her father's house.

CHAPTER 19

A rapping on the door awakened him. George lay there for
a moment, confused, the facts from the past few days
rapidly assaulting him. They were like remnants from a dream
except that they were real, underlined by the knocks coming
from the other room. No one in his previous life would come
unannounced to his door, especially early on a Tuesday morning.

He put on a robe despite the fact that his skin was still damp
and sticky from his humid room. In his exhaustion the night
before, he had forgotten to put his air conditioner on; the air
throughout the apartment had the thick quality of a sauna. As
he walked through his living room his head and stomach both
felt light; he couldn't remember when he had last eaten. There
was another loud knock, seven exasperated raps; he hoped it was
the police and not Bernie MacDonald or Liana coming to finish
the job.

"Who is it?" he asked through the locked door.

"Karin Boyd." It took a moment for him to place the name,

not because he'd forgotten MacLean's niece but because he was still swimming up from the deep sweaty grip of last night's sleep. He opened the door and was about to invite Karin in, but she pushed through and entered on her own. "I've been out here twenty minutes," she said.

"I'm sorry. Come on in," he said and shut the door.

Her face was flushed a deep red, and her jaw seemed locked in place. "You heard what happened to DJ," George said.

"I saw him this morning. He's lucky to be alive." The tone of her voice suggested George was the one who had run him over with a car.

"I heard he has a concussion. Does he remember what happened?"

"He remembers following you and finding you. He said that you were going to tell him everything you knew, but then he doesn't remember anything. The police said you were attacked."

"We were attacked by the man who probably killed your uncle. Look, I need to get myself a coffee, and I need to sit down. Come in and have a seat. I'm not going to give you the runaround. I'm on your side now." In middle school he'd suffered an entire year under the tyrannical rule of a female bully a year ahead of him. She used to glare at him with the same unchecked aggression that Karin Boyd was currently expressing. George moved away from her and toward the kitchen. "Sit anywhere," he said and was relieved when she followed and perched herself on the edge of one of his Nora-shredded easy chairs. "Can I get you anything? A glass of water?"

Karin declined, and he went into the kitchen, filled a pint glass with water, and drank it down. The pot of coffee, still on its hot plate, held four fingers of black liquid that was several days old. He poured it into the pint glass, then added ice and milk before returning to the living room. Karin was looking around his space with what looked like disdain, or maybe that was just her regular expression.

"Just like your uncle's place," he said, then immediately regretted it.

She raised an eyebrow. "It's a good location," she said, apparently unfazed by George's attempt at a joke.

"Yeah, it is. How did you find out about DJ?" he asked, sitting down.

"He was supposed to check in with me yesterday, but I never heard from him. I finally got through to Detective James late last night, and she filled me in. She said she'd had you in for questioning but released you. I came directly here from the hospital to hear what you were going to say to Donald." Karin crossed and uncrossed and recrossed her legs while she spoke. She was more casually dressed than the last time George had seen her—a short black skirt and a faded blue polo. Her hair was pulled back into a ponytail, and her face was not made up. As she talked, color gathered on her chest and on her cheeks. Her skin was the delicate bluey white of skimmed milk, and George imagined she avoided the sun.

"You'll probably be disappointed. I don't have a lot to tell, but I'll tell you what I know. I already told the police everything."

"I take it you didn't tell the police where Jane Byrne currently is?"

"I would've if I knew. I have no idea. My guess is she took everything that was in your uncle's safe and now she's far, far away. The only reason I think that might not be the case is that her partner is still around."

"He's the one who attacked you last night?"

"I think so. I mean, I know so, but I didn't see him."

"How do you know it wasn't Jane?"

"The car was the car I'd seen this guy in before. . . . Should I start at the beginning?"

"Okay."

For the third time in twenty-four hours, George told the whole story, everything that had happened to him since seeing Liana again on Friday night. Like Detective James, Karin was particularly interested in the abandoned cottage in New Essex and the other house down the lane where he'd met the strung-out-looking young woman.

"Do you think that's where they're hiding?" Karin asked. She was still perched on the edge of the chair. During the course of his story the sun had edged westward enough to sneak through one of the narrow living room windows and light half her face, making one of her tiny ears seem almost translucent in the glare.

"As I said, I can't see any reason why they'd be hiding around here at all, unless one of them screwed over the other one. I think it's possible that the house near the cottage was where they were staying. It makes sense. Let's say one of them knows who lives there. They find the rotting cottage and use it as a staging place where I could meet Bernie MacDonald pretending to work for your uncle. He'd scare me enough that I would agree to help Liana . . . Jane. If anyone went back there, as I did, they'd just see a dump by the water."

"Will you take me there?"

George knew the question was coming but hadn't decided yet how to answer. Despite a full night's sleep, he was exhausted and his nerves were shot. Although he was still curious as to the whereabouts of Liana and the diamonds from the safe, he felt relieved in his decision to hand over everything he knew to the authorities. "I can tell you where it is," he said. "Or better yet, we could tell the detectives what we're thinking. Let them go."

"But you already told them everything, right? You told them about the cottage and the house that's near it. If they want to go, they'll go."

"So we'll let them go instead of us," George said.

"It's a long shot, right? It's probably nothing. It can't hurt for us to check it out."

"I can tell you where it is."

"I don't think I want to go there alone. I'd feel more comfortable if you came along."

"Look—"

"I think you owe me. My uncle is dead, and you're partly responsible. If Donald were well enough, I would just go with him, but you're responsible for that too." Her voice was rising in pitch, and George realized that, rightly or not, she had cast him as a primary player in the crime that had occurred.

"I'll take you," he said. "But if anyone's there or I see a suspicious car, we turn around immediately and call the police."

"Okay."

"I need some time to get ready. I have to make a couple of phone calls."

Karin checked her watch, as though deciding whether to allow him the few minutes he'd asked for. "I'll wait," she said.

George brushed his teeth in the bathroom, ran wet hands through his hair, and applied an extra amount of deodorant in lieu of a shower. In the bedroom, while dressing, he called his office first, got hold of the receptionist, and told her that he was still feeling sick and wouldn't be coming in. Then he called Irene's cell phone; after several rings she picked up. "Where are you?" he asked.

"On the road. My sister and her kids are actually visiting my dad in Rochester, so that's where I'm headed. You put my life in danger at a good time." She sounded relentlessly cheerful, and he chose not to mention the incident that had happened outside her apartment building the night before.

"Drive safe, okay?"

"I will. Everything okay on your end?"

"Dull as dishwater. I called in sick to work, but only because I'm exhausted. Say hi to your family for me."

"I will."

Karin had parked her car, a metallic gray Audi, in front of George's building in a resident-only spot. George slid gingerly into the passenger-side bucket seat, still tender where Bernie had punched him. It was a perfect late-summer day, the temperature having dropped about ten degrees and the humidity suddenly not uncomfortable. Karin started the car and electronically lowered both windows before pulling out of the spot.

"You know how to get to New Essex?" he asked.

"I can get to the town center. You can direct me from there."

They were both quiet as Karin negotiated her way through the Monday morning ant farm that was Boston traffic. There was a sluggish jam where 93 North spilled onto 95, and Karin cursed and hissed at it as though New Essex were due to disappear at any moment. But once they were safely onto 95, the roads cleared and the silence in the car became noticeable.

"How's Mrs. MacLean?" George asked. "I'm sorry. I don't remember her full name."

"It's Teresa. She's rebounded slightly. Still dying, of course, but temporarily pretty lucid. It's actually a huge shame, because we had to tell her that her husband was dead. We chose not to tell her that he was murdered in their own house. We said he had a heart attack, and now we're just praying she doesn't get well enough to want to start looking at newspapers or watching television. She's still in pain, and she's still dying, but now she can feel grief-stricken as well."

"You're close to both of them?"

"I was close to my uncle. I was the smart child he never had, the one who got an MBA. I was actually working for Lehman Brothers during the crash. My uncle, probably out of guilt, offered me the job as his assistant when I couldn't find work. It was a nice bridge, I guess."

"What do you mean, 'out of guilt'?"

There was a discernible pause before Karin spoke. "I'm not sure my uncle did anything illegal, but in the economic climate before the mortgage crisis he made a ridiculous amount of money. It's possible some people got hurt while he got rich. So there might have been some guilt involved. I'm saying too much."

"He ran a Ponzi scheme?"

"Where did you hear that?"

"I didn't," George lied. "It just sounded like the type of thing you were describing."

"More or less, I guess. This is all off the record, I trust."

"I have no stake in this. I don't really care how your uncle made his money."

They were talking over the hiss of rushing air that came through their open windows. Karin hit a button to make both windows rise and seal. Suddenly the car was an almost noiseless space. Karin fiddled with the temperature controls, putting the AC on low. She was quiet again. George sensed that she was uncomfortable talking about her uncle's wealth, but he was interested. It was MacLean's money, after all, that was at the root of everything that had happened. "Did your uncle keep all of his diamonds in the safe in Newton?" he asked.

"God, no. A lot of them, though. We begged him not to, to put them in a safe-deposit box in a bank, but it had become a passion of his, those diamonds, and he liked to take them out and look at them. He was collecting them by color; they come in many colors, you know, not just white."

"All I know about diamonds is that they cost a lot of money."

"Yes, and they're easy to steal, and fairly easy to sell."

"And they are an easy way to hide how much money you have."

"Look, even if some of his methods were less than ethical, my uncle made plenty of money legitimately, through his furniture outlets and through his investments. You don't think I'm just pursuing this because of the money that was in the safe?"

"I figured that was part of it."

"My uncle got set up, robbed, and murdered. I want to find the scum that did it. I'd still be doing this if all he had in that safe was his childhood train set."

"I understand. I'd feel the same way."

"It's not my money, anyway, if we get it back. The money goes to his wife, and God only knows what her will stipulates."

As Karin's voice rose in pitch George noticed a corresponding increase in the speed of the Audi. They were easily cresting ninety miles per hour when he pointed out the exit to New Essex. She expertly crossed three lanes of traffic and downshifted into the hairpin curve of the off-ramp. He directed her toward and then away from New Essex center. Once they were on Beach Road, he told her to look out for the stone church. She rolled both windows down again, and the car was filled with the briny smell of ocean air. George looked toward the Atlantic, pinpricked with sunspots and glossily blue. Even though it was a Tuesday, a multitude of sailboats were out, pleasure boaters taking advantage of the high-pressure system that had swept away a week's worth of smothering humidity.

George was suddenly scared. While he believed that the house and cottage down Captain Sawyer Lane were probably dead ends, he considered the possibility that they weren't, and that Bernie MacDonald would be waiting for them, armed with his shotgun. He reminded himself that if there were signs of habitation at either the house or the cottage—Bernie's car, for instance—they would turn around and leave. Call the police. But something else was driving George, and he realized that it was Liana. There was a chance he would see her again, a small chance that she was being held against her will by Bernie Mac-Donald, and George, despite the lack of any evidence, still held out some hope that Liana might actually need him.

It was a hope he had nourished for two decades.

They passed the church, its small lot empty of cars. George pointed out Captain Sawyer Lane, and Karin slowed down and made the sharp turn. Even with the brightness of the day, the lane was dark under its canopy of trees. Karin hit one of the ruts too hard, and the bottom of her car scraped the road. She slowed to a crawl.

"Do you want to see the cottage?" he asked.

"The abandoned place?"

"Yeah, down by the water."

"No. Let's go straight to the house where you saw the girl. If it's a dead end, we can check out the cottage."

He pointed out the driveway, and she turned onto it. As before, high weeds sprouted from the broken gravel and dirt. The deckhouse was as dark and unreadable as ever. The garage was closed, and no cars were parked in the driveway; the windows seemed as brown and blank as the walls, and except for its relatively good condition, it looked as abandoned as the cottage by the water.

"When you were last here, was there a car out front?" Karin asked, and her voice had the tiniest waver to it. The dark woods had unnerved her.

"No. It looked just like this."

They parked, and both got out of the car. George had expected it to be even cooler in the piney darkness of the woods, but the air felt muggy, as though the humidity of the past week had somehow been trapped beneath the close-knit trees. Despite being so near to the ocean, there was no discernible breeze. They walked toward the door together, and George rang the bell. As before, he heard a deep gong from inside the house. They waited, silently, for half a minute. He rang the bell again and pressed his face to one of the narrow windows that ran the length of the door. The house was a split-level; a carpeted landing led to two short stairwells, one going up and one going down. Nothing moved.

Karin reached for the door latch, but it was locked. They looked at each other. "Should we peer through other windows?" he asked.

"I was going to suggest we break in."

"Let's just walk around the house, see if anything's open, or if anyone's here. Do you want to go that way and I'll go the other and we can meet on the other side?"

"Why don't we stick together?" Karin said. "This place gives me the creeps."

They began to circle the house, moving clockwise. The garage door was locked, so they rounded the corner. There was a short stretch of yard that separated the house's dark siding from the encroaching woods, but the yard had probably not been tended to since winter: its grass was knee-high, and it was filled with weedy flowers. George waded into the grass, walking splay-footed to press it down while he walked. Small clouds of bugs rose from the undergrowth. Karin, close behind him, said, "I fucking hate nature."

"All of it?" George asked.

"I don't mind looking at it, but I don't want to be in it."

There was only one window along this side of the house, a horizontal rectangle fronted by a mossy wooden window box with some scrappy vegetation protruding from it. Propped along the foundation were several faded plastic milk crates and a wooden pallet that was black with rot and mildew. "If I stand on a crate," George said, "I could probably look into the window."

He lifted one of the crates, exposing some wet black soil where it had rested for a very long time. A small green snake darted away into a fissure in the foundation. Karin let out a single choked scream and grabbed George's arm. "It's just a garter snake," he said. "Our official state reptile."

"I don't care. I'm wearing sandals. Let's go around to the back and see if there's a lower window to look through."

George agreed and put the milk crate down.

The small yard at the back was equally overgrown, with a brick patio extending the length of the house. Scattered over the mostly broken bricks was all the detritus of a once-furnished patio. A glass-topped circular table was covered with a thin scrim of black water; two of the chairs were tipped over on their sides. A large Weber grill had been left out for way too long; its metal handles and legs were spotted with rust, and an abandoned bee-hive was nestled in the joint of one of its legs. Between the patio and the house was a wide pair of sliding-glass doors. Karin went over and tried them, but they were locked. They both looked through the glass into the living room of the house. The state of the patio had led George to believe that the house's interior might be equally derelict, but the living room looked habitable. It was a low-ceilinged room with several large pieces of uphol-stered furniture, a bookcase-lined wall, and a brick fireplace. A low table in front of the sofa was cluttered with glasses, ashtrays, and dirty plates.

"It gives a little," Karin said, tugging at the door again.

"I think we should probably just leave," George said.

"Why? There's no one here. If we find anything that makes it look like your friends were staying here, we'll call the police."

George grasped the handle and pulled hard. It didn't feel locked so much as obstructed; he was able to pull the door open about half an inch, enough to see that it was unlatched. He crouched and looked at the interior track. A thin wooden dowel had been placed inside of it. Telling Karin to pull extra hard on the door, he watched as the dowel bent up and out of the track. Knowing that he was being foolish, George decided that it would be okay if they briefly looked in the house. "I think we can break it," he said, "if we pull hard enough."

They each got a hand around the door handle, planted their feet, and leaned all of their mutual weight into snapping the thin wooden security measure. It held for a brief moment before there was a surprisingly loud snap and the door slid open. George fell backward onto the patio, and Karin fell on top of him. She rolled awkwardly off as they both laughed nervously.

George shouted "Hello" into the dim interior of the house, even though he felt certain that the house was empty. He stepped inside, Karin right behind him, and let his eyes adjust for a moment. The air had a stale smell with something behind it, a tang of rot. He walked toward the low coffee table, covered with several dirty dishes, some smeared with what looked like the remains of food and some cigarette butts and ash. On top of a cigar box was a pair of spoons, each with blackened hollows in which, George assumed, heroin or cocaine had been cooked. He was tempted to move the spoons and open the cigar box, but some instinct cautioned him to touch nothing in the room.

Karin had entered the kitchen, which led directly off the living room. George could see her through a pass-through window. She was standing still and looking around. "What's in the kitchen?" he asked.

"It's disgusting," she said.

"No uncut diamonds?"

"Not in plain sight."

George flicked a light switch to see if the electricity was still on in the house. An overhead fan began to stir, and he switched it off. "Electricity works," he said. "You want to search up here, and I'll go down a level?"

Karin walked back into the living room. Her arms were held tightly to her sides, as though lifting them might expose them to the filth of the house. "Why do you keep suggesting we split up? I'm not walking around this house by myself. Let's look up here first."

A hallway led directly from the living room. Without windows, it was close to pitch-dark, and when George flipped a switch, two of the three recessed lights built into the hallway's low ceiling turned on. The walls were painted a dull industrial gray, and there were no pictures on them. The carpet, which, as far as he could tell, covered the entire top floor of the house, was a deep forest green. He could only imagine the dirt and grime hidden by its dark color. At the end of the hallway, two doors faced each other. One was open, and George leaned in to look. It was a bedroom, wallpapered in a print of tiny flowers and covered with pinned-up posters and framed photographs. He stepped inside, and Karin followed. It appeared to have been a teenage girl's room. The posters on the walls were band posters, and the framed photographs were group shots of girls in prom dresses or field hockey uniforms. There was a small pine desk in one corner and above it a bulletin board that was overrun with pictures cut out of glamour magazines. In the opposite corner was a narrow single bed, but instead of being made up with sheets and blankets, it had just a puffy sleeping bag and a single pillow without a cover.

"You saw the woman who lives here," Karin said. "How old do you think she is?"

"It was hard to tell. She's some kind of drug addict, so for all I know she's in her early twenties and looks forty. She's not a teenager, though. I'm pretty sure of that."

Karin was at the desk. She had picked up a spiral-bound notebook and was looking at its cover. "Does the name Kathryn Aller mean anything to you?"

George told her it didn't.

Karin put the notebook down. "Should we keep looking around the house?"

They went back into the hallway, where George opened the door across from the bedroom. They were immediately assaulted by a rank smell. It was a small laundry room, filthier than anything else they'd seen in the house. Besides a grimy washer and dryer, the tiled room was filled with several large trash barrels, all overflowing with trash bags. One of the overstuffed bags had fallen onto the floor and split open. Unidentifiable black ooze had spread from the tear, surrounded by large clumsy flies. "I guess this is the trash room," George said.

"Why doesn't she put it outside?"

"I don't know."

Without quite stepping into the room, George cupped a hand around his nose and mouth and leaned in to get a better look. Between the washer and dryer was a deep cube-shaped sink of white plastic, flecked in black mold. Flies buzzed around the sink. Against the far wall was a cylindrical roll of clear plastic sheeting the size of a large rolled rug, about six feet long. Each end of the roll was tied securely with yellow nylon rope. The effect was of a giant Tootsie Roll, with the wrapper still on. The room was well illuminated by a window above the sink, but George slid his hand along the wall to look for a light switch anyway. When he couldn't find one, he held his breath, stepped farther into the room, and pulled the string that hung from an overhead fluorescent light; the room was more hideous in its flat, harsh light. "What're you doing?" Karin asked from behind him. As he had moved into the room she had stepped farther back into the hall.

"I want to see what this carpet thing is."

He crouched beside the roll of plastic sheeting. More flies were disturbed, and they bounced erratically around the small enclosure, sputtering like live wires. There were many layers of plastic sheeting, but he could make out a dark form at the center, about five or six feet in length. He knew with sudden certainty what it was.

"What did you find?" Karin asked from the hallway.

"I don't know yet," he said, and the intake of breath from the act of speaking made him start to gag.

George willed himself to lean over the top of the plastic cylinder and pressed a hand down on the dark form beneath. As the plastic sheeting came together the image of what was contained came swimming up. A dark face, the forehead visible, plus the shadows of the eye sockets. He could also make out the fanned hair around the head. George pulled his hands away from the plastic, but the disturbance of the body, in its temporary coffin, had caused a full rank smell of decomposition to flood the tiny laundry room. He stood and bolted toward the hallway, then stopped when he realized he wasn't going to make it. He leaned over the deep plastic sink and vomited. Karin was oddly silent from the hallway, but when he had finished, she murmured, "What's in there? It's a dead body?"

"Yes," he said. "Wrapped in plastic. We have to call the police."

He turned the tap on, and it sputtered several times before emitting a thin stream of water. He knew he shouldn't be disturbing the crime scene, but he desperately wanted to swish some water into his mouth before getting as far away from this house as possible. He bent and took in a mouthful of the rusty-tasting water, then spit it into the sink. He emerged from the laundry room into the hallway. Karin had moved a couple of steps away; there was a dull, glossy look to her eyes, and he wondered if she was in shock.

"We need to call the police," he said again.

"Right." Karin looked around the hallway as though a phone might magically appear.

"Do you have your cell?"

"I left it in the car. In my purse."

"I saw a phone in the kitchen. Let's check it."

Karin followed him toward the kitchen. Having thrown up, he now felt not just purged of his nausea but somehow purged of all his fear. Future events unfolded before him with a deep clarity. They would call the police and await their arrival in the car, being careful to not disturb the scene any more. He would also try to get in touch with Detective Roberta James as soon as possible. He was sure she would want to view an undisturbed murder scene. The phone in the kitchen was wall-mounted. He placed the pink handset to his ear, but there was no dial tone. He wasn't surprised. "We'll have to call from your cell," he said to Karin. Her face, in the light of the open kitchen area, was flushed of color. Her lips silently opened and closed like a goldfish staring dumbly at its own reflection. She turned and went down the four steps toward the front door. He thought it would be best to leave the way they had come but decided to let that go and follow her. She unlatched the heavy door and pulled it inward and they found themselves facing the white Dodge parked behind Karin's Audi, blocking its exit, and Bernie MacDonald/Donnie Jenks walking toward them with a long rifle held casually by his side.

CHAPTER 20

The day after seeing *Liana at Palm's Lounge, George woke at just past dawn. Liana was coming at noon, and he wondered if he could wait that long to see her.*

After showering and getting dressed, he walked to Shoney's and got a large coffee and a Danish to go. He also bought a fresh pack of cigarettes. Liana wasn't due at the motel for another five hours, but George wasn't going to take any chances on missing her. He pulled open the shades in his room and cracked the door. He drank the coffee and ate half the Danish, then peeled the cellophane off the Camel Lights. When noon came and went, he wondered if he should go to the Emporium, borrow the Buick he had come to think of as his own, and swing by Liana's father's house. By one in the afternoon, George was in a full-blown panic, pacing the motel room, and almost halfway through his pack of Camels. He tried the phone number at the father's house, and there was no answer.

He decided to get the car, but as he stepped out into the warm, overcast day a dark gray Crown Victoria slid into the parking lot. George recognized Detective Chalfant behind the wheel.

Chalfant parked, turned the engine off, and stepped out onto the pavement. He was alone. "George, do you have a moment?"

They went back into the motel room, where the air was thick with the smell of cigarettes and unwashed clothes. George perched on the edge of the unmade bed, while Chalfant sat on the room's one chair. He smoothed out his trousers, then picked something off his knee. "Cat hair," he said and smiled toward George. "I'd like to ask a few questions, and then I have a favor to ask. Do you have a minute? It looked like you were going somewhere?"

"I was going to see if I could get a car from next door. Drive around maybe."

"I don't suppose you were planning on returning to Chinkapin, going back to Eighth Street, seeing if you could find Liana?"

George said nothing.

"That's okay," Chalfant said after a moment. "You don't need to tell me what we already know. I should be thanking you. You did our legwork for us, even though I like to think we'd have gotten there ourselves. Officer Wilson followed you from the station yesterday to Chinkapin. He called in the address that you were at, and we got the name Decter. The yearbook did the rest. I need to ask: Have you made contact with Liana? Have you seen her?"

George hesitated, thinking hard about how much to tell. "I've spoken with her. She called me here. We were supposed to meet today at noon."

"Has she called today?"

"No. Just yesterday. She's scared. She knows that people found out about the switch with Audrey Beck."

Chalfant breathed in through his nose. "George, I'm sorry to

*have to tell you that we have a warrant out for her arrest. If you
have any information on her whereabouts—"*

"What's the warrant for? I know she lied about who she was,
but that's more of a school issue, don't you think?"

"It's not for that. You're right. That is hardly a police matter.
The warrant is for suspicion of murder. We don't believe that
Audrey Beck committed suicide. There's compelling evidence that
someone else was in the car with her in the garage on the night
that she died."

"It wasn't Liana. I spoke with her about that. She was with her
earlier that night, at a bar, but they left separately." George realized
that he was speaking rapidly, his voice rising in pitch.

"George, relax. If you're right about that, and I hope that you
are, then finding Liana will make it that much easier to clear up.
There's no evidence, specifically, that Liana was in the car with
Audrey in the garage, but there was someone else besides Audrey
in that car. We know that much. We also know that Liana and
Audrey drove to Palm's Lounge together, so it makes sense that they
left together."

"How do you know they drove there together?"

"Audrey's brother, Billy, saw them leave. He identified Liana
by the yearbook photograph that we have. George, you can help me
out here. If you are so convinced that Liana's innocent, and I'm sure
you're right about that, then the best thing for her to do is to turn
herself in, clear this mess up."

"You looked for her at her father's house?"

Chalfant's eyes shifted a little, following a black fly that was
buzzing at the windowpane. "She hasn't been back to that house
since early yesterday evening. We have reason to believe she's fled.
Now, if you have any information on her whereabouts, or where

you think she might be going, then you're going to need to tell us that information. Otherwise, you'll be aiding and abetting. Do you understand that?"

"I have no idea where she would go, or why she would suddenly take off."

"She didn't tell you anything when you spoke with her? She didn't mention a person or a place she might go to?"

"No. Like I said, she was supposed to be coming here at noon to see me."

"I believe you, George. I believe that's what you think. But we're pretty sure that she's no longer in the area."

"Why would she do that?"

George watched Chalfant's eyes shift again, just a little. He was pretty sure that Chalfant had not lied to him before. Why did it seem he was lying to him now? "Is she okay? Does this have any-thing to do with Dale?" George asked.

Chalfant looked up. "What can you tell me about Dale Ryan?"

"Not much. I didn't even know that was his last name. He was at the house in Chinkapin yesterday."

"Okay, George. I am going to tell you what's going to happen. I need you to come to the station with me and answer some ques-tions. Just what we've been talking about here. Nothing to worry about. You aren't in any trouble. Then I'm going to need you to pack your things and head back up to college. Liana isn't coming back here, but there is a chance that she will be heading toward Connecticut. You need to be there in case she makes contact. And you need to let me know as soon as that happens. Can you do that for me?"

Listening to the detective talk, George began to feel a sense of comfort and safety that he hadn't felt in days. Chalfant was an *adult, and he was telling George what to do. The decision was out of his hands. And suddenly he wanted to be back at Mather with an almost painful intensity. It wasn't just that Liana might show up there looking for him. It was that Mather, even without Liana, felt like his home. George could feel the tightened muscles in his back and neck relax.* "Okay," *he said to Chalfant and stood.*

Together they went once again to the Sweetgum police station.

And afterward, George returned to college to wait for Liana Decter.

Chapter 21

In one fluid, almost casual motion, Bernie MacDonald lifted the rifle by his side. There was no sound, but George registered a rapidly approaching projectile, a streak of red making its way toward Karin and him. Then there was a hideous sound, like a small ax hitting wood, and Karin collapsed by his side. MacDonald altered the angle of the gun, and George slammed the door and latched it.

He dropped to his knees and looked at Karin. She was scratching at her throat, making small sounds like stifled yawns. He moved her hands away. There was a dart, not much bigger than a golf tee, stuck in the dead center of her neck. Grasping it by its red conical tail he pulled it free. It left a puffy mark and a tiny bubble of blood the size of a pushpin on a map. Karin sucked in a ragged breath, then groaned, moving her head back and forth.

"It's a dart," George said. "A tranquilizer, I think. How do you feel?"

Karin sat upright, put a hand to her neck. The puffiness was quickly turning to a welt, and she rubbed at it, smudging the blood. George was aware that they had left the sliding doors unlocked in the living room, and if he had any chance of escaping from MacDonald, he needed to get to those doors.

"I need you to stay calm," he said to Karin, "while I lock the back door and find a way to get to a phone. Okay? Just lean up against this wall. Everything will be okay." To his own ears, his voice sounded reasonable and calm, as though he were telling a colleague that he needed to send a fax and would be right back.

He maneuvered Karin so that she was leaning back against the hallway wall. Her eyes had a frenzied, animal look to them, but he thought that the lids were starting to sag a little. "I was shot?" she asked.

"Just with a tranquilizer. You'll probably fall asleep, but you're going to be okay."

She took her fingers away from her neck and looked at the smeary traces of blood on their tips. "I'll be right back," George said and bolted up the half stairway to the second level. He looked across the living area and through the sliding-glass doors. There was no sign of MacDonald in the backyard or on the patio. He pulled the doors tight and twisted the latch so that it locked, then stepped back into the center of the living room. It occurred to him that locking the doors was most likely futile. It was clear that this house, with its corpse wrapped in plastic, was directly linked to MacDonald and Liana. MacDonald would have a key, and if he didn't, he would simply break the glass doors.

George ran back toward Karin. She was still slumped in the position he'd left her in, but her eyes had closed, and she was already breathing heavily through a slack mouth. The hand she had been looking at, with its bloody fingers, still hovered in front of her face, her arm somehow staying bent and upright. She looked like a marionette, all strings cut but one.

George crouched. It felt like an hour since he'd discovered the body in the laundry room, but it had probably only been a few minutes. He could hear no sounds, neither inside the house nor outside. What would MacDonald do? If he came into the house, he'd run the risk that George would hear him and be able to bolt out another exit and run for it. George wouldn't be able to use the car, since MacDonald had blocked it in the driveway, but he could run into the woods and hide. His chances would be slim, but there'd be a chance.

George tried to calculate how many exits and entrances there were in the house. He knew of at least three. There was the front door, the sliding-glass doors in the living room, and there had been sliding-glass doors in the bedroom. There would also be some sort of entrance to the garage, probably down the stairs from where he was then crouched. Why hadn't Bernie made his move?

George decided to position himself in the darkened hallway on the second level of the house where MacDonald wouldn't be able to see him through a window. He came out of his crouch, the joints in his knees popping loudly. Karin remained in her position, her arm still raised as though her elbow had locked. George bent back down and gently grasped her wrist, lowering her arm so that it lay by her side. Now she looked like a drunk at a party who had fallen asleep standing up and slid down the wall. It was a small improvement.

He tried to walk casually, neither too fast nor too slow, up to the second level. He glanced through the glass into the backyard again, saw nothing, then entered the hallway, flicking the switch off so that the hall darkened. He leaned against the wall and listened again. A minute passed. His skin had felt charged and tingly, but now it was turning slack and cold. He ran a hand through his hair and was startled by how much sweat coated it. Something made a faint ticking sound in the house, and his legs started to buckle. He realized that whatever bravery and resourcefulness had gotten him this far was draining away, as fast as water emptying from a sink. Instead of imagining his escape from the house, he was imagining Bernie MacDonald suddenly appearing out of the darkness of the hallway. He saw himself stiffening in place like a statue while Bernie shot a dart, or worse, into his neck.

George thought, *Why isn't Bernie worried that I'm calling the cops? He obviously knows the landline isn't working, but how can he be sure I don't have a cell? Does he know that there's no service here, in the deep woods on the edge of the ocean?* If that was the case, then there was no reason for Bernie to hurry, and George knew that the longer he was in the house, the higher the probability that he would lose his nerve.

George decided to pick a direction and make a break for it. It would give him a fifty-fifty chance of escape. The advantage to the back of the house was the proximity of the woods, which began just a few feet from the patio. George tried to remember what the woods had looked like; he could picture a low-lying, impenetrable brush of rhododendrons and rosebushes toward the side of the house, but couldn't remember exactly what he had seen bordering the patio. If it was more of the same, then he wouldn't stand a chance.

The advantage to the front of the house was that he knew

exactly where to go—straight down the gravel driveway, staying close to the edge so that the trees could provide a little bit of cover, then making his way to Captain Sawyer Lane. He would be more exposed at the front of the house, but he could move faster.

George formulated a plan. He would move swiftly but calmly toward the front door, peer out toward the driveway, scanning for any sign of MacDonald. If he was still there, by his car with his rifle in hand, then he would turn and bolt out the back, moving as fast as possible, and take his chance with the woods in back. If he saw nothing, then he would unlatch the door and move through it as fast as possible, racing for Captain Sawyer Lane.

He willed himself to start walking toward the front door. He carefully took the few steps down to the landing, past Karin, who still lay slumped against the wall, her position unchanged. The skin of her face was turning an alarming gray. He stopped at the narrow side window and looked out into the world. There was no sign of MacDonald. His car was still there, parked behind Karin's Audi. A crow hopped along the gravel driveway, pecking at something. He looked as far as he could along the sight lines to either side and saw nothing.

He unlocked the door and swung it inward. He stepped outside, looking to either side: no sign of Bernie MacDonald. He ran toward the cars. The crow did a little stutter-step and lifted itself up and away on its ragged-looking wings. He ran past Karin's Audi, then MacDonald's Dodge, taking a quick look into its interior as he passed it. Lying across the Dodge's backseat was a woman. George slowed to a halt to take a better look; it was Liana, on her back, both legs bent to allow her to stretch fully across the length of the seat. Her head leaned against the back of the seat, her hair plastered to one cheek, and as George's shadow crossed her, he thought he saw a flickering of her pale lids. He stepped closer. Despite her awkward position on the backseat, her clothes were fairly neat. She wore the purple skirt he'd seen her in before and what looked like a cotton turtle-neck sweater. Her sweater had pulled up slightly at her midriff, revealing a sliver of white skin. One flat-soled shoe was on the floor of the car, and one hung from her slender foot. George pulled at the door handle, but it was locked. He gently rocked the car, trying not to make too much noise, but she was clearly out, no doubt tranquilized by whatever drug MacDonald had loaded his rifle with. George was glad to have seen the twitch of her eyelids, to know at least that she was still alive.

He felt a sting in his shoulder, grasped it, and pulled a tiny dart out, then flung it away as if it were a live wasp. MacDonald was walking toward him with a relaxed grace, the rifle already by his side again. He was coming around from the back of the house. George had guessed right: he had been at the back. George started running again, toward the road. *Maybe I can reach the woods, find a hiding place, and crawl into it,* he thought. *Maybe he won't find me. Maybe I've pulled out the dart before the poison has had a chance to get into my blood.*

But as he ran, passing in and out of shafts of sunlight coming through the breaks in the trees, the earth under his feet began to shift, tilting violently to his right. He tried to adjust his gait, but his feet tangled, and he went down face-first onto the forest floor. He got to his knees, and the world tilted again, the trees whirling around like sped-up film. He lay back down. The floor of the forest was a soft bed of fallen pine needles. He closed his eyes, and the spinning stopped.

Chapter 22

George sometimes wondered if the limited banks of his memory were entirely filled with details of Liana, all used up on the first semester of college, those sixteen heady weeks. Despite the lack of photographs, he could clearly remember most of Liana's outfits, the exact dimensions and decorations of her dorm room, the way she held a pen, the way she smoked a cigarette, the exact taste of her mouth. He remembered these details because in his mind he had returned again and again to those moments, allowing most everything that had happened to him since to float by unobserved and unanalyzed. And he was aware that every time he returned to those memories of Liana he was re-creating them in his mind, tinkering with them, falsifying them. He knew that he should not trust those memories anymore, that they were stories told to him through the distortion of time, like phrases passed along in a game of telephone.

But there were memories of one night, in the dark beginnings of December, that he did trust. He'd been over that evening so many times in his mind, and the conversation never changed; for that reason he believed it to be true. They'd been to Trumbull Arts Cinema, a student-run movie theater housed in an ornate refurbished lecture hall on the east side of the quad. They'd seen *Something Wild,* the Jonathan Demme film with Jeff Daniels and Melanie Griffith; though George hadn't seen this film since, he could remember it almost scene by scene, just as he could remember the slightly ratty balcony seats that they'd sat in and the way the flesh of her palm felt in his as they held hands while watching the film.

It was Friday night, and there was a party they were planning on going to afterward. The party was at Zach Grossman's quad; Zach was a friend of theirs, and the current boyfriend of Liana's roommate, Emily. He was local, the youngest of three brothers, and therefore a reliable supplier of kegs for freshman parties. As they neared the party, UB40 thudding loudly through the open windows, Liana squeezed George's hand and said, "I have a better idea."

"Yeah?"

"Let's go check out the new science building."

They walked against a cold prickly wind toward the far north of campus, where construction had begun on a four-story science building. It was being built on a gently sloping parcel of land that abutted the school's largest parking lot. The foundation had been laid, and the structural beams and girders were all in place, rising four stories. It reminded George of something created from a massive erector set. An orange plastic fence had been haphazardly strung around the site.

Liana led George to a section of sagging fence where a stake had been uprooted from the earth. She stepped over the fence, pulling George along with her.

"Where are we going?" he asked.

"Let's go inside. I've been dying to do this."

George followed her into the building. They stood on the poured concrete floor and let their eyes adjust to the dark. A half-finished stairwell, with rudimentary planks stretched across to create steps, led up to the top floor. Some sections of some of the floors were finished, but most were not, and looking up, George could see the purple night sky, the sprinkling of stars.

"I'm not going up there," he said.

"Why not?"

Before he could stop her, Liana sprinted up the steps, rattling the planks on the girders. George followed, swallowing his fear. At the third floor, Liana crossed a temporary walkway that led to a section of what seemed to be permanent flooring in the southwest corner of the building. She sat, and George gratefully sank beside her. Ratty blue tarps had been tacked up in place of walls, and they crackled and whipped in the sharp wind. "It feels like we're on a ship," George said.

"It does," Liana said, lying backward to look up at the sky. George turned toward campus. He could make out the low slate roofs of the dorms that surrounded the quad, then the chapel's steeple, lit up by its pale spotlight. The city flickered in the distance.

"All right," he admitted. "This was a good idea." He lay down next to Liana. The wind and the rattling tarp obliterated any other sounds from campus.

"Do you think Lulu was being dishonest?" Liana asked.

It took George a moment to realize that she was talking about the film they had just seen.

"Well, yeah," he said.

"Because she was pretending to be someone else? Because she wasn't telling him her whole story?"

"Both those things."

"But that implies that every time we meet someone we are somehow required to divulge our entire past, as if that would somehow be the most honest thing to do."

"There's a big difference between divulging your entire past and using your real name."

"But that kid in your dorm," she said, "the one who calls himself Chevy. That was a nickname he gave himself when he got to college. That's no different from what Lulu did in the movie." Liana's normally measured monotone was speeding up, not alarmingly, but enough to be noticeable. Although he couldn't say what it was, George had thought at the time that she was revealing something of herself to him. He sat up a little, cupped his hands around his lighter, and lit a cigarette.

"I guess," he said.

"All I'm saying is this: if someone reinvents herself, like Lulu did in the film, isn't it possible that the person she's become is more honest . . . more truly herself . . . than the person she was born as? No one can choose the family he was born into. No one can choose his own name, or how he looks, or what kind of parents he has. But as we get older we get to choose, and we can become the person that we were meant to be."

"You're about to tell me your real name is Bob and you come from Canada?"

"No, but I also don't feel at all related to my parents, or to Florida, where I come from. I might as well have changed my name. Do you know what I mean?"

"I understand. I'm not sure I entirely agree, but I get what you're saying."

"What do you mean you don't agree?"

"You make it sound as though human beings are free to change themselves entirely at a whim. It just doesn't work that way. We may not like who we were born as, but that doesn't change anything—it's still who we are."

"It has nothing to do with freedom to change. All I'm saying is that maybe the people we change into are the reality of who we are. Like in the movie—Lulu is truly who that character was. Even though she had made it all up."

"But that wasn't what the movie was saying. The movie was saying that we can't escape our past."

"I know. I'm telling you what *I* think."

"There's still something you're saying that I don't quite agree with."

"You're just arguing for the sake of arguing."

"I'm not. I get what you're saying. You're saying that as we get older we have the opportunity to become the people we were meant to be. I just think, in general, that people who try to escape from their past, or try to divorce themselves from their parents, they're kidding themselves. It doesn't happen that way. Maybe on the outside, maybe in the way that others see them, but down deep everyone is the product of their past."

"So you don't think people can change?"

"I'm not saying that. I'm just saying that no one can ever completely shed his beginnings. Like it or not." George flicked his cigarette over the edge of the building. Watching the orange sparks get whipped away by the wind made his stomach feel a little hollow. He had never liked heights.

"Blood will out," Liana said. Her voice sounded resigned.

"Something like that."

Liana was quiet, staring up through the skeletal frame of the building. George turned onto his side and stared at her profile, a black cutout against the distant lights of the parking lot.

"You're just saying that because you like where you came from," Liana said. "You like your parents and your hometown and New England. You chose to go to fucking college less than two hours from where you live. I don't think you really understand what it's like to feel like a stranger in your own family."

"Okay. Granted. Calm down. I'm not really disagreeing with you about anything. I just think . . . that when you say . . . that when you say that the people we become later in life are more truthful than the people we were at the beginning of our lives, I don't entirely agree with that. No, wait. Hear me out. I just think that there is truth in both aspects of a person. You can't discount where we come from even if you'd like to. It's still always there. It's still the truth of who we are."

Liana was quiet again. In retrospect, George recognized that she was defeated. The conversation ended, but over the years George had returned to it in his mind again and again. He'd long since realized that Liana Decter was asking for permission to become Audrey Beck permanently. She'd been this new person for less than three months, but she must have seen the genuine possibility that she could entirely shed her previous skin and start new.

They stayed in the half-finished building another hour, getting colder. They had turned onto their sides and wrapped their arms around each other for warmth. George remembered the pain in his hip and how Liana had started shaking with the cold

before he did. They'd kissed, and George had been able to see a
wet glint of light in one of Liana's open eyes. They touched each
other through their clothes. George asked if they should go back
to one of their dorm rooms.

"No."

George stayed on his side while she moved down the length
of him, unzipped his jeans, and took him in her mouth. Liana
had done this before, but it had always been a brief precursor
to something else, with her not quite knowing what to do and
George struggling not to come. That night George was relaxed
enough to pay attention to the feeling. He let his head fall back
onto the cold floor and stared into the night sky. After he had
come, Liana kept him in her mouth while he softened. That act,
like the conversation that led to it, had been keeping house in his
memory banks ever since.

Liana had slid back up and kissed him. He had now begun
to shake as well, but they stayed side by side for another fifteen
minutes before admitting defeat.

And now, when George woke, nauseous and groggy from
the tranquilizer, and found himself on his side, face-to-face with
Liana, he thought initially that he was dreaming, or that he was
dead and had been returned to the happiest moment of his life.
But then Liana's eyes opened, and he saw the fear in them and
became aware of the rope-bite at his wrists and ankles and the
hard surface that he was lying on that was bucking up and down.
He smelled gasoline and heard the rhythmic whine of a motor
and the slap of water. They were under a green tarp, translucent
enough so that he could sense the daylight above them and make
out the shadowy features of Liana's face.

"Where are we?" he said in a grainy voice he barely recog-

nized. The act of speaking unloosed something in his head, and
the world, already lifting and falling, tilted even more precari-
ously, as though he were tumbling unmoored through space. He
heaved violently, his body straining against whatever was holding
him in place. His wrists felt like they were being scored by razor-
sharp glass.

After retching, he broke into a coughing fit, tears streaming
from his shut eyes. When he finished coughing and his breathing returned to a sort of normalcy, he looked again at Liana. She
had managed to slide a little ways away from him, and George
realized that she was bound up like he was, immobile beneath
the tarp.

"You okay?" she asked.

George's throat and mouth felt coated in bile. Another wave
of nausea passed through him, and he shut his eyes to fend it off.

"You were shot by a tranquilizer gun," Liana said.

"I know," he said and reopened his eyes. "Where are we?"

"We're on Donnie's boat. Or I guess you know his real name
now."

"Bernie."

"That's right. He's going to kill us."

The boat banked sharply, cresting a wave and slapping down
hard on the water. George felt what seemed to be another body rolling up against his backside. He tried to turn his head, but all he
could see was the tarp pressing down on them. "Who's behind me?"

"Your friend. I don't know who she is."

"Karin Boyd. She's Gerry MacLean's niece. Jesus."

"She's dead, George."

"How do you know?"

"I watched him drag all three of you onto the boat. Bernie

told me she died from the tranquilizers. Not that it matters. He's going to kill us all anyway."

"The other body's on this boat as well?"

"Katie Aller?"

"The woman who was living in that house?"

"Yeah, that's Katie Aller. Bernie killed her last night."

"Who is she?"

"It's a long story and we don't have time. I need you to try something. He tied your hands in front, right?"

"Uh-huh."

"Before I got nabbed, I managed to grab a steak knife and slide it under my skirt. It's in the band of my underwear. I've been trying, but I can't get to it."

"It's in the front?"

"Uh-huh."

George scooched forward as much as he could so that his knees and Liana's knees were touching and their faces were side by side. The tarp moved with him but still covered them entirely. Even though he couldn't see the system that Bernie had used to hog-tie him, he knew that his ankles were secured, as were his wrists. It also felt as though the rope had been wrapped around his waist and tied to his wrists so that his hands were pinned to where his belt buckle would be. His fingers were tingly and numb, but he could move them. He got close enough so that he could touch Liana's fingers. He could also feel what felt like nylon rope tied tightly around her wrists, plus stickiness on her skin that was either sweat or blood. "You need to slide yourself lower down," she said.

He did what she said. It was hard work. Bernie had tied the rope tight at every juncture, and he could feel the damage at both his ankles and wrists where the nylon was cutting into his skin. Once his hands were below Liana's, she pulled herself in closer to him so that his fingers pressed against the tops of her thighs. He could feel the fabric of her skirt, the line of her underwear along one hip. He couldn't feel a knife.

"To the right," she said. He rolled forward enough so that his hands slid an inch toward her crotch, and suddenly he could feel the hard protuberance of what was probably the dull end of the knife.

"I'm going to have to pull up your skirt," George said. "Can you get your hip off the ground?" George had bunched some of the fabric of Liana's skirt in his fingers and was able to tug it toward him. Liana lifted her hip off the deck. He grabbed another handful of fabric and bunched it in his fingers. A jolt of the boat caused Liana's hip to come down hard. She grunted. It took about three excruciating minutes, but they did it, Liana arching her body to get her hip off the deck, while George worked the fabric toward him a half inch at a time. His wrists were screaming, and his fingers were cramping, but he didn't dare say anything to Liana. It was clearly extremely painful for her to lift herself off the deck. He listened to her breathing become pinched and ragged. Finally, when his fingers touched the hem of her skirt, he gave one last violent yank on the fabric, then slid his fingers past the hem. He was now touching Liana's naked thighs. "Thank God," she said, letting her body relax.

Her thighs were damp with sweat, and George walked his fingers up to the edge of her underwear. "This job has its benefits," he said, and she emitted a single tired laugh.

George hooked a finger onto the edge of her cotton underwear, inching further up, feeling her prickly pubic hair through the fabric, then pulled himself closer to her and lifted his hands so that they found the knife, secured horizontally beneath the elastic band. He pulled down on her underwear till he could feel the exposed wooden handle, getting a thumb and forefinger securely on it. As he rolled back the knife came free, nearly snagging on her bunched-up skirt, but he held on, changing his grip so that he had it securely in the palm of his right hand.

"You got it?" she asked.

"Yep."

"Can you cut through the rope?"

"Yours or mine?"

"Work on yours. It will be easier. My arms are completely numb."

"Give me a moment." George felt as though the boat had changed course and now the hard midday sun was directly hitting the green tarp that covered them. Sweat was running in steady rivulets from under his hairline. He could smell the fear in his own body odor, mixed with the brine of the ocean air and with something else—the smell of rot, the smell he remembered from the laundry room in the house on Captain Sawyer Lane. Katie Aller, in her shroud of plastic.

He maneuvered the knife so that he was holding its wooden grip in the four fingers of his right hand, its serrated edge pointing down. He rocked his wrist forward and felt the knife snag on the rope around his wrists. He did it several more times and the knife snagged a little less, sawed a little more.

"It's working, I think," he said to Liana.

"Thank God. If you can get your hands free, there's a plastic tackle box that keeps sliding around and hitting the top of my head. I'm nearly positive there's a gun in there. It's a revolver."

"You want me to shoot Bernie?" It seemed an obvious question, but even as George asked it he could feel a tremor of itchy fear in his stomach. He remembered how he'd felt standing in that hallway, waiting for Bernie to stroll toward him with his rifle, and he wondered how much bravery he had left.

"If you can get to the gun, point it at Bernie, tell him to dive out of the boat into the water. He won't do it, but you'll have given him a chance. He's going to try and find a way to talk you into screwing up. Don't give him the chance. Tell him to go in the water. If he hesitates or does anything different, then aim at his center and fire. It's him or us, George. You know that. How's that rope coming?"

"It's coming." The boat motor revved down to a mosquitoey whine, and George's heart hammered at the thought that Bernie had found his dumping ground before he'd had a chance to saw through even a single knot, but then the motor picked up again. "What's he waiting for?"

"My guess is there're lots of boats out today. He's looking for open ocean."

"You want to tell me how we wound up here like this?"

Liana blew out a steady breath, her breath stale and warm. "I'm not proud of this, obviously."

"This whole trip, your being here, was all a scam to get those diamonds from MacLean's safe." George didn't ask it. He said it. *If these are my last moments on earth,* he thought, *I have no interest in being lied to anymore by Liana.*

"Yes," she said. "But I didn't know Bernie was going to kill anyone. I promise you that. He was just supposed to knock MacLean out, take the diamonds, and run."

"How'd Bernie get into the house?"

"We knew that there would be gardeners on Sunday and

timed it to coincide with their being there. I drove to a street where Bernie could walk through the woods and onto the property. He was dressed to look like a gardener, so if he got spotted coming in from the woods it wouldn't look too suspicious. He'd scouted the house and knew that there was usually a half-open window above the back porch roof. He brought a short stepladder with him. It was easy. He would get into Gerry's study on the second floor and wait for him. After he got the diamonds from the safe, he would just carry them back through the woods, where I would be waiting for him."

"Why did you need me?"

"I really did not want to show up at MacLean's house myself. What I told you about our relationship was true. His wife was dying, and he was probably unstable. It made much more sense to send a neutral party. Plus, if you went, that meant I could drive the car. Bernie didn't want to leave a strange car on a street in some tony neighborhood in Newton for three hours. It would attract too much attention. How's that rope coming?"

George was still sawing, but he had felt what Liana had probably felt: Bernie taking the boat in a wide circle, the motor revving down into an idle. Had he found his dumping spot?

"I feel like I'm cutting through rope but my hands haven't loosened up any. Why did you come and meet me at the Kowloon? You didn't need to."

"I thought it made sense to check in on you one last time before Bernie and I made our getaway in the morning, but Bernie freaked out. I didn't realize how convinced he was that you and I were in it together and were going to screw him over. That's why he went and threatened your girlfriend and why he started killing witnesses. He snapped."

George felt the nylon rope weakening. He yanked with his wrists, but they were still securely tied. He angled the knife differently and connected with another piece of nylon. He started to saw again.

"We can get out of this," Liana said, but to George, her voice sounded less than sure.

"Keep telling me things. It helps."

"Like what?"

"Where were you all yesterday?"

"In New Essex mostly. At the house you found. I was trying to reason with Bernie and get him to just leave town with me. He was convinced we left too many witnesses. You, of course. Katie Aller . . ."

"Who was she?"

"I met her down in the islands. She was a drug addict who was burning through her parents' money. They're dead, and that's their land and property all up and down Captain Sawyer Lane. I got in touch with her when I knew that Bernie and I'd be coming up. She let us stay in her house—"

"And use her cottage."

"—and use her cottage, yes, and—"

"And this must be her boat."

"It is. Look, George, I could say this a thousand times, and I know it wouldn't make a difference, so I'll only say it once. I am so sorry for dragging you into this. I had no idea that there would be any danger involved. You have to believe me on that. I deserve to die today, but you don't."

George was beginning to sense a loosening in the rope. Blood was rushing back into his fingers, and he could swivel his right wrist at least forty-five degrees. The new freedom allowed him to change the angle of the knife and get better purchase. He made two strong cuts, and the rope popped loose, freeing his right hand. His left hand was still bound and held by the rope that was wrapped around his midriff.

"My hand's free," he said.

"Both of them?"

"Just my right hand, but I think—"

The boat made a thunking sound, as though something had bumped up along its side. "What was that?" he asked. Now that he had one hand free, his fear had ratcheted up a notch. Hopelessness had been replaced by a small amount of hope. A surge of adrenaline made his head swim. He squeezed his eyes shut to let the feeling pass.

Liana said, "Shit," and he opened his eyes. She was straining her head back, her eyes looking upward as though she could see through the tarp. He was about to ask her what was going on, but suddenly he felt it too. The boat was slowing down, almost to a stop. The motor had stopped droning; it burbled and stuttered a little before turning off completely. The boat rocked forward then back in the open water, and the sudden silence felt overwhelming. Like a kid playing hide-and-seek, George squeezed his eyes shut again and stayed quiet, as though Bernie might forget the two live humans under the tarp.

"Rise and shine," came the nasally voice, shockingly loud in the new silence. Bernie pulled the tarp halfway down their bodies as though it were a sheet. George peered up, but the sun, high in the cloudless sky, was blinding, and all he could see was an obscured figure looming above them, an outline of shimmery black that erased their last vestige of hope.

CHAPTER 23

S ay your good-byes, you two," Bernie said.

"Bernie, please, hold up for just a moment," Liana said, her voice unnaturally high. "Think about what you're doing. This isn't you."

Bernie, still a dark, unfeatured figure blocking the high sun, fanned his arms out as though he were trying to stretch a knot in his back. "Remember when you convinced me to come along on this ride?" he said. "How you told me that breaking and entering another man's house, knocking him out, stealing those diamonds, would be child's play? That it would only be difficult the first time? You were right. It wasn't difficult at all breaking into his house, but it was a little bit difficult hitting him with that hammer."

Bernie laughed, awkwardly, the way someone might laugh at his own unfunny joke at a cocktail party. "I thought that hitting someone on the head with a hammer would be like hitting a block of wood, but it wasn't," he continued. "It was like hitting a piece of fruit. The head of the hammer went right in. It even stuck there for a moment. Do you know what that was like?"

"Bernie, you know I didn't ask you to do that."

"You told me to knock him unconscious."

"Not with a goddamn hammer. Jesus, Bernie, think for a moment what you're about to do. You can have the diamonds. You can go away. We'll dump these other bodies. No one will be any the wiser."

"Yeah, I'll dump the bodies," Bernie said and moved out of the path of the sun. Its midday force hit George's face, and he squinted, wondering, for one nonsensical moment, where his sunglasses were. Bernie bent, and George heard a dragging sound, like a heavy piece of furniture being pulled along a floor. His eyes were adjusting to the flat cloudless glare, and he could make out that Bernie had pulled something heavy parallel with Liana. She was arching backward to try to see what he was doing.

"Bernie, stop it," she said, using a new tone of voice, trying to approximate a motherly authority, but all George heard, and all Bernie probably heard, was a desperate attempt to try something new, to try anything, that might stop what now seemed inevitable.

George sawed as fast and hard as he could with his freed right hand, working on the tight nylon that bound his left wrist to the loop around his waist. He was acutely aware of the sudden quiet of the open ocean and knew that he needed to work at his restraints without making a sound or drawing attention to himself.

Bernie got hold of Liana by the rope around her waist and hoisted her up slightly, then rolled her onto her front. The motion caused her to exhale sharply, then groan. The tarp slid off her lower half, and Bernie looked down at her hiked-up skirt, her exposed legs and buttocks. "What's this?" Bernie said. "Did you give your boyfriend one last feel? Jesus, Jane, that's perverted." He reared back and made his barking laugh, the one George had heard a few days earlier when he'd first encountered him outside the cottage in New Essex. Hearing him call her Jane, George realized how little Bernie knew about the woman he was preparing to murder.

"Think what you're doing," Liana said, the tone of her voice changing again.

"I have thought about it. I thought about hitting you on the head with a hammer like I hit that old man and then dumping you into the ocean. But then I thought that was too good for you." Bernie was bent over Liana's body, and George could now see what he was doing. He had dragged over a cement block, about a square foot, and he was tying it to Liana. "No, I think I'll just dump you into the sea as is, let you think about what you did as you drown." Bernie was working fast, and as he finished speaking, he straightened up and tightened the knot he had just made. Liana twisted her head toward George. Hair obscured half her face, but George could see one scared and red-rimmed eye. Bernie tugged Liana toward the edge of the boat, her exposed skin squeaking on the boat's linoleum deck.

George had nearly cut through the rope that constrained his left hand, but it wasn't going to be enough. Even if he cut all the way through before Bernie tipped Liana into the ocean, his ankles were still tied together. His hands would be free, but there was almost no chance that he could maneuver his way to the tackle box, remove the gun, and shoot Bernie, not with the lower half of his body still hog-tied.

Bernie tugged violently at Liana again, pulling her up against the edge of the boat.

"Stop," George shouted, and Bernie turned, an almost-surprised grin on his face, his grayish-purple teeth exposed.

"The boyfriend speaks," he said.

"I called the police before you shot me," George said. "I told them your plan to dump us in the ocean. They'll probably be searching the area now, with planes."

"Oh, yeah. How did you know I was going to do that?"

"I saw the boat earlier, at the cottage. Where else would you dump the bodies?"

Bernie looked at him with some interest. He had lifted the cement block and dropped it over the edge of the boat. The rope attached to Liana was taut. All Bernie had to do now was lift her body and roll her into the water. "If that's the case," he said, "then I ought to work faster. When those search planes fly overhead, I wouldn't want to have any evidence still on the boat."

Bernie turned back to Liana. She was now struggling, bending her body back and forth against the restraints. Bernie planted one foot near her head and one near her waist and bent to lift her. George yelled out "Help" as loud as he could on the off chance that another boat had drifted toward them. All he heard in return was the raspy squawk of a circling gull. George yelled again as Bernie grabbed hold and began to lift Liana. They could see each other through Bernie's spread legs, and Liana shook her head at George. The ocean breeze had caught her hair and pulled it off her face so that he could see both her eyes. They were now flushed of their panic, resigned. George stopped yelling.

"George, I'm sorry," she said. "I love you."

"Audrey," George said.

As George tore frantically at his still-bound left wrist, Bernie rolled Liana's body up and over the edge of the boat. George heard a single hard splash, then nothing. The cement block had dragged her instantly under the water.

Bernie turned and leaned against the edge of the boat, placed both of his large hands flat on his thighs. "That was harder than I thought," he said, his voice coming out a little breathlessly. George couldn't look at him. Exhausted, he rested his forehead on the sticky deck, focusing on Bernie's shoes, a pair of tasseled loafers. One of the cuffs of his suit pants fluttered in the breeze. George breathed deeply through his nose and took in the acrid coppery smell coming off the deck of the boat. A large emptiness swallowed him. Knowing how soon death was coming, he felt deeply alone. An image of his father flashed into his thoughts.

George heard the scuffed sound of Bernie standing up. *He'll remove the tarp from me,* George thought, *see the knife in my swollen fingers, and take it away. He will find the severed rope and laugh at my feeble attempt to escape, then retie the rope and give me my own personal cement block to take with me to the ocean floor.*

With his head still plastered to the deck, George watched Bernie move toward the front of the boat. George lowered his chin down to his chest and could see three more blocks of cement nestled behind the forward seats. Bernie picked one up with one hand and moved out of his vision. "You're awfully quiet, George. I'm saving you for last, so you've bought a little time. Feel free to talk. I wouldn't mind some conversation."

George felt Bernie's feet move along the deck, the tarp rustling but staying in place. A soft thud made George think he'd lowered the cement block, then he felt two hands, one on his lower back and one on the backs of his thighs, shove him forward a couple of feet. The knife, still gripped in his freed right hand, scraped along the textured decking, and George thought for sure that Bernie would have heard it, but all he said was, "Stay right there, will ya?"

George looked down at his body. The tarp was still over him. Bernie would be busy for a few minutes securing cement blocks to Karin Boyd and Katie Aller before dumping their bodies. He fingered the rope, finding the frayed edge where he'd cut almost three-quarters of the way through. He repositioned the blade and started sawing again.

"I was surprised by this one," Bernie said. "MacLean's niece. You do attract the pretty ladies, George, although I can't say I know why that is. I loaded my darts with just enough juice to knock out someone your size—it's not an easy science, you know, but it was a little much for this one. Put her to sleep for good."

George had just managed to cut all the way through the rope around his left wrist, and his arm, its muscles deadened, dropped to the deck. He faked a coughing fit to cover the sound, buckling over and rubbing his numb, stinging hands together. The fake coughing fit soon turned into a real one, the spasms of his diaphragm causing his near-empty stomach to produce its last teaspoonful of bile. He spit it onto the deck.

"This'll all be over soon," Bernie said. George couldn't see him, but it sounded like he was hoisting Karin Boyd's body over the edge of the boat. Hoping that Bernie was turned away, he quickly moved his hands over his midriff and found a double loop that went relatively loosely around his waist. There was a knuckle-size knot just over his left hip. George knew nothing about knots. He ran his fingers over it, noting only that it seemed extremely tight and that he couldn't locate any frayed ends to work free. The knot secured a length of rope that was tightly drawn across his thigh and between his legs. If he could sever the rope, although his ankles would still be bound, he would be able to stretch out his body and his hands would be free. He'd have a chance to make it to the gun inside the tackle box.

George heard a splash—Karin Boyd going to her watery grave—and then he heard a deep exhalation from Bernie. Was he getting tired? He was strong, that much George knew, but even though the day was relatively cool, the sun was at its peak and Bernie was dressed in dark suit pants and a shimmery gray silk shirt.

"Ah, Katie," Bernie said as George heard the sound of rustling plastic. He imagined she was still rolled up and bound like a carpet, the way he'd seen her in the house on Captain Sawyer Lane. "You didn't really know Katie, did you?"

"I met her," George said, wanting to keep Bernie talking. George had gotten the blade of the knife under the taut rope that connected his waist to his ankles.

"Then you probably know that I didn't so much kill her as beat her to the punch. Do you know how old she was? Twenty-two going on eighty-two. She'd been a drug addict for less than a year, but what a year." Bernie barked out a laugh. "You know who introduced her to drugs, don't you? Your precious Jane. She had a real knack with the ladies, just like you."

George was starting to feel weak, his head swimming, sweat slicking his entire body, and he needed all the energy he could muster to cut his way through the last few pieces of rope. The sun hitting his face made him feel like a piece of meat under a broiler.

He heard Bernie grunt a little, and the plastic rustled again. "People are heavier when they're dead, you know that? I hurled this thing around a couple of times when she was still alive, and she didn't weigh a whole lot more than a rag doll, but now, Jesus, I'm getting old."

The rope George was working on split in two and his legs were freed. He was still bound at the ankles, but he was no longer trussed like a turkey. It was all he could do to stop himself from stretching out the cramped, numb muscles of his legs, but he didn't know where Bernie was looking. Stretching his head back as far as possible, he could see only the sky, now streaked with a few scudding clouds. He heard the splash as Katie Aller was dropped into the sea. He was now alone with Bernie on the boat, and he realized that there was no way he was going to be able to cut through the rope binding his ankles. He twisted his head the other way, looking back toward the spot where Liana, bound up, had been lying. Bumping up against the side of the boat was the tackle box she had mentioned. Next to it was a bright red life vest, and George wondered if it wouldn't be better to simply grab the vest and dive into the water, take his chances there.

He heard the scrape of Bernie's shoes on the deck behind him. He tried to take a deep breath, but the air he pulled into his lungs felt thin and deficient. *Any moment now, Bernie will rip the tarp away from me,* he thought, *see how I've worked my way free from the rope, and then I will have to act, striking out at him with a knife designed to cut through nothing tougher than a New York strip.*

Bernie made a sound behind him, a brief humming noise in his throat that sounded like a question, then took three steps toward the helm. George watched him bend and unlatch a compartment, pull out a pair of binoculars. He brought them to his eyes and stared into the distance. George had been given his chance.

With as much speed as he could muster, George rolled from his side onto his hands and knees, then pushed himself forward from his knees and toward the tackle box. His muscles felt slow and stiff, as though he'd been tied for days instead of hours. He unsnapped the box's lid and dumped its contents onto the deck. Tools, fishing gear, and several flairs spilled out, along with a black revolver that had been wrapped in a greasy cloth. George grabbed it with his right hand and rolled back into a sitting position. Bernie was still calmly standing at the helm, the pair of binoculars in his hand. There was a slight quizzical smile on his lips, and George watched Bernie's eyes move from his face to the gun in his hand and back to his face.

"It's not loaded," Bernie said.

"You sure?" George asked and pulled the hammer back. It clicked into place easier than he thought it would. His arm was shaking, out of both fear and fatigue, but he didn't care.

"Go ahead and fire it," Bernie said. "It really isn't loaded. Why don't you just take that life jacket and—"

George pulled the trigger. A slight recoil bucked his hand, and the gun issued a sharp bang that sounded like a firecracker. Bernie dropped his binoculars onto the deck and lifted his right hand to his neck. A terrible burbling sound came out of him, and a dark sheet of blood spread down his front, soaking his satiny shirt.

Bernie squeezed his neck harder, but blood coursed over his knuckles, slicking the back of his hand. He reached out with his other hand and grasped the back of the pilot's swivel seat, lowering himself into it like an old man with joint problems.

Bernie's eyes stayed on George. There seemed to be no fear or anger in them—just confusion, as though he were wondering why his neck had suddenly sprung a leak, and what that might have to do with the gun that George was still holding. Bernie slouched in the chair, still turned toward George, and his blood-covered hand dropped to his thigh. The entire front of his shirt was drenched in blood, and his drained face had turned a ghostly white. His eyes no longer looked confused. They looked like nothing. He had died.

George turned away and looked around at the surrounding ocean. He expected to see a boat on the horizon, or whatever it was that had distracted Bernie, but all he saw was a horizon line that extended in all directions. A gull bobbed on the blue swell about twenty yards away, but that was the only sign of life.

He closed his eyes and tried to clear his mind for a moment, tried to comprehend what it was that had just occurred. The harsh sun itched at his skin and the deck tilted. Dream images flirted at the edge of his consciousness, and for a brief hallucinatory moment George almost allowed himself to fall asleep.

When he opened his eyes, nothing had changed. He was alone on the deck of the boat with the spilled contents of the tackle box and a cement block that had been meant for him. The revolver thrummed in his hand. Bernie lolled in the pilot's seat, swaying back and forth in rhythm with the gentle swell of the sea.

CHAPTER 24

George returned to Mather College. Even though his trip down to Sweetgum had felt like a lifetime, in reality he was back in his dorm room less than a week after he'd left. He told his roommate, Kevin, and anyone else who asked, that he had gone home for a few days. Back to Massachusetts to be with his parents. No one questioned him.

He felt guilty lying, but told himself that he was protecting Liana.

George had decided that Chalfant was right. That there was a chance that Liana would come back to Mather to look for him. She couldn't go back to Florida. She had no other family. Where else would she go? And George had decided that if Liana came to him he would help her, at whatever cost. He might try to convince her to turn herself in, but if that didn't work, then he would be willing to do whatever it took to make sure she wasn't caught. And to make sure that he had some part in her life.

George had not been particularly social his first semester of *college, mostly because of Liana, but he became even less outgoing that second semester. He never went to parties, and he stopped regularly hanging out with the guys in the quad at the end of his hall. He often ate alone in the dining hall, tucked behind a copy of the school newspaper. He walked from class to class alone, hunched in his winter coat, a constant cigarette between his lips. His free time was spent in the same isolated carrel in the library, on the basement level. It was quiet there, even by library standards, the only sounds the click and hiss of an ancient radiator. He studied hard, trying to make up for the unspectacular grades he'd received first semester. He could tell that the other freshmen from his hall, Kevin in particular, felt hurt by his sudden distance. But he was protected by the death of Audrey, by what they perceived as his grief.*

That winter was the coldest on record for over fifty years, with temperatures in the single digits for weeks on end. As the shortened days crawled by the cold and the dark made George's time in Florida, and also the previous semester, seem like a dream of another world. Still, whenever the phone rang in the dorm room he shared with Kevin, a small jolt in George's stomach would make him wonder if Liana was making contact. But it was never her.

For February break George returned home. His mother never mentioned Audrey, but his father did, asking George how he was doing after the sad news. George told him he'd been better, and his father offered him a scotch and water, the first time George had ever been offered an alcoholic drink in his home. He accepted, and they sat together, quietly, in his father's den and drank.

"How do you like it?"

"Maybe it's an acquired taste."

His father laughed, showing yellowed teeth from a longtime pipe-smoking habit. "I should have made yours with ginger ale."

"No, this is fine. It's growing on me."

Back at school, the days grew longer and the temperatures warmed up. George missed the anonymity that his hooded winter coat had provided him. Walking across campus, he felt eyes rest on him a little longer than was necessary. He knew what people were thinking: There's George Foss. His girlfriend committed suicide over Christmas break, and now he hardly talks to anyone. Just keeps to himself. *George didn't particularly mind. He was lonely, but the thought that Liana might one day show up or call kept his hopes alive.*

When a phone call finally came, it was from Detective Chalfant. Kevin took it, one Saturday morning when George was at the dining hall.

"You in trouble?" Kevin said after delivering the message and a number to call back.

"He's a family friend. Calls himself 'detective.' Kind of a joke."

Instead of calling back from his room phone, George brought a calling card to one of the phone booths in the student center. No one used that particular bank of phones, and George knew he'd have privacy. He lit a cigarette, inhaled deeply, then dialed the number.

Chalfant picked up on the second ring.

"It's George Foss, returning your call."

"Hi, George. How are you?"

"Fine."

"Any word from our mutual friend?"

"Uh, no. I haven't heard from her. I thought maybe you had news."

"I'm afraid not. We haven't turned up anything. She's well and truly disappeared." George listened to a shuffling sound, as though

Chalfant had transferred the phone from one hand to another. "George, I want to give you a heads-up. I don't know if you've been following our local news down here, but Liana Decter's father is dead. He died on the night that Liana took off from Chinkapin. I didn't tell you then because I didn't want to muddy the waters, and truth is, we didn't know what we had on our hands at that point in time. But now there's a second warrant out for Liana's arrest. It's a first-degree murder warrant, George, for her father's murder."

"What?"

"It's pretty clear-cut. And it's starting to make some splashy news around here, and nationally too, we suspect. That's why I wanted to call you. I wanted you to hear it from me first."

"Why would she kill her father?"

Chalfant sighed. "The reason it took us so long to issue a second warrant was because we had reason to believe that Kurt Decter was killed by a bookie he owed money to."

"Dale."

"Yes. Dale Ryan. I forgot you knew about him. We held him for questioning, and he admitted that Decter owed him money, but said he had nothing to do with his death. He had a strong alibi and nothing came up forensically, so we let him go. We are now operating under the assumption that Liana killed her own father before fleeing in order to . . . this is just a theory, of course . . . but in order to protect him from Dale. It seemed that occasionally Liana would perform sexual favors in order to pay back some of her father's debts."

Chalfant paused, but George said nothing. Even though he already had this information, hearing it again from another source caused a slight tightening in his stomach.

"We think that when Liana decided to leave town, she knew

that her father would be at the mercy of the men he owed money to. She probably did what she did because she knew he was doomed."

"How did he die?"

"He was killed in his house, by a knife wound to the throat."

Chalfant did not provide more details. He reminded George, once again, that if Liana contacted him, it was his legal responsibility to alert the authorities. George promised to call if Liana made an appearance.

Later that year, during one of George's compulsive visits to the periodical section of Mather's library, he found a long article on the case that had been published in the magazine section of a major Florida newspaper. It was highly speculative, mainly based on an interview with Officer Robert Wilson, who apparently was no longer working for the Sweetgum Police Department.

George read the article so many times that he felt as though he'd memorized it.

The body of Kurt Decter had been discovered in the living room of the house on Eighth Street. "It was the ugliest house on a street of ugly houses," Wilson said. Both detectives, Chalfant and Wilson, had come to the house together to issue their warrant for the arrest of Liana Decter. They had known that they were at a crime scene even before they pushed open the door and the pungent smell reached them. Folks in Chinkapin didn't leave their houses unlocked in the middle of the morning.

It had taken a moment for their eyes to adjust to the dark interior. The body was upright on a faded brown couch in the middle of the living room. Head fallen forward, chin on chest. Baggy cargo shorts, legs spread, hands resting almost casually by the thighs. At first they thought that Decter was wearing a black tank top, but then it became clear, from the shoulder straps, that the shirt had been white and the front was stained dark brown from spilled blood. Black flies battered and buzzed around the corpse.

There had been no need to check for a pulse. Decter's throat had been slit, deep and wide enough that the skin flapped open on either side of his jaw. The blood had not only soaked his shirt but pooled in his lap. An arterial spray had crossed the glass-topped coffee table and spattered the beige shag on the other side of it.

Neither Chalfant nor Wilson had known what Kurt Decter looked like, but based on the skinny, liver-spotted arms and the sun-damaged bald patch, they judged the dead man to be about seventy years old. The remote control was tucked by his hip, and his feet were bare. The coffee table was littered with empty cans of Coors. A large ceramic ashtray, made to look like a curled-up alligator, was filled with cigarette butts and the stubby ends of several joints. Next to the ashtray was a small open baggy containing a few buds of pot.

A kitchen knife had been laid flat on the back cushion of the couch, its dark brown handle blending in with the plaid fabric. Both detectives had circled and stood behind the couch, careful to not touch anything before scene-of-the-crime officers arrived. Wilson told the reporter that the sight of the knife carefully laid next to the victim, like a knife left on a cutting board next to a chopped carrot, had somehow been more horrifying to him than Kurt Decter's slit throat.

Chalfant had searched the other rooms while Wilson stood behind the body and took in more of the scene. The massive boxy television was turned off, but it was still pulled out from the cheap-looking entertainment center, tilted toward Decter's eye-line. A dusty-looking golf bag leaned up against the wall. On the floor was a bowl of water and, next to it, a pile of dry cat food that had been *poured into an empty TV dinner tray. A line of ants ran between the food and a deep crack at the base of the wall. There was a dirty plate on the table, the remains of a T-bone steak still on it, the plate smeared with bright red juices. A fat black fly gracefully arced from the dead man's lap to land on a piece of gristle.*

Wilson remembered thinking that Kurt Decter, high and drunk, his stomach filled with an expensive cut of steak, had died a happy man.

George understood, intellectually, why Liana had killed her father. It was punishment, of course, for being who he was: a weak-willed degenerate willing to pimp out his daughter in order to erase his debts. But it was also a mercy killing. Liana was prepared to leave town forever, to never see her father again. She knew her father would continue to gamble and continue to lose, and without Liana there to protect him, Dale would keep calling. Kurt Decter was a dead man walking, and he was going to check out painfully. Liana was just speeding up the process, taking him out with one swift cut of a knife.

But understanding what had happened the night Audrey died was a different story. The article stated that there was definitive proof that Liana had been in the car with Audrey. George imagined that they had fought at the bar. He believed what Liana had told him—that Audrey wanted to end the arrangement, that she wanted her life and name back. He also believed that Audrey had probably gotten completely incapacitated at Palm's Lounge. Liana drove them back to the Beck house, where her own car was waiting. When Audrey's car was nestled back inside its closed garage—the engine still idling, Audrey passed out next to her—Liana must have made the decision to leave Audrey in the car to die from asphyxiation. Had she thought that letting Audrey die would allow her to go on living Audrey's life? She couldn't have. It made no sense. Maybe she had thought that, with Audrey dead, she would have a fresh start, that the clock she had instead of a heart would fully stop and she would never have to confront the life she had left behind and the lies she had told. It would be a clean break.

George had wrecked that plan by showing up for a funeral.

Chapter 25

George brought Irene her coffee, placing it carefully on the table in front of her. Nora, also on the table, sniffed at the brew, then twitched her head back in disapproval. She gracefully leapt onto the floor, strutting toward the kitchen to survey her food bowl.

"Thanks," Irene said. "We could've gone out for coffee, you know."

"Nice try," George said.

"You *can* go out for coffee, you know," she said with a kind of mock exaggeration that was grating in its transparency. "You're not a total shut-in yet, are you?"

"I go out," he said.

It was technically true. In the ten days since he'd shot Bernie MacDonald, George had occasionally left his apartment, most often on forays to the corner grocery store or the liquor store conveniently located right next to it. He had also visited several police departments at their request. He was not becoming an agoraphobic, at least he told himself he wasn't, it was just that the sight of normal people behaving normally—or worse, enjoying themselves—filled him with a sense of unease that bordered on horror. He had come to accept that in his current state his mind was a movie screen that would play only one movie, a movie of that Tuesday afternoon in New Essex on the boat with Bernie. He didn't wake up in cold sweats, or scream in his sleep, or cower at unfamiliar sounds, but he couldn't stop seeing again and again what had happened. He was reminded of a period during his junior year of college when he had become hopelessly addicted to Tetris on his computer, to the point where those six colored shapes floated constantly in his mind's eye, even infiltrating his dreams.

"We'll go out for coffee sometime," Irene said and pressed her lips together in a sympathetic frown.

"That expression on your face is not helping," he said. "Besides, I never liked going out for coffee. You know that."

"I wouldn't pester you like this if you'd agree to see someone." Irene cupped her hands around her coffee mug as though it were winter. August had ended, but the city was still trapped in a combustible heat, and George's apartment, cooled only by his window air conditioner, was in the high seventies. The someone she was referring to was the therapist she wanted George to see. She'd done research and found a man she thought was perfect. George had agreed with her in theory, but not yet in practice.

"I will," he said. "When I'm ready. It's only been two weeks. You took longer than that to get over *Silence of the Lambs*."

She smiled, put her coffee back down on the table, then stretched out along his couch. She wore black capris and a sleeveless polka-dot shirt. The bruise that had been left by Bernie

MacDonald's fist had almost completely healed. George could detect a faint yellow sheen, but maybe he was only imagining it. "Fine. You win today because I'm too tired to argue with you. How would you like to hear about my puny problems?"

"I'd love to," he said.

She told him about the disastrous date she'd agreed to with the divorced editor, how he had taken her to a microbrewery and lectured her on the pleasures of barley wine, then had gotten drunk and sobbed in his car on the way home. George listened and made sarcastic remarks, but as was always the case these days, his mind was still on that blank expanse of death, the images turning and falling like Tetris pieces.

After shooting Bernie, he had turned his attention to slicing through the rope around his ankles. His hands had begun to shake violently, like someone trying to raise a plastic cup to his lips on an airplane being tossed around in turbulence. He somehow managed, keeping his head down, eyes on the task. When his feet were finally free, he pushed himself backward and leaned against the stern. Bernie hadn't moved, was still sitting in the gently swiveling pilot's chair, his chin on his chest as though he were asleep, except that his chest was painted with his blood, now darkening from a bright red to a muddy brown. A large fly of some sort buzzed around Bernie's lowered head. How had it gotten here so fast, in the middle of nowhere? George had a sudden fear that it had taken him hours to unshackle his feet instead of just minutes. He stared at the sun, trying to imagine the hour of the day. How soon would night come, and would he still be bobbing on the ocean with a corpse?

It was that thought that propelled him into action. He stood on numb legs and attempted to walk toward the bow, but his trembling muscles forced him down on his knees, and he crawled toward Bernie. Reaching the body, George prodded the shin with a finger and cowered back, still afraid that Bernie might be alive. When nothing happened, he managed to stand, pushed Bernie off the chair, and took his place. The body landed with a heavy thud and the horrific sound of gas escaping. George didn't look, but smelled the sharp odor of shit mixed in with the brine and blood.

He stared out at the empty sea. It was a calm day, but the surface rippled here and there, white breakers shimmering in the sun. He looked in all directions. Everything was the same, the ocean dropping away along the curve of the earth. The thought occurred to him that he would never find land, that he would die in the middle of this nothingness. The sun, high up in the sky, neither rising nor sinking, seemed to mock him with its own lack of meaning. He looked at the controls on the boat, and there, attached to the console, was a compass, an instrument he probably hadn't laid eyes on since his failed year as a Cub Scout. It was covered with saltwater; when he wiped it clean, its arrow told him that the boat was pointed north. All he knew was that he needed to go west, back toward land. Just getting within view of other boats would be enough. In the land of the living, he might be arrested for murder, but that would also mean that they would take him off this boat, away from the nauseating pitch of the sea. And away from Bernie, lying in his own blood and excrement.

He found the ignition key, attached by a coiled cord to a piece of marlin-shaped foam. He turned the key. Nothing happened, and his chest constricted with fear. Then he fiddled with the throttle, securing it in neutral, and tried again. The motor coughed into life. George had never steered a boat in his life, but he managed to move the throttle to get the boat moving at a speed he was happy with. Then, after turning the wheel till the compass told him he was moving westward, he held steady.

After about ten minutes George spotted what looked like a decent-size craft to the north of his position. He considered keeping the boat pointed toward land, but he didn't know how much gas was left and thought he would rather take the first opportunity to get himself clear of Bernie's dead body. He whipped the wheel around too fast, and the boat seemed to skip on the flat water, bucking and sending a sheet of spray that rainbowed in the sun.

As he approached the other vessel he was relieved to see that it was immobile in the water. It gleamed impossibly white, a large sport fishing boat with what looked like a satellite system attached to its cabin roof. He could see two figures standing on its deck, tall fishing poles in front of them. At about fifty yards away, he watched both men turn in his direction and saw two women rise from chairs to see what was approaching. George slowed the boat and waved both arms in what he hoped looked like a combination of "I need help" and "I am harmless." He suddenly wished he had covered Bernie's corpse with the tarp.

As he got closer he could see that the men were both middle-aged, with deep leathery tans. Each held a can of beer in a cozy. Both women, equally brown, were rapidly pulling on bikini tops; they had been sunbathing topless.

George edged up close to the boat, toggling the throttle to avoid ramming them. He cut the engine when he was about ten yards away, and the boat drifted, thunking into their side. One of the men, who had a gut the size of a medicine ball, said, "Jesus Christ, asshole."

George held up his arms again, said, "Sorry. I need help."

One of the women, her bikini black and gold, peered over the edge of the fishing boat, saw Bernie's body, and let out a weird keening scream. "There's been an accident," he said, which was as close to the truth as he was willing to get. "Can you call the Coast Guard, please?"

"Is that man dead?" said the second woman, who had come to the rail as well. She appeared to be younger than anyone else in the party by at least twenty years and had just lit a fresh cigarette. The smell drifted down to George, a heavenly smell, briefly masking the stench of blood and salt in the air.

"He's dead," George said. "I can explain after you call the Coast Guard. Can I come aboard?"

The man with the protruding gut had moved toward the helm, and George watched him lift a radio transmitter from its complex console. The other three looked at one another as though silently deciding whether to allow what was clearly a crazed murderer aboard their boat. George watched their eyes survey his deck and saw the younger woman spot the revolver George had discarded. "I'm not armed," he said and held his palms face out. "I was abducted by this man. If you don't want to let me on the boat, then please, can I have some water?"

Till he asked for a drink he hadn't realized just how thirsty he was. His mouth tasted of metal and blood. The younger woman, who wore a bright yellow bikini, turned to the other man, who hadn't spoken yet. "He can come up, can't he?" she asked.

He turned back to his fellow fisherman, still fiddling with the transmitter, then turned back toward George. "I guess so. Let me get the drop-ladder."

The Coast Guard arrived within fifteen minutes of George's

boarding the *Reel Time*. While waiting, he'd accepted a deck chair, chugged water, and rubbed at his wrists and ankles, till he realized that he was making it worse, ripping at the loosened skin and causing fresh blood to spring up and spatter to the deck of the boat. The men kept their distance, but the younger woman, who introduced herself as Melanie, asked him what had happened. He tried to speak, but he began to shake so badly that he had to put the water bottle down. Suddenly cold, a distant voice, his own, told him that he was going into shock. When the Coast Guard vessel arrived and took him on board, he was given a blanket. That small act of kindness led him into a fit of crying.

In the days that followed George told his story countless times to countless law enforcement agents. He could sense in the different attitudes and the leading questions that there was a dispute over whether to arrest him or not. He had shot a man in the neck, and he had been directly linked to the deaths of four other people. He had also been directly linked to an enormous theft, and it was increasingly clear from the questions aimed at him that the diamonds taken from MacLean's safe were still missing. He came to believe that Detective Roberta James was the one who was protecting him, the one who believed every word of his story. Certainly, she was the only detective who routinely provided him with information, letting him know that no bodies had been recovered from the depths of the Atlantic, volunteering the information that MacLean's wife had finally died and that, as far as the detective knew, she had never been told about her husband's murder.

In retrospect, George hadn't minded the constant interrogations. Telling his story again and again seemed to make it manageable. It was only after one whole day passed when the police did not contact him, a day when he never left his apartment, that he began to feel the enormity of what had happened. Certain images—Bernie slouched on the pilot's chair, Karin Boyd turning gray in Katie Aller's house, the look on Liana's face as she was tipped over into the sea—never left his mind. Reading did not help, and neither did television. When he left his apartment, the world that had always seemed relatively benign looked to him like a disaster waiting to happen. Buildings teetered as though they were about to fall, cars careened dangerously around corners, and violent strangers eyed him as though they could read the terrible thoughts in his head. Any thought of the ocean filled him with an empty dread.

He had spoken to the human resources department at the magazine and had conditionally been granted a "family care and crisis" leave. All they needed was for his personal doctor to fill out a form and fax it to them. Every day he thought about calling his doctor and arranging an appointment. And every day he didn't call. His office sent him emails he didn't answer.

Irene's visits didn't particularly help, but they didn't hurt either. They filled time during the day, although getting through the day was not his biggest problem. Getting through the endless hours of the night was.

"I thought he hated his wife?"

"Oh, you *were* listening," Irene said, sitting up to drink the remains of her coffee. "So he says." She shrugged.

"No second date, then."

"God, no. My experiment with broken men is officially over." As soon as she said it her face reddened with regret. "I didn't . . ."

"Except for me, of course."

"I don't consider you a broken man."

"Thanks. Bloody but unbowed. That's me. Whatever doesn't break you makes you stronger. By the way, whoever said that should be cast out to sea with the ghost of Bernie MacDonald."

"I'll find out who said it and take care of that." She picked one of Nora's hairs off a shoulder and shifted forward.

"You're going?" George asked.

"Unless you beg me not to."

He walked Irene to the door, where she kissed him, as she always did, on the lips. "I think you're going to be fine."

After Irene left, George straightened his bedroom closet, filling a paper grocery bag with shirts he didn't think he'd wear again. Maybe later he'd walk the bag the two blocks to the Goodwill. It could be his outing for the day.

He refilled his coffee cup, resisting the urge to add a slug of bourbon to it, and went back to his living room to work on what he was secretly calling his "death journal." It had been a suggestion from Detective James, the last time they'd spoken. She'd walked him out of the police station, as she always did. While they stood for a moment in the gray city dusk, he'd thanked her for her kindness.

"What for?" she'd asked.

"Believing my story. Not arresting me. Not looking at me the way the other policemen . . . policewomen . . . do."

"I'm not doing you any favors. Truth is, I actually believe your story."

"But you keep bringing me back here."

"I'm hoping you remember something new. There are lots of questions still."

"You haven't found the diamonds yet, have you?"

"Nope."

George lit a cigarette, having resumed the habit since re-gaining land. He took a deep, lung-expanding hit, then exhaled away from Detective James, but the evening wind picked up the smoke and sent it into her face. He apologized.

"No worries. Smells good. I'm one of those ex-smokers who still likes vicarious smoke. I even miss it in bars."

"Sometimes I think you're my perfect woman, detective."

She laughed, explosively. "That's not something I hear every day."

"You're just hanging out with the wrong people."

"Tell me about it."

He took another long drag on his cigarette. "You think you'll need me here again?"

"Probably. I'm still not convinced that you've remembered everything you can."

"It's because I'm trying to forget everything I can."

"I have a suggestion for you," she said as she rubbed the back of her neck, then straightened the collar of her shirt. She wore no nail polish. In fact, except for maybe rouge, George didn't think Roberta James wore any makeup at all.

"What's that?" he asked.

"I think you should try to write everything down."

"I thought that's what you guys were doing."

"I think there's more you could write. Write down every little detail of what happened. Try and describe things. I'm still convinced we're missing something. It could help us sort out what happened, but I was also thinking it might help you . . . in processing things."

"You think I'm fucked up."

"No, but I think a pretty fucked-up thing happened to you.

It can't hurt to write things out. I wouldn't suggest it if I didn't think it was something you should do."

Taking the suggestion, he had found an old blank notebook stashed on his bookshelf and begun to write, in his cramped, nearly illegible script, the events that had transpired. He wasn't writing things down in chronological order. He would just think of something that happened and try to describe it. It wasn't pleasant, but it did pass the time.

Lately he was focusing on his attempted escape from Bernie MacDonald at Katie Aller's house. He described the interior of the house, the look of the laundry room where Katie's body had been stashed. He tried to remember his thoughts and questions at the time. *How did Bernie know we're here? Did he follow us in the Dodge, and if so, why has he waited so long to approach us with the tranquilizer gun? Why hasn't he been worried that we might call the police from our cell phones in the house?*

He wrote about his decision to make a run for it out the front of the house, and about the way Karin Boyd looked as he passed her in the hall. The gray of her skin, and the awkward, slumped position of her body. She must already have been dead, or dying, the tranquilizer dose too much for her body size. Then he wrote about seeing Liana in the backseat of the Dodge, how she had been sprawled unconscious. He remembered knowing that she was alive because . . . because of the flickering of her eyelids. It was something that he had been returning to again and again, that slight movement he had witnessed. Had he seen an involuntary twitch or had he seen Liana quickly shutting her eyes when she realized that someone was passing by the car? At the time he remembered thinking that it was involuntary, that she had been knocked out, or tranquilized as well, and that her lids had twitched. Why was he now convincing himself that Liana had been fully conscious in the backseat of the Dodge, pretending to be otherwise?

Was it because it fit with what he kept thinking? That Liana and Bernie had been working together from the very beginning and that everything, including the trip on the boat out to sea, had been orchestrated?

And if that was the case, then why were they both dead and he was still alive? How had Liana allowed Bernie to dump her overboard? Why was Bernie so convinced that the gun from the tackle box wasn't loaded?

All he knew was that it was helping to write everything down. The more details he recorded the clearer it became to him what had actually transpired over that long weekend. He felt he was getting closer to the truth.

He flipped to the back of the journal, where he had begun sketching. He had drawn several pictures of the boat, trying to remember everything that was on it. This time he drew a sketch from above, showing the positions of the four bodies, two alive and two dead. He stared at it till his focus went blurry, only turning away when he heard the sound of church bells in the distance telling him it was noon.

He got up and went to the kitchen, where he poured the rest of the coffee from its pot into his mug. This time he did add a slug of bourbon.

CHAPTER 26

The police arrived the following morning, a Wednesday, just after nine o'clock. George had begun to brew a pot of coffee and was considering what to do with the long day ahead of him.

There were three loud raps on his door, followed by the shouted words: "Police. Open up." A male voice. George, fully expecting to be arrested, opened his door and was greeted by O'Clair, accompanied by two uniformed officers. "George Foss. Detective John O'Clair of the Boston Police Department. I have a search warrant for these premises." He held up two folded pieces of paper. He looked like he'd won big on a scratch ticket and was holding it in the air.

George sat on the couch, drinking coffee, reading his copy of the warrant, while the two uniformed police officers worked their way from the kitchen area through the living room and toward the bedroom. Nora, interested, followed them, zigzagging between their legs and staring into the opened cabinets. O'Clair didn't take part in the search but stood in the living room, in his

shiny gray suit, bouncing on the balls of his feet and occasionally checking his cell phone. "Where's Detective James?" George
asked.

"Oh, she's apprised of the situation."

"What are you looking for exactly?"

O'Clair didn't respond.

George thought of the money that Liana had given him that
he had yet to mention to the cops. He had moved the cash to
the basement of the building, wrapping it in a rag and tucking it
underneath a dryer unit. He had wondered at the time if he was
being overcautious, but now he was very glad that he wouldn't
have to explain ten thousand in cash to the Boston PD.

"Detective, we found something," one of the uniforms said
from the bedroom.

O'Clair, doing nothing to suppress the pleased look on his
face, told George to stay where he was and entered the bedroom.
George racked his brain, trying to imagine what they might have
found that would implicate him in any further way. He wished
he'd made his bed and picked up the pile of dirty clothes that
had accumulated in a corner. Flashes of light came from the
bedroom, photos being taken. George stood, just as O'Clair
emerged from the room, accompanied by one of the uniformed
cops, a short Hispanic woman with Frida Kahlo eyebrows. She
wore white rubber gloves and held out an unfolded piece of white
paper on top of which were two small rocks, one with a greenish
tint, the other pink.

"Can you identify these?" O'Clair asked.

"I've never seen them before. Where did you find them?"
Even though they looked like rocks, George knew they must be
diamonds. The back of his neck prickled.

"We'll be impounding these as evidence. You're going to have to come with us to the station."

G eorge waited in one of the interrogation rooms. He'd been there alone for over an hour after telling O'Clair that he was waiving his right to have a lawyer present. George wondered if he'd now been in every interrogation room in the Boston Police Department. This one actually had a window, covered with bars. George could make out the Zakim Bridge and, in the distance, the Bunker Hill Monument in Charlestown. The sky was a washed-out blue, or maybe it was the grimy window that made it look that way.

"Hi, George."

He turned at the familiar voice, happy to see Detective James. She wore a black suit over a silky white shirt, the collars spread out over the lapels of the suit. If George did eventually get arrested, he was hoping she would be the one who cuffed him and not O'Clair, who would undoubtedly have a smug look on his face.

"Detective," George said.

"My partner informed me you're waiving your right to have a lawyer present. Is that still the case?"

George told her it was.

"Okay. Have a seat. I need to let you know that this conversation is being recorded." She indicated the small camera in the corner of the room. George nodded.

After identifying herself, then George, then the time and the location of the interrogation, James said, "Do you want to tell us about the diamonds we found?"

"I'd never seen them before."

"Then how do you think they got into your clothes drawer?"

"Are they MacLean's diamonds?"

"I don't know. You tell us."

"I don't know either. But I think it would be a pretty big co-incidence if they weren't."

"So how did they get into your drawer?"

"Liana Decter put them there. On the day MacLean was murdered, the night that she spent in my apartment."

"And you didn't know about this at the time?"

"No, I didn't."

"And why would she do that and not let you know about it?"

"I can think of two reasons. One, she was thanking me for my help in ripping off MacLean. Not that I knew I was helping her."

"And what would be the other reason?"

"She was framing me."

"And why would she do that?"

"Do you have a while?"

Detective James smiled. "I have all day. And I would love to hear why Liana Decter would frame you."

"She would frame me because I'm the only one who knows that she's alive and if I'm in jail I can't come after her."

"Previously, you told us that you witnessed Liana Decter being killed by Bernie MacDonald."

"I'd like to change my story."

"So you didn't see her strapped to a cement block and thrown into the ocean?"

"No, I'm saying that I saw that happen, and I still think she's alive."

"How would that be possible?"

"I'm not sure exactly how she did it, but in my gut I don't think she drowned that day."

James stretched her neck one way, then the other, like she was preparing for a boxing match. "Why don't you start at the beginning?"

"You sure?"

"As I said, I have all day."

"Okay," George began. The words came easily. He'd been rehearsing this speech in his head for the past several days. "For lack of a better starting point, I'm going to say that this all started down in Barbados. We know for a fact that Liana, or Jane Byrne, as she was going by, was working at the Cockle Bay Resort, and that's where she met Gerry MacLean. She knew he was rich, and she knew he was corrupt, meaning that he probably had cash assets. He was a mark, and she conned him. She knew what his two wives looked like. She copied their look and seduced him, won him over enough so that he brought her up to Atlanta to be his mistress. Gave her a job—or she asked for one—and that gave her access to his business records. Then, one way or another, she discovered that he had converted a lot of his cash into diamonds and that they were in a safe up here in Massachusetts.

"So how do you break into a safe? She came up with a perfect plan. She'd steal money from him, which was easy because he regularly sent cash down to the islands and she had access to it. She'd take one of these shipments for herself and skip town. He'd be upset, but she knew, because of the nature of the shipments, that he wouldn't contact the police. She probably knew that he'd sic his regular investigator, Donnie Jenks, on her. Then all she would need to do would be to contrive a way to return the stash to him up here in Boston. And when someone brings cash to your house—a lot of cash—what do you do? You open your safe and put the money in there. That's what she was counting on.

"She needed some help, so she recruited a local bartender in Atlanta by the name of Bernie MacDonald. And then she recruited Katie Aller, or contacted her at least. Katie was someone she knew from working at one of the resorts in the Caribbean. I've found out a lot about her. She was an only child, and both her parents were killed in a boating accident when Katie was eighteen. They were loaded, and it all went to her. They owned the land with the house and cottage on it in New Essex, plus they owned some property in Florida and Mexico. Her father had sold luxury yachts out of Fort Lauderdale. Katie was a drug addict, maybe because of Liana's influence, and maybe not. When Liana knew that she and Bernie needed a place to stay in Boston, she got in touch with Katie. My guess is, she brought Katie up here with her, got her installed in her old home with enough drugs to keep her happy, and used the property. It turned out to be a perfect place to stage my meeting with Bernie, or as I knew him initially, Donnie Jenks."

"Why did he pretend to be Donald Jenks? It seems pretty obvious that you would figure it out."

"It didn't matter if I figured it out eventually. She always knew that I would cotton on to the fact that I'd been used to get at MacLean's diamonds. I figure that Donnie Jenks's name was the easiest to use since he already worked for MacLean. Maybe I would try and check it out before agreeing to the money drop. I don't really know, but I know that what Liana needed to do was to convince me to help out by bringing the money to MacLean.

Liana wasn't sure she could do that herself, so she figured, if I was introduced to Bernie and he seemed genuinely terrifying, then my protective instinct might kick in and I would agree to deliver the money to MacLean."

"I understand why she needed Bernie and why she needed Katie, but why did she actually need you?"

"She didn't really. At least not for the first part of the plan. She probably could have gone to MacLean's house herself, or she could have even sent Katie to do it. The only reason she wanted me to deliver the money was to get me involved. She needed me to be a witness when she was dumped into the sea. Everything was leading up to that. Taking the money from MacLean was just the beginning. But she had a bigger plan. She not only wanted the diamonds, she wanted a completely clean getaway, a closed case in which she'd be dead."

"So you think that you were meant to survive the day on the boat?"

"I do. Not only do I think I was meant to survive, I think Bernie knew I was supposed to survive as well. He was in on it. What Bernie didn't know was that *he* was supposed to die."

"Back up some. Why did Bernie threaten your friend . . . Irene, was it? Why did he threaten her, and why did he take that shot at you from the car?"

"It had to look as though Bernie had gotten paranoid, that he had gone a little crazy and wanted to either shut me up or kill everyone who was involved in the heist. And it was crucial that I know this story because I was the one who would be telling it. The basic story would be that Liana, instead of leaving town with Bernie immediately after the diamonds were stolen, wanted to see me one more time and this was what drove Bernie into his paranoiac rage. It was a stretch, I know, but I believed it for a while. I think Liana was playing on my vanity, assuming that I would choose to believe she would stay around an extra night to be with me."

"You're talking about Sunday night?"

"Right. After Bernie stole the diamonds, it would have made perfect sense for the two of them to get as far away as possible. Instead, Liana met me at the Kowloon, then came back to my apartment and spent the night. Before leaving, she planted two of the diamonds in my clothes drawer, hidden away where I wouldn't immediately find them. She was cutting it very close, knowing that MacLean's body would be found and the police would start looking for me. I think that she was willing to take that risk and that it was important to her plan to spend the night with me—to keep me hooked, to plant the diamonds, and also to provide a plausible motive for Bernie MacDonald to go off the reservation.

"Bernie pretending to freak out was crucial to the second part of the plan. The first was to get the diamonds from MacLean—which was easy enough, as it turned out—and the second was to fake her death and eliminate Bernie. Then all the diamonds would go to her and people would stop looking, because she would be dead. She *knew* she could pull off the first plan, and the second plan was just gravy. This part is crucial to understanding what happened, what I believe happened. Everything that happened after the robbery was like a quarterback taking a shot at the end zone. A Hail Mary at the end of the second half when your team already has the lead. Is this making any sense to you?"

"What is this football that you speak of? No, go on, I got it."

"Okay. It was far too complicated for her to know that she could get away with it. It was a Hail Mary, but if it didn't work out—if, for example, I instantly decided to turn her over to you guys, or if I was unable to kill Bernie on the boat—then she would still have the diamonds and she would still disappear. Thinking about it this way is the only way it makes sense."

"So talk about what happened on the boat."

"The way I see it is that Liana must have told Bernie that the plan was to keep me alive as a witness to her death. Why he went along with it, I don't exactly know, but I assume he was at least partly under Liana's spell and wanted to please her. She must have convinced him that she needed to disappear forever. So all along the idea was to get me onto the Allers' boat, which was tied up by the cottage, and then take it out to sea. I made it relatively easy for them by showing up at Katie Aller's house, although unfortunately I showed up with Karin Boyd and she became collateral damage."

"What if you hadn't come out to the house?"

"Then Bernie would have found some other way of kidnapping me. He was clearly following me. He followed me the night I went to visit Irene in Cambridge, the night he fired a shotgun at me and ran over the real Donald Jenks. He could have killed me then, but that wasn't the plan. He was still play-acting. The real plan was to take me alive, and that's why he had the tranquilizer rifle. Why else would he have such a thing?"

"We traced that gun, by the way, back to a zoo in Atlanta. It had been reported stolen. Seems Bernie might have had a friend who worked there."

"Which goes to show that this plan was in effect for a while. The gun was a chance to take me alive, which was crucial. Karin was a wrinkle in the plan, but it only meant that Bernie had to take us both out. He'd mixed the tranq dart to knock a man of my size unconscious, but it was too much for Karin and she died from an overdose. Not that it would have made any difference since she would have been killed anyway.

"While this was happening, while Bernie had me cornered in Katie Aller's house, Liana was waiting in the car. The way I see it now, she was fully conscious, lying on the backseat pretending to be knocked out, on the odd chance that I would race by the car and see her. Which I did. I was fairly convinced that I was looking at an unconscious woman, but I did see her eyes move, I'm sure of it. At the time I thought it was just a side effect, some sort of tic from being knocked out, but now I remember it differently. What I think I saw was Liana quickly closing her eyes when I appeared at the window of her car."

"That's not what you said in your signed statement."

"I know. I've changed my mind. Maybe I've thought about it too much and I can no longer see it clearly, but I think she was simply lying in the backseat of the car. She was waiting for Bernie to catch me. While Bernie went after me, Liana locked the car and lay down on the backseat. If I saw her, I'd assume that Bernie had gotten to her as well. And I did see her. And that's exactly what I thought."

"But if you hadn't seen her, you might not have hesitated and you might have gotten away."

"That's true. I could have made it into the woods and then out onto the road. If that had happened, then I believe that Liana and Bernie would simply have quit and taken off. Remember, this whole thing was a Hail Mary."

"And Liana was the quarterback," she said.

"Yes, you got it. Liana's the quarterback. Bernie's a lineman, at best."

The detective laughed. "All right, I got it. I think you're underestimating the value of a good lineman, but I understand what you're saying. Keep going."

"So once I was knocked out, it was simply a matter of getting all the bodies onto the boat. We were driven down to the cottage, where the boat was tied up. Liana would have helped, then allowed herself to be tied up by Bernie. We were laid face-to-face under the tarp. He would have then cruised out to open ocean and circled around till I came to. Once that happened, Liana went into action, telling me about the knife she'd smuggled and basically allowing me to cut through the rope I was tied with. This part was all about the timing. It was crucial that I get free, but not until after Liana had been dumped overboard. I think that they had some sort of signal so that Liana could let Bernie know when to stop the boat and begin dumping bodies. I think the signal was that she would kick the side of the boat. I heard it at the time and thought it was the sound of the boat stopping because, immediately after that, Bernie grabbed Liana and threw her overboard. But a boat doesn't make a thumping sound when it stops. Not unless something falls over. Liana signaled Bernie that it was time for me to witness her dying. I wouldn't be able to do anything about it, but I would be left with a knife, and Bernie would take his time dumping the other two bodies. He was stalling, giving me time to cut through the rest of the rope."

"And to get to the gun," Detective James said.

"Well, no. Bernie didn't know about the gun. He might have known there was a gun in the tackle box, but he was sure it wasn't loaded. No, he thought I was supposed to get free and grab the life vest and take my chances in the ocean."

"You'd have been a sitting duck. He had a boat. He could have just run you down."

"But he wasn't supposed to run me down. He was supposed to let me get away. What Bernie didn't know was that she gave me a way to shoot him. She left me a loaded gun. My killing Bernie was what she wanted to happen. That way there would be no one left alive who knew *she* was still alive. I would report to the world that she was dead, and even though a body would never be found, or the diamonds for that matter, there would be no real reason to keep looking for her. It was perfect."

"It's just so improbable. There were far too many things that could have gone wrong. What if the tranquilizer shot had killed you as well as Karin Boyd? What if you hadn't been able to get out of your ropes? What if Bernie had lived? I could go on and on."

"If Bernie had lived, it wouldn't have been the end of the world for Liana. He wasn't going to rat her out. All she'd have to do would be to share the money with him. As you said, there was plenty of it, and who knew—my guess is she'd have found some way to kill him off later. He trusted her. It wouldn't have been hard."

Detective James looked skeptical, her lips pressed together.

"I used to have all the same doubts and questions till I began to think of it a different way," George said. "As I said before, there were two plans. The first plan was foolproof, or as close to foolproof as a million-dollar robbery can be. That was the plan to get MacLean's diamonds. The second plan was a pipe dream—a way to get the diamonds, to get rid of Bernie, and to disappear permanently. That plan could've gone wrong, in all the ways you said, plus many others. Katie Aller could have been pulled in by you guys instantly after the murder of MacLean if you'd made the connection sooner. I could have left town. Bernie could have accidentally shot me with the shotgun outside of Irene's place. If any of those things had happened, then Liana was prepared to cut bait. She'd have been out of town before you guys even knew her full name. But she stuck around to make it perfect, and she pulled it off.

"Have the diamonds showed up anywhere? Doesn't that tell you something?" George continued.

"Well, as you know, some of them have shown up."

"I mean most of them. I'm sure there were more than two."

"Let's say you're right," James said, "and Liana planned the whole thing. How did she get away after Bernie dumped her in the water? You said she was tied up. You watched Bernie tie a cement block to her."

"That I don't know. My guess is that she wasn't tied up but just looked like she was. I'm sure it was a real cement block, but maybe he tied it to her in a way that it would just break loose once it was in the water."

"You said you heard one splash and then nothing."

"That's what I remember. Maybe she swam underwater for a while, coming up far enough away that I wouldn't hear her. Maybe there was another boat nearby, or some sort of flotation device. I was still tied up on the deck at this point—I couldn't see anything outside of the boat."

"I don't know, George," Detective James said.

"I admit that I have a tough time with this part as well. It was open ocean. I was up in the boat pretty soon after Liana went into the water, and I didn't see a thing. But if anyone could swim away into a new life, it would be her. I don't know how she did it, but she did it. It was a magic trick."

"A pretty impossible magic trick. You were miles from land."

"I know it sounds ridiculous, but it's ridiculous no matter how you look at it. I keep thinking back to my time on that boat. Everything was staged so that I would be a witness. It was too convenient. Liana smuggled a knife on board that I could get to. When I got hold of the knife, I asked her if she wanted me to cut her free, and she said no. Then Bernie finds his dumping ground as soon as my hands are free. He chooses to dump Liana overboard first, but then he doesn't immediately dump me overboard. That doesn't make any sense. He would want to get rid of the two live bodies and then deal with the dead ones. All of this was set up so that I could cut myself free and escape. So I could be a witness."

"But even if you got into the water, there was no guarantee that you would survive."

"There was no guarantee of anything. It was all a Hail Mary. I know it sounds improbable, but do you think it's probable that Liana let Bernie get the better of her and that they're both now dead and the diamonds have gone completely missing?"

"I don't think any of this is probable. I think it's just as probable . . . and I'm not the only one . . . that you have all the diamonds."

"If I had all the diamonds, why would I leave two of them in my underwear drawer?"

"Maybe you did it to back up your story, to make it look like you got framed."

"I think you're mistaking me for a criminal mastermind. You're giving me far too much credit, Detective."

"You're not the only one who thinks that."

After the interrogation, George was left alone for another hour. He imagined the conversation that would be taking place outside of the soundproof room, a decision being made on whether he would be booked now or booked later. He tried to care, but kept thinking about those diamonds left in his drawer. Were they a thank-you from Liana? Or were they a final *fuck you?*

Detective James reentered the room and said, "You're free to go, Mr. Foss. We're done here for now."

George stood. "You'll walk me out?"

Once outside, George lit a cigarette. "I was pretty sure I was going to be arrested in there," he said to Detective James, who'd come out to the brick steps of department headquarters with him.

"You've got this department tied in knots. But you will be arrested. It's just a matter of what charges, and when."

"Thanks for the heads-up."

"There's a general belief that you'll lead us to Liana Decter."

"So someone agrees with me that she didn't drown at sea."

"No, I think the consensus is that she was never on that boat. At least, there's no proof she ever was."

"Just my word."

"Just your word."

"I guess I'll try and enjoy my freedom while I have it."

"Oh, and don't leave town. I'd like to be on record for having said that."

"Why do you still trust me?" George asked.

"I don't know if I trust you, but I believe you're telling the truth. I listen to a lot of lies from a lot of liars in my job. I believe you when you say that you were acting in good faith when you returned the money to MacLean, and that you were conned by Liana and Bernie. I don't think you knew about the diamonds in your bedroom. And I believe that you think Liana's still alive."

"But you don't think she is."

"You know Occam's razor?"

George nodded.

"The simplest solution to this is that Liana Decter and Bernie MacDonald stole a lot of diamonds. Bernie got greedy, or jealous, or both, and decided to kill everyone who was involved. He almost succeeded but got killed himself. The diamonds . . . who knows? They could be anywhere."

"Then why am I here? If Bernie really wanted to kill me, he could have. How is it possible I got the best of him?"

"I think you got lucky," she said. "Very, very lucky."

CHAPTER 27

B ack at his apartment, George knew what he had to do.
It was late afternoon. He fed Nora, then got the keys
to his Saab and headed out the door. He had decided to return
to New Essex, convinced that Liana had left something behind.

I'll know what I'm looking for when I find it.

As he drove through the rotary in the town center his heart
rate seemed to double and he became light-headed. On Beach
Road he pulled into the church parking lot before reaching Captain Sawyer Lane. He rolled down his window and gulped at the
briny air. For some reason, he remembered the slumped figure
he'd seen on the church bench the first time he'd driven out to
the cottage by the marsh. He remembered looking at the sleeping man and thinking that maybe he had died on that bench
and no one had noticed because he just looked like some elderly
parishioner taking in the sun.

George, his heart returning to normal, put the car back in
gear and turned out of the church parking lot. He took a right

onto Captain Sawyer Lane, then an immediate right onto the rutted driveway of the Aller house. Dusk had come, and it was dark in the piney woods, but he could make out the perimeter of yellow tape that still circled the property.

After finding Liana's copy of *Rebecca,* with the postcard from Mexico tucked into its pages, George drove back to Boston in the darkness. He kept the air conditioning on and his window cracked so that he could blow cigarette smoke out into the night. He didn't know exactly what the book meant—had it been left specifically for him, the way the diamonds were, or was it simply a mistake on Liana's part?—but he knew what the book meant *for* him. It was a clue, a piece of information that he, and no one else, now had.

Returning home, George sat on his couch and flipped through the book. There were many marked passages, all boxed in with a blue pen, the way Liana always wrote in her books. He ran his finger along the pen-marks, their precise angles, and perfectly straight lines. He turned back to page 6, where the postcard of the Mayan ruins had been inserted, and read the marked passage: "But I have had enough melodrama in this life, and would willingly give my five senses if they could ensure us our present peace and security. Happiness is not a possession to be prized, it is a quality of thought, a state of mind."

That night George didn't sleep. Liana haunted his every thought, till he became convinced that her constant presence in his mind was further proof that she was alive somewhere. But where had she gone after her resurrection from the ocean? She would have the diamonds—that much he knew for sure—and she would have a new identity. New name. New hair. Living somewhere far away. That was her gift. Transformation. She had told him that that was her curse, but it wasn't. It was a gift, a specialty, a talent. She could become someone else, and she could then just as easily kill what she became, taking out whoever happened to be in the way. And if transformation was her special talent, then George knew that what had attracted Liana to him was that he was someone who would never transform. He would always be the same.

And that is why she looked for me in Boston, George thought. Not because she needed closure, or wanted to see him again, or needed his help in a time of need. She came back to him because he could play a part—a tiny walk-on role—and getting him to play that part would be as simple as showing up at a bar, looking beautiful, and acting scared.

Dawn light began to fill George's bedroom window. He heard the *Globe* delivery truck rumble by on the street below. Even though he hadn't slept, George felt wide-awake. He knew what he had to do.

"Irene Dimas."

"Hi, it's me."

"Oh. I didn't recognize the number. Where are you?"

"I'm actually away. For a little while. I was wondering if you'd do me a favor."

"Okay. Sure." George could hear the busy sounds of Irene's workplace in the background. He'd managed to catch her at her desk, even though it was just past five on a Friday.

"I need you to look after Nora."

"I can do that. How long are you going to be gone?"

"I was actually hoping you'd take her back to your place. I might be gone for a while."

Irene's voice rose in pitch. "Have you been arrested? Where are you calling from?"

"No, no. Not yet anyway. I'm out of town. I just don't know how long it will take. I'll feel better knowing that Nora's with you."

"Please tell me that you're not looking for her."

"Okay. I'm not looking for her."

"I don't believe you. You need to leave this to the police."

"The police aren't looking for Liana. They're watching me. They found some of the missing diamonds in my apartment."

"When? How?"

"I have to go. Can you just make sure that Nora's okay?"

"Sure. Of course. You can't tell me where you are?"

"I can't. I'm sorry."

"What are you going to do if you find her?"

"I have to go. Take care of Nora. I'll be back."

George hung up before Irene could ask more questions.

If he did find Liana, what would he do? The truth was, he didn't know exactly. He wished he could tell himself that he would make her pay for what she had done. But he wasn't sure. All he knew was that if he didn't find Liana Decter and prove to the world that she was guilty, he was going to be arrested and sent away for a long time. And he knew that everything that happened in Boston, from her appearance at Jack Crow's to the bloodbath aboard Bernie's boat, had unfolded exactly the way it was supposed to, exactly the way Liana had planned it.

He wrapped the cheap disposable phone up in the bag it had come in and shoved it down into the garbage can next to the picnic table. A black bird with yellow eyes swept down and perched on the garbage can's edge, wondering if he'd disposed of food. George stood, slinging the strap of his messenger bag over his shoulder, ten thousand dollars wrapped in yesterday's *Boston Globe* in the zippered inside pocket. It was all he'd brought with him, besides his passport and a few changes of clothes, as he'd left his apartment the day before. Knowing that the police might be watching him, he didn't dare bring a larger bag.

Emerging from his apartment into the cool dawn, he saw nothing suspicious, just one yellow cab idling on the corner. Still, he walked to his garage where he kept his Saab, entered through the front door, then slipped by the night attendant sleeping at his desk and made his way out the rear entrance to a garbage-strewn alleyway. From there he walked to the nearest T station and took the subway to South Station. He was sure that if he went to Logan and tried to take a departing flight he'd be stopped. But he thought he might have a chance from an airport in Canada. There was no train service to Montreal, so George bought a one-way bus ticket.

The Canadian agent at the border stamped his passport and barely looked at him. It was the same at Montréal-Trudeau Airport, where he bought a ticket to Cancun. George had been so sure that he'd be questioned at security, or that his messenger bag would be searched and the cash discovered, that he could hardly believe it when the three-quarters-full plane lifted over downtown Montreal and the St. Lawrence River on its way to Mexico.

A dilapidated bus took him an hour south of Cancún to Tulum. He'd need to get a hotel room, someplace cheap that would take cash without asking questions. But first he bought a phone and headed toward the Mayan site.

It's just like the postcard, George thought as he looked at the gray ruins that spread out along the bluff and, in the distance, the quiet, sun-flecked surface of the sea. And George knew, with absolute certainty, that Liana wasn't resting on the bottom of the Atlantic. She was alive.

ACKNOWLEDGMENTS

This book wouldn't exist without my agent, Nat Sobel, who read a story about a couple of college freshmen and wondered what would happen if they met twenty years later. He coached me all the way to the finish line. Every time I thought I'd done something perfect, Nat would let me know that it could be a whole lot better. He was right every time.

A heartfelt thanks also goes to Joe DeMarco, who first published *The Girl with a Clock for a Heart* in novella form in Mysterical-E. Very few literary journals, and even fewer online journals, are interested in stories over ten thousand words. Not only did Joe read the long story I sent him, he gave it a home. And thank you to *Spinetingler Magazine* for nominating my story for Best Short Story on the Web.

Thank you to David Highfill, my editor at William Morrow. David's intelligence and enthusiasm made the editing process so much less painful than I thought it would be. Angus Cargill, my editor at Faber and Faber, offered astute suggestions, all of which improved the book. And thanks to the entire Sobel Weber team—Judith, Adia, Julie, and Kirsten—whose professionalism was only exceeded by their kindness.

Myriam Steinback is the rarest of combinations—a great boss and a close friend. Over the sixteen years that we have worked together in teacher training, she has accommodated my schedule to allow me time to write, and has offered constant encouragement, both for the work I do as a project manager, and the writing that I do in my spare time. Thank you.

And a final heart-shaped thank-you to Charlene, my first reader, biggest fan, and toughest critic. Thank you for letting me shut the office door as often as I do.